NARROW GIRLS
ON A BLUE PROFOUND STAGE

LISA L. SELLGE

PROPERTIUS
PRESS

"Time Long Past," by Percy Bysshe Shelley. Transcribed by Shelley in a copy of Leigh Hunt's "Literary Pocket-Book" for 1819 presented by him to Miss Sophia Stacey, December 29, 1820.
"What's the Buzz," by Tim Rice and Andrew Lloyd Webber. © MCA Music, Ltd., 1973.
"They Call the Wind Maria," by Alan Jay Lerner and Frederick Loewe © Warner Chappell Music, Inc., 1951.
"Never Mind," by Harry Dent and Tom Goldburn. Published by Francis, Day & Hunter Ltd., London, ca. 1913.
"Toe Dancers," by George Dillon, c. 1927.

ISBN print: 978-1-4583-0646-3

Propertius Press
Lynchburg, Virginia
www.propertiuspress.com
email: propertiuspress@gmail.com

NARROW GIRLS ON A BLUE PROFOUND STAGE is available in print and as an ebook wherever books are sold.

for my sisters

She was usually laughing. How can I explain this now? I don't know what the years may have done to her but even then, it wasn't beauty that made her bewitching. I think it was her grace. Not the grace of a ballerina but the grace in her hands. The way she would thread a needle, or operate the manual shift of her car, or trace the lifeline on your open palm. I'm writing this as if she has passed away but as far as I know she's still occupying the planet somewhere. I would describe her to you but what good are physical traits when not accompanied by chemistry or history? Instead, think of someone whose spirit is intoxicating. Someone who cannot be ignored, through no fault of her own. Let that person, for you, be Rebecca.

If there is anything to be gained from looking back, perhaps it is the knowledge that decades pass, but people who shaped us still live in our psyches. So will we remain in the lives we influence today, or did so years ago, with the things we said or did. As I flipped through old journals and photographs, I began to reconstruct the birth of it, the crescendo, the aftermath. There is no need to right any wrongs or excuse interactions that challenge all that is sane in the world. But to look away would be to deny the story. Mostly, I simply wanted to remember. Condensing time to its most resonant moments, reading the map that brought me through adolescence and into the adult world I wanted so desperately to inhabit.

You may wonder what the big allure was. I can answer that with one simple word: freedom.

Chapter 1

Look at this photograph. This is me. I'm coming off the stage at the Westwood Theater, throwing a heavy gym bag over my shoulder. My eyes are squinting with laughter, my lips are deep red. One arm encircles long-stemmed roses thrust toward me as I emerged from the wings.

The flash of a camera.

In glitter to darkness. Then, the mellow lights of the theater, where the seats sweep up toward the control booth. Empty like a playground after children have left it, tether balls still clanging on the posts, swings still rippling on their chains.

You may not remember how it feels to be fifteen. Or perhaps, for some, the blooming begins at a different age. But I became still at fifteen and opened inside like an anemone. I was that quiet, too.

* * *

Rebecca held the edge of tulle against my hip and pulled until the bolster hit the floor. Pins stuck between her teeth, she mumbled quiet commands. I turned little by little as she wove pins into the tulle. A car pulled into the parking lot in front of the studio and I craned my neck to see.

"Damn it, Anneliese, if you don't hold still, I'm gonna stick you!"

"Who's coming?"

"Looks like…" Rebecca squinted, "looks like Paddy and Allison."

I didn't care. Allison was too old to be a ballerina. Paddy wasn't so cute. He was just a salesman who followed her around like a dog. I went back to staring and turning.

"Are you going to audition?" Rebecca mumbled through pins. The Civic Light Theater was doing *West Side Story* this year.

"Don't know," I said. It depended on who else would be there. "Are you?"

"Maybe," she said. "I can sing. Think they'll take me?"

I watched her remove another pin from her lips and weave it through the fabric that was evolving into my costume for the *Romeo and Juliet* "*Lovers*" *pas de deux*. Rebecca was ten years older than I. An actual adult. But not so old that responsibilities anchored her anywhere she did not wish to be. Her decisions were her own. Her lack of concern for anyone's approval, her immunity to anyone's list of rules, beguiled me. I imagined her taking up the stage, confident energy glowing, her voice filling the hollow space.

"You could be *Rosalia*," I said.

I twisted to inspect the tutu, its white layers stiff but weighted, falling elegantly at a slight angle from my hips. I rolled to the tips of my pointe shoes, appreciating my reflection in the shop window. "I don't care about being *Maria*," I said, "but I can't wait to dance in this."

* * *

Pacific Crest High School had released us early on Thursday so there was still an hour to kill before class. The afternoon sun glowed through the studio windows. I walked into the warm and empty reception office. No one labored over paperwork at the front desk, though its disheveled contents suggested late-night brainstorming along with multiple cigarettes and cups of coffee. I passed through swinging barn doors into the dressing room and dropped my gym bag on the bench. The faint sound of trumpets lured me into Studio A where I found Christopher counting out the steps to his *Romeo* solo, the record player turned low.

"What's shakin', Anneliese?" he said, without stopping the strong, steady movements that took his body over, under, down, around. He was a substantial man for a dancer, muscles bulging rather than rippling from behind his shoulders. He wore an old, white tank top, arm holes intentionally ripped open to the waist, with ratty blue jeans. His soft, lace-up black oxfords spun before the mirror and he struck the end of a *pirouette* like a gymnast. He grabbed a towel from the music podium, wiped his face and brown stringy hair, then smiled at me, waiting for a reply. I simply shrugged and returned his smile.

"Well, I need a beer," he said, and lifted the needle from the record player. In the next studio we heard the peppy beats of Michael Jackson's *Pretty Young Thing*. Ricky Preston was choreographing for his evening class. Christopher knocked twice on the adjoining door before we passed through his domain from the ballet side. Ricky blew him a kiss and Christopher caught it, placing it on his cheek as we continued into Rebecca's shop.

On the blue industrial carpet, Christopher glided to the floor, stretching effortlessly into the splits. I sat in one of the white plastic chairs lining the glass wall. Rebecca looked up from her sewing machine.

"Mess up my patterns and I'll wring your neck," she barked at him. Christopher twisted, just now noticing the tissue representations of costumes strewn about the low-pile industrial carpet like crime scene outlines.

"I won't hurt anything," he protested.

Ricky appeared from Studio B, sweat dripping from the tips of his red hair. His tall, thin body gave off mists of exertion. One glance at Christopher sent him in a bee-line across the room where Ricky planted a loud kiss on Christopher's smiling lips.

"Now that you've all disturbed me," said Rebecca, getting up and grabbing a pack of cigarettes from her desk, "you might as well hand me a beer." She ran her fingers through blonde curls that touched her shoulders. She twisted her back and it popped like packing bubbles. "I've been sitting for hours," she complained. Heavy silver bangles slid up and down her wrists as she stretched and contorted her spine.

"At your service, Cinderella." Christopher extended a toe and flipped open a small refrigerator disguised behind a row of costumes. He sat up and grabbed several bottles from its shelves, handing one to Rebecca, one to Ricky, and keeping one for himself. Lids were popped with a succession of vaporous whispers. Rebecca stood before me and brushed newly cut bangs from my eyes. I'd wanted them to look just like my new instructor, Jade's. They did not.

"Hey, Anneliese," Rebecca said.

Younger than all of them by a decade, I was out of my league and accepted her attention gratefully. Rebecca flicked her lighter, igniting the cigarette between long fingers. I watched enraptured as she put the paper end between her lips. She sucked, and smiled, immensely pleased.

Jade was next to appear at the shop door, this time from the parking lot. She stretched one arm high along the frame like a pinup girl. She was a tall, narrow woman, whose elegance permeated every inch of her. Dudley had brought her to the studio, he said, to widen the scope of our training and she added a new level of discipline we'd escaped before her arrival. Jade had been a soloist with the Canadian Royal Ballet but developed extreme stage fright. I assumed there was a deeper story, but she never told us what happened. I loved the stage and couldn't imagine leaving it. These days Jade made her living pushing our boundaries beyond what we thought possible. And you'd never guess, looking at her now, that she was ever afraid of anything.

"You all know what's better than beer?" she asked, dressed in her customary white leotard, in which she moved like poetry in the afternoon sunlight. Christopher looked up from the floor, intrigued by her seductive tone. Rebecca shot a warning glance at Jade. I followed her stare. Stringy blonde bangs fell long beyond Jade's amber eyes to her high cheekbones. She blew them out of the way, but they instantly fell back. For a few seconds, no one spoke, their inside knowledge hovering like a swarm of bees in the room. From beneath heavily blackened lashes, Jade surveyed the group, a queen addressing peasants. I sat in my chair and tried to appear older than I was. And invisible. All eyes drifted toward me, the suddenly unwelcome guest.

"Can I bum a smoke?" Ricky asked. Rebecca tossed him her pack of clove cigarettes which he caught, then collapsed next to Christopher on the floor, laying a sinewy hand across his broad shoulders. I breathed relief at the interruption.

Jade relinquished her door-jamb pose, swinging her hips as she entered, and cast a skeptical look in my direction. From her gym bag she produced a sandwich bag and a small, rectangular mirror. She knelt to the floor, her face near the carpet, like someone from the far east deep in prayer. Onto the mirror she poured a fine, white mound. She concentrated intently on her task. "Does anyone have a razor blade?" She demanded more than asked.

"Does anyone have a razor blade, Jaybird?" Rebecca mocked, using the nickname reserved for Jade's closest friends. "Well, it just so happens, I have one right here." She rifled through the mess on her desk, producing, sure enough, a razor blade, as if it had been waiting for this moment all along.

Jade reached her fingers high in the air behind her until the blade was received in the tips of her long, purple fingernails. She carefully carved several neat, narrow lines in the powder. Christopher and Ricky leaned in to observe her masterpiece.

"Shouldn't you be getting ready for class?" Jade asked, still kneeling but jutting her chin in my direction. I opened my mouth, ready to protest that there was still plenty of time, but Rebecca moved between us so Jade's critical gaze was eclipsed.

"Anneliese is with me," Rebecca said. She reached for my hand and pulled me from the chair. "Aren't you?" she added. Her hand moved to my waist, fingers resting on my hip bone. I met her eyes, conspiratorial, searching. Any potential response from me evaporated. I glanced at Ricky, now absorbed and communing with his cigarette, then at Christopher who returned a raised eyebrow.

Rebecca drew me into the circle of smoke and thin, white cocaine.

"She's just a child," Christopher said, "leave her alone." But there was teasing in his tone. Jade sat up and lit a cigarette while Christopher put his nose to the mirror, inhaling deeply.

"Anneliese was never a child," said Rebecca, smiling, her face very near mine. I breathed her clove cigarette breath as she spoke. I wanted to be her favorite.

Jade looked sideways at us, her own smoke escaping in a thin wisp from the side of her lips and held her gaze. When her disapproval failed to stir me, she focused instead on Christopher and Ricky, draped over each other and giggling. Ricky grabbed his beer from one of the white plastic chairs and guzzled until he drained it. Christopher twirled Ricky's penny colored hair, his smile fading to a curved line, stage presence beginning to wane from his face as the drug wore down. Then it was Jade's turn. She covered one nostril and sucked in like a trucker preparing to spit.

"Come and get it, Anneliese," she taunted as she righted herself. She knew I would not.

"Not tonight," I said and shifted my weight to lean against Rebecca who leaned back into me.

"As you wish, dear," said Christopher. He snorted my share and sat up smiling. Jade stepped over me, through the door, and onto the wooden floor of Studio B.

"I need to stretch before class," she said. "You might think about it too, Anneliese."

I ignored her, looking to Rebecca, who returned a questioning eyebrow. I said nothing.

"What?" she prompted.

"Will you be here after class?"

"Might be."

Christopher's eyes darted back and forth between us, a beer-wet smile on his lips. "Uh-oh," he said.

"Uh-oh, what?" laughed Rebecca.

"As if you don't know," he said, turning back to Ricky. "She's a hot one and you know it, Bec."

Rebecca's voice turned low now and satin-smooth. "I know," said Rebecca. "She's got a body that won't quit."

"Mm-m-m," said Christopher, still smiling. Not that he had any interest for a second.

So, this is how I fit among them. I stood casually and headed into class, aware of the eyes following me. I would not be fifteen within these walls.

Studio B was empty now. I walked through to Studio A and then through the swinging barn doors where I found Jade not stretching, but shuffling papers behind the front office desk. She was writing furiously when Dudley walked in the office door. She looked up to greet him.

"Your eyes, Jade, what's wrong?" Dudley asked, staring hard at her.

"Must be allergies," she said, without missing a beat.

I laughed to remind her I had been among them minutes ago. I wouldn't let her think for a second, I belonged to the clan of baby ballerinas gathering in the studio. I belonged among them: Rebecca, Christopher, Ricky....

"You belong in class," she said to me.

"On my way," I said.

Her stern tone at once chilled me and made me laugh. Twenty-seven and Canadian Ballet-trained. My instructor. But not my confidante. Though I would never expose their habits, her face told its own tales: purple spidery veins appeared on the end of her nose. I wondered if Dudley recognized them. If he did, he wasn't concerned. No one was concerned.

Dudley smashed the end of his cigarette in the tin tray on the desk where it joined his last dozen.

"Well," he said, "best do as you're told. Class will begin soon."

Back through the barn doors, then, where coffee stained the ancient green dressing room carpet. The painted benches peeled and exposed old wood. Long-ago-white walls were marred and scuffed by dancers' feet. It was what it was, and I cared for all of it with my entire soul. Our studio dripped with an ozone of sweat and passion. It vibrated from floor to warped tin ceiling.

I did as I was told. I had nothing to prove to Dudley. He loved me without question, a grandfather watching his long-whittled piece of wood develop into something of his vision. Pleased, so far, with the results of our years together, he could not guess who I was becoming. At least, I hoped he would not.

Chapter 2

On my mother's kitchen counter, dark red wine sat tempting me in a glass. I put my nose over the rim and breathed it in. Still, the tingle of a long class on my damp skin. Still, the stirring planted in my brain from the words they had allowed me to hear, things they had let me know without telling me to my face. They were safe. They hadn't touched. They hadn't really even flirted. Only commented, really. I raised the glass to my lips and sipped. I thought it should taste the way smoke smelled coming out of Rebecca's cigarette. Why she should haunt me like this I wasn't sure. I swallowed. Not a foreign taste, even at fifteen. At my house, we were allowed. Wine was part of the food we ate.

Mother had her back to me while she cooked. Her own wine glass at the ready and frying pan sizzling something with onions. She rarely asked me about ballet. She asked instead of the people there, some delicate sense in her maternal brain setting off alarms.

"Is Dudley still using a cane with his bad knee?"

"Yes, still."

"Poor old Dudley. I should call him."

My mother never talked with Dudley. Not since I was a six-year-old in a square-looking black leotard and the only student in black shoes. She hated pink. What was the use of putting a black-haired daughter in a pink ballet outfit when she looked better in black? I wanted the pink. I didn't say so.

"You should call him." I tried to sound nonchalant. He would be surprised, I thought. Would they talk about me? Or his knee? I hoped the latter.

"Did you have Jade's class tonight?"

"Yeah." We sipped.

"Are she and Rebecca friends?"

"I guess."

She let minutes pass in silence. Only the crackle of her frying pan and the smell of onions and red wine filled the space.

"You know, Rebecca's a little strange..."

"I guess. How do you mean?"

"I don't know." She sipped her wine. She did know. She hoped I did not. "How old is Rebecca?"

"Twenty-five."

"And Jade?"

"Twenty-seven."

I wasn't sure where she was going with these questions. But I would have told her anything she asked. Just about. I would have told her the things I understood. For instance, Jade (nicknamed "Jaybird" because she talked so much) had the most perfect *développé à la seconde*, the most fluid *arabesque*, the most elegant *pirouettes*. I would have told her that Jade drove us to the point of exhaustion and exhilaration. That I adored her classes and that she knew I would not stop no matter how hard she pushed me. That I would compete with her when given the chance and I would not stop until she did, waving me away with a brush of her hand, "Alright, Anneliese, let it go."

But Mother didn't want to know about ballet. She sipped her wine.

"How are your grades?"

"They're okay. Did you know Hannah's mother pulls her out of ballet if she drops below a B?"

"Is that what I need to do with you?"

"It wouldn't work with me."

It would have worked. Anything that threatened to keep me from the studio would have done wonders for my academic success. But she took me at my word, which she found frightening enough in its certainty. And I would have been a frenzied energy to deal with. She decided not to. We sipped.

"Is Christopher still with Ricky?" she asked.

"Christopher will always be with Ricky," I said.

It was strange to hear my mother acknowledge Christopher and Ricky as lovers. She tried to sound natural and comfortable with the subject, yet I could tell from the tense gathering between her shoulders as she sautéed onions, the tight-throated tone, even siphoned through wine, that the thought of male lovers made her squirm. She was searching.

"Aren't they worried? About AIDS?"

"I've never asked them. They don't seem to be."

It was a lie. Here is what I remember about the night Christopher talked. Another studio floor scene. This time, the wood beneath us all, exhausted but waiting for the night to feel as if it were over. No one wanted to go home. Or we were all together, in another home.

"I just finished reading *And the Band Played On*," Dudley had told us. "It was quite worrisome. All about AIDS, where it came from. It did not have a hopeful ending. I urge you all to read it." He was looking at Christopher and Ricky.

"Yes, *dad*," said Christopher, drawing the vowel out long and sassy.

Dudley had packed his classical albums and his choreography notes into a burlap sack, which he slung over his shoulder. He did not smile. He placed his reading glasses on his nose, took his cane, and headed for the swinging barn doors that led through the office and into the parking lot.

"Good night, all!" he said. A slight British lilt was still present. We all smiled as we looked after him. He stopped at the front door and looked back. "Is someone coming for you, Anneliese?"

I felt my face heat up. I was the only dancer in the room for whom someone needed to come. Why was he concerned? Jade smiled smugly in my direction.

"My dad will be here." I answered quickly, wishing I had a more interesting answer. Perhaps a mysterious man on a motorcycle with whom they would all witness me disappear onto the highway, without explanation, leaving them to wonder, if they cared to. Dudley nodded and continued to the parking lot. The heavy door of a Buick slammed, the engine turned, and we relaxed. Christopher lit two clove cigarettes, side by side, in his mouth, inhaled, and handed one to Rebecca.

If you had been a spirit that day and looked down upon the circle of friends, all collapsed on the floor, some leaning against one another and others in their own space, you would have seen a light around Christopher. You would have heard him sigh in resignation and you would have seen death dancing lightly about the edges of his body. No one else that night would have a glow such as his.

"Why would I want to get tested?" said Christopher. "I already know I have it."

I looked in his eyes for fear. For truth. It was all there.

"I wouldn't want to know," said Ricky.

"And the awful truth, my love, is that if I go, you will go with me."

"Could be," said Ricky. "No one knows for sure how it spreads."

"Yeah," said Rebecca, "they know."

"Oh, what do you know, Princess?" said Christopher. He threw a sweaty towel at her. I wondered how he could be so unconcerned. Rebecca blew the smoke from the corner of her lips, eyes locked on Christopher's. I knew that look. She cared for him. She cared for us all. She wished we all loved each other the way she loved each of us. But for Rebecca, to love us was to know each of us, all the way inside out. It made us all jealous.

Not many years later, there would be a snapshot of Christopher in a mermaid costume reclined in a wheelchair. A Halloween party full of dancers leaning on him with wide smiles. Exuberance would still stream from his face. Green and sparkling scales would encase legs that no longer worked. I knew without being told that Rebecca made the costume for him. She was a master of such things.

"Well," said my mother, tossing the onions, swallowing wine, "I hope they are all right."

"Me, too," I said.

"Do you think she, Rebecca, well ..."

"What?"

"Is she like them?"

"Like Christopher and Ricky? No. Maybe. I don't think so. She dates men."

"She likes you an awful lot, doesn't she?"

"I guess so. She likes everyone an awful lot."

I went to bed early. I hadn't thought about Rebecca that way, really. I thought of the women in my family. They were strong and passionate. Too emotional, my father said on many occasions. We were a sort of coven to which only men of our choosing could belong. Forever critical, my father drifted along the edges of our acceptance.

And there were not many men to be trusted. Except maybe Dudley, who had nurtured me from childhood and smiled when I succeeded. I wished my own father had been like that. But when you're fifteen, when there are questions, there must be someone to ask. Someone who won't gasp and fear for your life. For me, there was Rebecca.

Chapter 3

Jade and Rebecca stood in a narrow open doorway at the back of the studio, smoking the remains of a joint. Strolling across the long wooden floor toward them, I tried to think of a reason to be there, too, where stacked portable barres were stowed during center practice, shoved aside among pulleys and ropes, large push-brooms and an old fan. The day was warm and the two women spoke in low, smoke-filled, sophisticated tones. I wanted to hear their words—the secrets that would certainly stop once I was within earshot. There had to be something necessary to tell Rebecca. Her eyes followed my approach while her lips continued to move in conversation. I could ask her something about my *Juliet* costume or the evening's painting project. I took the sweet cloud of smoke full-faced, breathing in, as Jade sent her strong exhalation deliberately in my direction.

The doorway where they leaned so casually, heads tilted together, one wispy blonde, the other tangled, the color of sand, led to the parking lot where the railroad tracks ran along an old wash, now full of weeds and dry clay. Jade's expression was not difficult to read. "*Here she comes,*" it said. But I didn't mind. Because Rebecca's eyes were soft. Welcoming. Waiting. She blew her smoke to the high tin ceiling and studied me, the edge of a smile beginning on her lips.

"Hey, Liese," she said, "what's going on?"

I spit out the easiest reply. "Will you paint with Dudley and me tonight?"

"Yeah, he mentioned that. Sounds fun."

On the long wall facing the mirrors, four eight-foot drapes hung in panels, each painted with a towering dancer in an elegant pose. Rebecca had created them in the colors of spring, summer, fall and winter, when we had danced Glazunov's *Four Seasons* the year before. I had danced my first *pas de deux* that Christmas. I was *lightning*. A 19-year-old boy named Craig was *thunder*. And I was amazed. Because when I jumped, he caught me easily. When I leaped into the air, he doubled the force of my lift. When I flipped, *tour jeté*, I was plucked from flight like a firefly. It was magic. When it was over, the four painted banners had been moved from the theater to the studio wall and had hung there ever since. Rebecca was an artist. She sketched designs for Dudley fully formed and perfectly proportioned. He would nod and they would emerge from her machine the same way. I will always think of her mumbling through pins.

"Dudley's out getting the paint," I told them. "Are you staying, Jaybird?" She raised an eyebrow at my casual toss of her nickname but she let it go.

"Hell no, I'm not getting that crap all over me." She tossed the now pitiful scrap of paper and tobacco out to the blacktop and pulled the door shut behind her. "Catch you later," she said to Rebecca, her tone flat and unreadable. She left the way I'd come, a little unsteady, across the maple wood.

"What's with her?" I asked.

"Oh, you know Jaybird," Rebecca said, "there's always something bugging her. Got class now?"

"Yeah, just barre, and then we paint," I said, eager to show off my calligraphy skills. Poppa had given me his old lettering book from England and I'd spent long summer hours tracing and learning to space properly, perfecting the long-tailed scroll at the end of the "Y" and the strange tilted cross at the center of an "S," neither of which I would be needing that night.

"I'll see ya after class then," she said, and headed toward Studio B, but turned back. "You are dressed to kill tonight, aren't you?" I wore the same black unitard I'd danced in as *lightning* last year. Mother had removed the silver sequined bolt that once wrapped around its torso and down the length of one leg.

"Am I?" I smiled.

"You know you are," she said and disappeared through the door, into the haven of her shop.

After class, Dudley sent me to fetch the newspapers he'd gathered and stowed behind his desk. He went to the parking lot and pulled a gallon of black paint from the trunk of his gold Buick, tottering against its weight without his cane. Rebecca appeared from behind him, whisking it away with ease, her other hand full of paintbrushes. I scanned their tips, hoping for one that matched the tilt of my calligraphy pen, and followed her back to the far end of the studio, where she had listened to Jade's words, their intimacy sparking something strange and jealous.

I began spreading newspaper at the base of the huge roll-up door. When open, except for the small exit door to its left, the entire back wall was gone. If it wasn't too hot or too cold, we could be dancing at the barre, staring out over the tracks, all the way to Saddleback Mountain. Or, when it rained and we had worked up sweat enough to steam, Dudley would open it, pulling dramatically on the rope, letting in a blast of cold, delicious air to revive us, while the sound of rain on the metal roof drowned out Vivaldi. But when it was down, it was simply industrial grey. Tonight, we would paint, beginning from high at the top: B – A – L – L – E – T, a panel of metal for each letter, one under the other, until the T hit the floor. Rebecca had planned it out and now she taped off the squares, high above me on a ladder, while I pried the lid from the paint can.

"Very good," said Dudley, standing in the middle of his studio, surveying our preparations. "You won't be needing me on that ladder, I hope."

"No way," Rebecca said from six feet above us, a roll of tape in her teeth, "You stay on the ground where you belong."

"Well then, I'll grab some supper I suppose. I'll just be across at the Deli," he said.

"Bye, Dudley," we chorused.

Next door in Studio B, Ricky's class still pulsed into the evening with a throbbing backbeat. His intermittent shouts of critique and encouragement penetrated the wall between us while Rebecca rocked out to the music.

"You'll fall, Bec!" I said, happy to be the only witness to her carefree exhibition.

"If I do, I'm gonna fall on you," she said.

Something caught my eye in the newspaper as I taped it to the floor. "What the heck?" I said. A grainy black and white photo showed the back parking lot of our studio, a group of young dancers in a line. Every year, on a day in spring, the patrons of *Mugs Away*, the local dive bar, would moon the train engineer as he came by. Standing in the lot across the tracks, they would line up, turn their backs and drop their pants, all the while swilling beer and toasting the train. When I was about ten, Dudley had decided his dancers should give the tradition a more appropriate flair. A few minutes before the train's scheduled approach, he lined us up in the back lot and gave us a minute or two of twenties-era chorus girl choreography. The local paper had gotten word of the new addition to *Mugs Away*'s theme and captured us that day, from behind, twelve girls in a row, our arms around each other's waists, high kicking toward the train as it roared past. The faint little man in the window of the train waved back in our direction. I remembered the day vaguely. He had blown his whistle for us.

"Bec," I said, "you have to see this."

"This better be good." she backed down the ladder still biting her tape roll, and crouched next to me, draping one arm across my back, peering over my shoulder, her chin resting there.

"I remember that day!" she said, "except I was at *Mugs Away* giving him the moon treatment."

"You did that?"

"Not just me. Christopher, Ricky, I don't remember who else. But I heard about Dudley's chorus line."

"Which one am I?" I traced along the backs of the heads, each in a ballet bun, each in the requisite leotard and tights, some with leg warmers and flats, others in pointe shoes, each perfectly turned out and angled to about thirty degrees, one arm extended in the air. Rebecca took my index finger and moved it to the middle of the row.

"This one," she said.

"Really?" I squinted.

"Yeah."

"How can you tell?"

"I'd know that... bun anywhere," she said. Her voice was smooth and low. Almost a smoky whisper. I looked at her. Something in her eyes, her slight smile, jolted something primal in my brain. She let her hand trail across my shoulders and I shivered, drawn like a magnet to her energy, wishing to remain just like that, shoulder to shoulder, sharing a secret. But she stood and returned to mount the ladder.

"Aren't you done with that?" I asked.

"Actually... why don't you go up to the top and start the B. I'm gonna grab a cigarette." Her tone had changed to something like confusion.

"Okay," I said, trotting to the paintbrushes tossed in a heap on the floor. But she didn't move from where she stood, mid-stride, leaning into one hip, considering.

"...that way I won't have to fight you for the ladder," she continued.

"Okay," I said, again. Still she remained, looking down at me.

"...not that I'd mind fighting you for it," she said.

I stopped and looked up at her, curious to confirm her double meaning. The smile was fading from her lips, now parted as if to say something else. I waited, a brush in my hand, unsure if I could speak.

"You make me crazy," she said.

* * *

"Who will it be, who will it be...?" Rebecca teased me as I sat waiting for her to finish sewing the bodice of my *Lovers pas de deux* costume. Two dancers would be cast in the role. Only one of us would dance the closing night when Jade and Dudley would sit in the audience. Jade couldn't miss my performance, I thought. I was not her favorite person, but I was her best dancer.

"Shut up, Bec."

"What's with you today?"

"I don't know."

"Got love on your mind, from the look in your eyes," she stopped to read my reaction. "And chapped lips... kissing in the wind?"

I wished. Rebecca and the others knew little of my life outside the studio. My sister, Ingrid, after whom I plodded to school each day, kept me in a circle of academic friends who seemed both worried for and frightened of me. I learned not to talk of my ballet life at school. And the reverse was also true. *You belong here*, Dudley had said.

"Love? Yeah, maybe."

"How old are you now?"

"I'll be sixteen next month."

"Finally."

"What?"

"Nothing. It's just that you... Sometimes I wish you'd hurry and grow up."

"Me, too."

She left her sewing machine and came to sit next to me. Windows that looked into hills of thistle and mustard weed behind the old industrial park surrounded her office. It calmed me to sit there. It calmed me to be with her. She took my hand in both of hers and trailed a fingernail along my palm.

"A good love line," she said, "I knew it! But don't fall in love. It's much more fun to fall in lust. That way you don't get hurt, know what I mean?"

I thought I knew. There was a boy, a junior in school. I liked him. He paid attention. And then he did not. If that was love, I was already a goner. *Too emotional*. But it was a badge I was comfortable with. Who would want to live unable to feel?

"If it helps any, I love you."

"Thanks, Rebecca," I said, assuming her claim as sisterly.

"Sometimes I think we should all just give up and become a big pack of lesbians."

I laughed. I hadn't heard that word used in conversation. It sounded absurd.

"Now get out and let me finish," Rebecca said. I left through her office door to Ricky's studio where he was choreographing to something poppy. I could never move like that. I stood in the doorway studying him.

"What are you staring at, Anneliese?" he yelled across the room as he danced, sweat flinging from his tall body. I didn't have an answer for him. If you can believe me, I was shy. And unsure of why I did anything. I followed an ache and sometimes a muse, and sometimes just curiosity. I didn't ask why or what. So how was I to answer him? He was just beautiful. So I stared. He shook his head at me.

When I first met Ricky Preston I was nine years old. Hannah and I had been side-by-side at the dressing room mirror, scraping our hair into tight twists. Ricky had come up behind us, peering between our faces, grinning at the reflection of the three of us: Hannah, blonde and fair; Me, dark and unruly; Ricky, a tall redhead with freckles. "When do you girls find time to play?" he'd said to us. Such casual familiarity from an adult surprised me.

"The studio is our playground," Hannah had said, unfazed. And it was true: we missed nothing of other childhoods. Everyone at our studio seemed ageless.

I passed through his studio to the ballet side. Dancers were assembling at the barre. I walked to the front. Everyone shifted back for me and I plopped to the floor to tie a pointe shoe. Wesley was behind me at the barre.

"Hey, Liese."

"Hey, Wesley."

"I saw you in the hall today."

"You did?"

"Yeah."

"Didn't see you."

Wesley was three years behind me in school. Two years before, when we needed a boy, he was an available brother. Once on stage, Wesley caught the bug and never left. Now he had the technique of one who was put on earth to dance.

"Are you doing *Lovers* today?"

"Probably at the end of class."

"Who's partnering you?"

"Christopher."

"Who's partnering Bridget?"

"Christopher."

"Don't you guys wish you could have a straight guy throw you around?"

"Someday." I smiled.

After an hour and a half of class, Jade called for the *pas de deux*. Christopher stood in the center of the room in white tights and customary loose tank top. He smiled at Bridget and me and clapped his hands.

"Who will be my first victim?" he asked.

I shrugged at Bridget.

"Go ahead, Bridget." Jade said. Her tired disinterest cautioned us to perfection. I leaned against the barre and watched while Wesley slid into splits at my side. Bridget was an effortless partner for Christopher, but they lacked chemistry. And twice she hadn't nailed the end of the partnered *pirouette*. I looked for Hannah across the room, expecting to witness a shadow of humor slide across her expression.

Only a week ago, Hannah and I had perched on the edge of my bathroom sink which we'd filled with hot water and Epsom salts.

"One—two—three!" Hannah had said. On three, we plunged our blistered feet into the salty, medicated water and breathed in short, quick gasps until the sting subsided. I looked at her reflection in the mirror, gaze cast down like something on the floor fascinated her.

"What's up?" I asked, knowing the answer would not be nothing.

Hannah looked up, meeting me squarely. "Why is everything so easy for you?" Hannah had a habit of turning long trails of thought into sudden conversation. As if she expected me to have heard all along. And perhaps I had. Our friendship had been cementing now for eight of our fifteen years.

"It's not fair that you have the good feet. You don't even care."

"Maybe working harder makes you a better dancer," I offered. "If I don't have to work, how far will I go? Besides, you have a better memory for choreography and Dudley always says you can't get anywhere always watching everyone else to see what's next. And who does that? Me!" Hannah ignored me.

"And you're so damn skinny," said Hannah, not dissuaded from her pouting. "Your stomach is concave."

"It's just in my genes," I said. My mother was an 85-pound pixie. "Besides, you're more graceful than I am!"

"Oh, come on. Who do you think will get to dance *pas de deux* with Christopher?"

I shrugged.

"Probably you," said Hannah.

"Probably Bridget," I said. "Dudley said we could learn the part, but I'm sure he's going to give the solo to an older dancer."

"Bitchy, Busty Bridget the Curious Chicken? A *Lover?*" Bridget was a strong and beautiful dancer. We couldn't let her get away with that. She'd been graced with the title because of her tendency to stick her neck out before attacking a step. I had whispered my catty observation to Hannah one day in class as we stood watching her, waiting for our turn to dance. Hannah had laughed so hard her face had turned beet-red trying to hide it. She'd added the part about *bitchy* and *busty*. True, Bridget was curvaceous for a ballerina, and a bit of a snob.

"Anyway," Hannah said, inspecting a loose flap of skin that hung precariously from an angry blister, "we're teenagers."

"I don't think fifteen qualifies as a lover," I said.

"Does sixteen?" asked Hannah. "We'll be sixteen by showtime."

"I think *Juliet* was actually fourteen in the Shakespeare play," I said.

"And Romeo didn't have to dance with a Curious Chicken!" Hannah added, and exploded in the deep and shameless laugh I knew from kindergarten.

But tonight, not a trace of that laughter graced her face as she watched the *pas de deux* unfold from across the studio, perhaps oblivious to my thoughts, perhaps not. I bit back my smile and watched Christopher partner Bridget, my cattiness fading.

The music was Prokofiev's Opus 64. *Romeo and Juliet* was Jade's signature piece. I felt the sublime choreography pulse through me even when I was the silent observer. When the music stopped, I was still staring.

"Anneliese, go ahead," said Jade.

"Come on, baby!" said Christopher.

I left the barre and stood opposite, four feet between us, which I would cover in one beat and then I'd be upon him. Two long violin bows stroked before I planted my hand in Christopher's and stood on *arabesque*. Jade lifted the needle from the record player with a zip of disgust.

"Again," she said.

I backed up the four steps and Christopher raised a single eyebrow. The violin stroke again. This time I covered the distance and took the *arabesque*, solid as a tree trunk. On the second stroke I let my weight shift into his arms as he took me off balance and back on again on the other side of him. I flew. He held my hips as I bent back, sweat dripping from my nose, then traveling down my forehead and falling to the floor. I was nowhere in time but here, never traveling farther than his arms would allow but everywhere in his presence, overhead and in between until the slight shove at the small of my back when I would run from him, turn, and jump. And he would never fail. I slid down, wrapping his contours behind me until the tips of my shoes touched the wood planking.

Jade lifted the needle. I was not yet awake. She clapped her hands once and called Bridget back in.

"Who wants what night?" she asked. She did not comment on the dance.

"I don't care," said Bridget.

I believe she did not care. As dedicated as she was, she avoided the woven studio cliques.

"I'll take Saturday night," I said, sounding what I hoped was casual.

"And the matinee?"

"Sure, both."

Jade looked at Bridget, who shrugged.

"Friday, Bridget," Christopher confirmed, "Sunday, Bridget?"

"If Anneliese wants," she said.

How could she be so calm?

"Okay," said Jade, "and who is driving to LA?"

Of course, I could not volunteer. Rebecca had appeared from Ricky's studio with our costumes.

"I have to bring these up anyway," she said, "I'll drive."

"I'm taking my car," said Bridget, "if anyone wants to drive with me." Bridget was on the verge of her own adulthood, graduating at the end of the year.

"Got room for Ricky?" Christopher asked.

"Sure."

"And Dudley will take the *corps de ballet* in the van," Jade continued. "Soloists, I want you there two hours early. Anneliese, who is driving you?" I gritted my teeth at the insult.

"I've got room," said Rebecca. Jade was less than enthusiastic. She looked at Dudley, waiting for him to insist I ride in the van with the other girls my age.

"I'll go with Rebecca," I said.

Still enraptured, entirely distracted, I didn't notice when Hannah left the room.

* * *

A small, beige, capsule-like Toyota had been Rebecca's car since she first arrived at the performing arts school five years earlier to sew costumes for the troupe. She was exciting even then, going to discos on Friday nights with blue tint at the tips of her hair and long dangling earrings. She was always surrounded by a flock of adoring fans, usually men. Back then, a ten-year-old longing to understand the adult world, I could not imagine who she was outside our walls.

Today, things were different. I opened the passenger door, threw my dance bag over the seat and got in next to her. She could do everything at once: hold a cigarette and shift the car into reverse, check the rear-view mirror, smile at me as if we had gotten away with something. My mother hadn't asked who was driving or I would have lied to avoid questions. I don't remember the hour of freeways, but the line of skyscrapers appeared in the morning fog as we moved north on the 5 freeway to Los Angeles. There was not the cylindrical building of today, but instead the old library tower, since burned down, which stood among urban sprawl, somewhere unseen. Not so tall, but elegant.

If I tried, I could not find that studio today. From the balcony I looked down into the huge, mirror-lined room with soft gray Marley floors we had not yet heard of in the suburbs far south of LA. High, old walls with peeling white paint and ancient black scuff marks could have been any dance school anywhere. I was stirring, the city infusing my brain. Energy everywhere bounced from wall to wall. We dropped our bags and I wound my hair into a tight, unmovable twist before a long, horizontal mirror.

Jade appeared looking serious and busy. And perfect. Rebecca hung costumes on a metal rack. It would be an early Saturday morning open-class attended by dancers from everywhere. After class we would drive to the Westwood Theater. Christopher and I would rehearse *Lovers* on the stage. I imagined narrow planks of black, hollow wood beneath our feet that would give and creak upon landing. But for now, I had to stay focused.

I trotted down the stairs to claim a good barre. It was odd to dance without Hannah by my side. She had blamed falling grades and her mother's wrath when she pulled out of the production. But perhaps there was more to it than she let me know. I hadn't pressed for details or begged her to stay.

Dancers filtered in, too self-involved to care who else was in the room. On the balcony, Rebecca observed the assembly like Evita presiding over her public. I tried to catch her eye from where I stood at my barre 20 feet below but her eyes seemed to dart everywhere else but on me. Stealing a furtive survey of the other dancers from the corner of my eye, it was clear I was not the queen here. I swallowed my fear, and donned nonchalance, the dancer's cloak. Christopher and Ricky swished in at the heels of Bridget, who made a straight shot for center floor. Christopher gave Ricky a peck on the cheek and took a corner with an ever-present small smile on his lips as if nothing could shake him. Ricky headed upstairs toward Rebecca to watch.

A small ballet-bred Madame entered the cavernous room with deliberate steps. All eyes turned to follow her in the sudden hush. So this was the legendary ballerina, Melissa Hayden, former principal of the New York City Ballet. We stared at her as she crossed the floor, lifted chin, to confer in staccato whispers with the pianist. She was gaunt, bony, maybe sixty-five. My heart was beating in my throat. I wondered whether she was a screamer or given to sarcasm and humiliation. It would be one of the two. Her mouth was set in a tight line. As she strolled to the front of the room, she sized us up. We tried hard not to shrink. She signaled the pianist with a subtle upsweep of her elegant hand.

From the balcony, Rebecca was making faces down at Christopher, determined to crack his serene expression. I tried to hear only the music, to remember the long sequence Madame Hayden had uttered without so much as a "good morning." Dudley sat on a stool in the corner with his cane between his knees. His eyes followed my balcony gaze and he raised a warning eyebrow in my direction. Sixteen beats later, I forgot Rebecca and danced.

Chapter 4

My grandmother sat at the kitchen table in the small apartment, resting her chin in her hands. Her little finger fell across her lips as it often did when she was thinking. I wondered if I would slip into that pose someday, far into the future. And if I did, would I be able to remember her clearly? See her before me as I saw her that day, round and silver, lilting and comfortable? She was sipping her tea at the table as I sketched a bird sitting on a bottlebrush tree outside her window. It was summertime, and evening came later and later. Though night had just begun to fall, the bird remained.

"I wish your Mother would get back," she said.

"She'll be here, Ma, don't worry."

"Your dad will have a drink and then drive them home."

She was right, of course, but my father was no different from anyone else's father, I supposed. They couldn't go calling a taxi every time he had a beer, could they?

"And she had to go and marry a German. Of all the men in the world, one of them."

"I guess nationality didn't have much to do with it."

"I suppose not."

Ma was from Truro on the coast of England. She wasn't British, but a Celt, born with a dirt floor and the smell of seaweed in the air. When she was young in the 1920s, she had loved a black man. She kept the poem he had given her in her wallet still, even though she'd married Pop long since.

She sipped the last of her tea and peered into her cup. Dark tea leaves sat at the bottom in a wet mound. Her gaze, though directed at the leaves, told of leaving the room and travelling far away. I didn't know how to read tea leaves but I thought someday it might come to me, just because I was her grandchild and it seemed right that it should.

I didn't speak, just sketched a folded wing, a spray of bottlebrush, and waited to hear if the leaves revealed anything.

The man Ma married had been a painter and a soldier from Penzance. Now plagued with shaking hands, he had given his oil paints to my mother, who gave them to me the year I was twelve. I loved the smell of linseed oil and imagined the strokes each stiffly-bristled brush would create: the fan-shaped brush for foliage, the flat edge for tracing mountains, the thin needle-nose top for the feathers of a bird. I could not make them behave the way he and my mother could, though I thought it must be inside me somewhere.

I heard Ma whispering a prayer. She returned her little finger to her lips. The evening had turned to black night and we heard the clock chime eleven. Ma peered at the clock as if it advanced on purpose to frighten her.

"It's okay, she didn't say she'd be back before midnight." I squinted at the little beak I'd drawn on the paper and looked out the window to compare it to the real one. The bird had long ago flown.

"I can't help it," she said.

"She's grown up, Ma."

"She's my youngest, and she doesn't always think. She's got a brain like a sieve."

I had heard that last comment from her often in my childhood. It made me laugh to think of my mother in any less than complete control. But I figured her own mother knew her best. My mother put on a pretty good act for her daughters. She never let us see anything but fierce conviction. Well-placed empathy. The value of dignity. I thought Ma probably had a much clearer picture of her than my sisters and I.

"Well, the good Lord will watch over her," she said. I smiled and said nothing.

"I believe I'll have a drop of brandy," Ma said, "but I won't go to sleep until she gets back. She isn't planning to drive home after she comes to get you?"

"I think she is, Ma."

"Oh, Lord."

"It's okay. We'll make it."

She came back to the table with her brandy and sipped.

"Having a drop of brandy, Flos?" said Poppa as he shuffled slowly from the bedroom.

"I'm just worried for Gwen, Pop."

He made his laborious way over to me and peered over my shoulder, scrutinizing my sketch.

"It's a bird," he said. *Oh good. Recognizable.*

"He was over there sittin' on the bottle-brush just this morning wasn't he, Flos?"

"I believe he was."

"Was he there again in the evening, Leesie?"

"Yep."

"He's a mockingbird. Maybe you got your mother's talent after all."

"Not really. Not like you, Poppa." He studied my bird another moment.

"Well, at least you sit up straight. You sit up real straight."

His eyes settled on the window, looking far off for a moment, then drifted back to his recliner, tipped it back and went into himself.

"Pop is tired," Ma said, "Do you wanna go and climb into bed with your sisters?"

My little sister, Katrine, who was ten, had fallen asleep on the couch hours before and Ma had roused her enough to lead her to the bedroom and tip her over on the sheets. Ingrid, one year my senior, had gone into Ma's room to read a romantic drugstore novel in the early evening and had fallen asleep even before Katrine. They couldn't stand each other and I found it quietly amusing that they ended up side by side in a double bed. Had they known, they'd have jumped up as fast as they could and taken opposite corners of the house even if it meant sleeping on the floor in a heap. I wished we were spending the whole night with Ma so I could witness the waking up of the side-by-side sisters.

As I was considering a bed, we heard footsteps on the porch and a jingling of keys. The door opened.

"Oh, Gwendolyn, you're back."

"Hi, Mom."

My father walked in behind her, smiling politely.

"Hiya, Flos."

"Hi yourself," she said, giving him a critical once-over. "Did you have too much to drink?"

"Of course not, Flossie," he said.

He was more patient with her than with anyone else on the planet. No one else could cross-examine my father and get away with it for a second. I wondered how she did it. Even more, I wondered if I could learn it. And I admired her for not being taken in by his strict demeanor.

I thought about leaving home someday. Maybe when I turned 18. Before then, he would not allow it. I would wait until there could be no argument. Then I would pack my things into whatever I could carry and I would move out. But I would be sorry to leave Ingrid.

My father went into the bedroom to wake Ingrid and carry Katrine to the car. I hugged Ma tightly before I followed him out the door.

"Be careful and keep him awake," she called to my mother.

"Relax, Flos!" he called back as he made his way down her front walkway.

I stared out the window at the night sky on our trip home. He drove carefully and perfectly, ever the engineer. In that space, I was not threatened, but solid and comfortable. I hadn't decided for sure where I would go when I moved out, but I thought Rebecca might take me in when the time came.

* * *

Stage doors whined as we exited into the dark alley. Rebecca's arms were full of costumes and a makeup case. Tonight, the *Lovers pas de deux* had been Bridget's. I danced in the *corps de ballet*, trying hard to remember counts, which I never bothered to learn. For the past six months only the *pas de deux* had concerned me. Tonight, I paid for my lack of attention.

Dudley caught the door as it closed and stopped us in the alley.

"Anneliese," he said, quietly, "a word with you."

He linked his arm under mine and strolled me away from Rebecca. She walked to the car to load the trunk.

"Was there a problem, dear?" he asked me with eyes cast to the concrete. He did not sound so concerned as he did suspicious.

"In the *corps*?" As if I had to ask.

"In the *corps*."

I said nothing. Across the parking lot Rebecca was busy packing and arranging.

"You can't have the limelight all the time," Dudley went on, planting his eyes in my line of sight and putting a stop to my wandering attention. "And when you're dancing in the *corps* you must move as one, with the other dancers."

"I'm sorry. I know."

"Tell me then, where was your head?"

I could not have told him that my brain was tangled in Rebecca. He would have wondered why. I wondered why. Not a moment had passed since we arrived in Hollywood three days earlier that I had not been at her heels, waiting for whatever words she would give me.

And I could not have described the dim theater wings, where heavy velvet curtains hid the waiting dancers, as I stood alert, staring at the well-lit stage. Or that my gaze continued across the black, wooden floor to the opposite wings where Rebecca made last-minute adjustments on the costume of a male dancer as the performers prepared to enter.

When she had finished sewing, she stood up to watch the *corps de ballet* enter and take their places. The dancer who needed adjusting moved behind her in the small dark space to peer over her head. Soon his hands found their way to her shoulders and his fingers rested there like birds. I fixated on them from across the vast space. I hadn't realized she was involved with him. Or she wasn't. Men always found reasons to put their hands on Rebecca.

In my wing, our ensemble huddled at the edge of the curtain. The violin crescendo told us we had four beats left. We counted off in a whisper, then ran, as one, to the center. I had forgotten, only in the instance of the downbeat, the knot in my stomach... the stirring in my brain. The glare from the lighting booth at the back of the theater disoriented me. I glanced to my left, to my right, to take my position in line. Panic was smearing the choreography into a messy jumble of positions.

I believe I would have found my place, picked up the step, until that moment when the choreography took me again to the shadows where the dancer had moved his hand from Rebecca's shoulder and replaced it with his lips. His fingers settled just beneath her chin, palm against her neck. She smiled as if it were nothing, an every-minute, any-man occurrence. I struggled with the chase of choreography. The *corps* was quick and united, but I had lost their rhythm. And in a wing upstage, watching his brood with a mixture of alarm and concern, stood Dudley.

"You were not present on that stage tonight," he continued. "If something is wrong, you ought to tell me."

"But it was nothing. Just a bad night."

His eyes met mine and narrowed.

"Among us," he said, "there are dancers, and then there are people who have *wished* to be dancers, but there were other things more important." *Was he referring to Rebecca?* "You are still young. You have some time. But not much time. Don't waste it."

"I won't."

But on that night, we both knew I would glory in the shadows of those for whom there were *things more important.*

Dudley nodded, sighed, patted my arm with resignation. How was he so wise? I was about to be lost to him. He turned to the stage door, walking tentatively without his cane. For a moment, I wanted to follow. To stroll beside him and feel again like his student, clean and black and white and comfortable and pure. I wanted to dance in his class with giggling girls while he smiled and clapped and said, "wonderful!" or "very good, my loves!" But I had nothing left to say. The heavy door closed behind him.

Chapter 5

Our final night at the Westwood Theater had been threatening to arrive all week. Three performances behind us, we drove to the Hollywood Motel with its dark corridors littered with cigarette butts and layered in soot. Inside the aqua-painted rooms, musty shag carpet crunched stiff and dirty underfoot. The high windows plunged below street level and feet walked by on the sloped sidewalk outside. A trash bag dragged at the heels of a homeless man. I lay beneath the sheets in one of the side-by-side double beds, hoping it would not dawn on someone to bend low and peer into the window. This evening, I was alone.

Down the open hall, in a room of his own, Dudley was probably working out lighting cues or scribbling notations on the libretto. The other young dancers had grouped off and shared rooms here and there. I had managed to work myself in with Christopher, Ricky, Jade and Rebecca. But the instant they dropped their dance bags on the rusty shag carpet they made quick plans to go to a local bar.

"Will you be alright?" Rebecca asked me as she left.

I was stunned by how quickly all this came about. I could not go with them and I had the feeling that Jade had engineered the whole thing to further her point.

"Sure," I said, "I'm pretty tired."

What could I have said? Should I have begged her not to go? And then what? I would have worn my age like an aura. Behind the door was the silence of the room, the hum of cars, the glow of the street lamps. The traffic light outside the window took the bare white walls on its ever-changing red, gold and green kaleidoscope. I slid out from the worn sheets and closed the curtains.

That night, the Santa Ana winds blew into Hollywood, clearing the night air and scattering the purple petals from the jacaranda trees. The sounds on the street morphed into a wild and anxious murmur of things displaced.

Past two a.m., I still listened for the door of the motel room to open. Listened for muffled giggles and sarcastic insults, all in the name of fun and booze, to pour back into the room and breathe life into it.

The first voice I heard outside the door was Jade's.

"Why should I be quiet? She belongs in the girls' room."

"Oh, get over it. Rebecca likes to hang out with her," said Christopher.

I waited for Rebecca's voice but it did not come. Keys rattled in the lock. I shut my eyes and turned to the window feigning sleep in case they divulged any more secrets. Ricky entered behind them. They didn't mention Rebecca and she did not return. Things were shuffled. Zipped. Water ran. I felt exposed in the room with them. Rebecca had always stood up for me. Without her, I was an outsider in their world. When the breathing around me became even and heavy, I got out of bed and opened the motel door.

At the end of the long corridor, I could see the black night with stars clear and glistening. Palm trees and jacarandas could not be still, buffeted by the constant wind. The restlessness of the night reminded me of Ma, and how she and I could talk sometimes without talking. I wondered if I was thinking of her because she was thinking of me. Perhaps she had been trying to contact me while my mind was wrapped around Rebecca and the *pas de deux*. I had the strange notion I had somehow betrayed her and tried to open a connection to her in the night.

Somewhere on the boulevard the sound of rubber screeching, long and troubled, on pavement shattered the steady hum of the city. It was followed by a sickening thud of metal against something immobile. My heart began to beat. I imagined the beige paint and twisted metal, and Rebecca against the steering wheel. I ran to the end of the corridor but the east wing of the motel blocked my view. I changed my mind and ran back to Dudley's room and banged on the door.

"Now what on earth makes you think it was Rebecca's car?" Dudley asked, rubbing his eyes. "It could have been a million different people."

I paced Dudley's hotel room from one end of the double bed to the other. "I don't know how I know, but she didn't come back when everyone else did." I tried to quiet my panic, measuring my breath with footsteps: four to breathe in, four to breathe out.

"Rebecca is a big girl. If she wants to keep crazy hours it's none of our business." There was a bit of stress on the word our. "I suggest you get back to bed yourself and stop concerning yourself where you're not concerned. Understood?"

"Okay," I said. He walked to the door and ushered me back outside, closing it behind me with an exasperated "Good night."

The wind was cool, blowing jacaranda blossoms down the corridor and sweeping them into swirling eddies. A few magenta bougainvillea petals joined in, kicking up a psychedelic dust devil. I stood outside Dudley's door, listening to the L.A. traffic, low and steady. Nothing but a few pale horns interrupted the din. In a minute, she came walking down the path, one hand to the back of her neck, the other to her forehead.

"Rebecca!" I ran to close the distance between us. "What happened? Are you okay?"

"I'm fine, I'm fine. Just a little banged up." She swayed, smelling of smoke and gin.

"Where's your car?"

"Towed by now, I imagine."

"Is it bad? Where are they taking it? How will we get home?"

"Will you stop? It's not bad. It's just bent a bit. I'm tired. Can we go to bed? I'll deal with it in the morning."

Dudley's door opened. "Ah," he said through a five-inch crack, "The prodigal daughter has returned."

"I'm sorry I woke everyone up," she said. "I thought I could just slink into bed but I guess not, eh?" They both looked at me. I looked down.

Dudley sighed and rubbed his eyes. He looked exhausted. "Rehearsal begins at 8:00 tomorrow morning," he said. "I will accept no less than one hundred percent from each of you. If you're going to fool around until all hours of the night, I won't stop you. But I'll certainly ask anyone to leave who doesn't wish to be here. Dancers and staff alike. Now, if it's all right with you, I'm going to get some sleep." The door closed with a sharp echo down the hallway.

As we slipped off to the other room, she offered few details. The cops had arrived and let her go with a warning, though she'd clearly been drinking. She had refused a ride to the hospital, claiming only a headache and stiff neck, all the while bemoaning the price of towing charges from LA back to our town. She could charm any man into giving her her way.

It would be easy to say that Rebecca seduced me. I could be the victim. A blameless child led astray. But that would not be fair, for I could not leave her in peace. We got into the bed under the sidewalk window and whispered.

"Are you sure you're alright?"

"I'm fine," she sounded curt and tired. We rested our heads on the overstuffed motel pillows. She stared at the ceiling. "Tomorrow's your birthday, isn't it?"

"Yeah."

"About time."

"Yeah."

"Go to sleep."

"*Lovers* is mine tomorrow."

"I know."

"Will you be in the wings or the audience?"

"What difference does it make?"

"I want you to be in the audience."

"I'll try."

"Sit with Jade. I want to know what she says."

"I'll try."

Rebecca got up again and opened the window. Warm wind blew into the room sending the curtains flying.

"What are you doing?"

"I need a joint."

"Now?"

43

"I won't be able to relax after what happened tonight."

She went into the small dressing area and turned on the bathroom light. She fumbled in her make-up case and took out rolling paper and a plastic zip lock bag. I lay back and decided to let it go. I didn't like the idea of marijuana, though I hadn't tried it. Mother had said I would lose control and that frightened me. But I supposed it wasn't so different from the wine we drank at home.

Rebecca sat on the edge of the bed near the open window. A bright flame from her Bic leapt into the darkness, then soft embers glowed as she inhaled. She passed it to me out of habit.

"No, thanks."

"It'll help you sleep."

"I'll sleep." I knew I would not.

Rebecca inhaled again and leaned over to me. She covered my mouth with hers, coaxing my lips apart with her own, and blew the smoke in. A warm rush spread over my body as she pulled back and sat up, looking at me. The lights from the street made her expression just readable: she was tired, she was confused, and now she was stoned.

"I didn't want it," I told her.

"Don't let me do you any favors," she said.

"I'm going to sleep. That better not affect me tomorrow," I said. I stared out the window at the traffic lights flickering through the blowing branches of a palm tree. But I could only think of her lips. I couldn't move. Or breathe. She puffed on into the night and I don't know when she finally went to sleep.

* * *

Los Angeles sparkled as it did maybe once a year. At seven a.m. it was already warm. Around me, everyone slept. I looked at the phone on the bedside table, knowing I should call home. Not wanting to call home. I thought of the questions I might have to answer. *Where had I slept? How late had we been out? What do the dancers talk about?* A small crevice that had begun to crack open between my life as a dancer and my life as a daughter suddenly widened into a chasm. I looked over at Rebecca who slept soundly. I decided to claim the shower first and slip out.

Dudley was in the courtyard with coffee and a cigarette, studying choreography notes or lighting cues. I kissed his cheek and sat next to him on the plastic and metal patio bench. Aqua, again.

"Good morning, love," he said without looking up, "did you get any sleep at all?"

"Some."

"Feeling ready for tonight, then?"

"Absolutely." I was already thinking of the Westwood stage. The heat from the spotlights, their colors spilling onto the floor like gems. Christopher would become, for me, merely a prop. And yet in that eight minutes, I would love him in a way that was reserved only for a man who could lift me and hold me suspended. One who could launch me, as if I were a bird, into flight. The anticipation of the coming night overtook even the memory of smoke and lips pressed to mine.

"Best get to the theater," said Dudley, gathering his loose papers. "Shall I drive you with me and the girls in the van?"

I hesitated for a moment. Dudley read me perfectly and glanced disapprovingly at the motel room door. I couldn't let his thoughts progress.

"Yeah, I'll go with you. Let me get my bag."

His face softened. But I had the feeling a talk was coming on that drive to the theater. I opened the motel room door quietly and went in.

"Liese?" said Rebecca, still groggy. "Where are you going?"

"With Dudley, to the theater."

"Already? Can't you wait for me?" I wanted to.

"No, he wants me to come now. You guys should get up. He'll be royally pissed if you're late, especially this morning."

"Oh, all right, I'll wake them." I wanted to exit before she did. Before anyone stirred in the other bed where Ricky lay facing away from Christopher, their lower backs connected, their shoulders veering away in a V. Jade had been the one to bunch blankets on the floor, pillows shoved uncomfortably under her ribs, her hips. But she slept soundly as I carefully stepped over her.

"Come here first," Rebecca said quietly.

I dropped my heavy bag back to the floor and went to the bed under the window.

"What?"

"Last night—did it bother you?"

"No, not really."

"It bothered me." Her eyes relaxed into mine, hypnotic and pale, unblinking.

"Why?"

"I'll tell you some time."

"Tell me now." I wanted words to go with such undefined emotions. Her words.

"Not now. Go on with Dudley."

She reached for my hand and squeezed it. But I did not turn and head for the door. Not yet. Even with tired eyes and old blotchy mascara she was bewitching. I could have stared at her for an hour.

"Don't look at me like that."

"Like what?"

"Do you expect me to believe you don't know what you're doing?"

"Rebecca, tell me what I'm doing."

"You stand there with your hair in your face, your—fuck-me eyes, and you're..."

She hesitated. I stared at her, enjoying the effect I was having on her.

"...You're sixteen today."

"I am," I said happily, though it hadn't been my first thought that morning. Perhaps my second. "Does that make you feel better?"

"A little," she laughed. "Listen, don't make more of this than it is."

I could feel a small fountain of pain beginning in my ribcage. To be told not to feel something I was feeling. I narrowed my eyes and took my hand back.

"Not at all," I said, flatly, and went out the door.

I could feel my steps falling heavier than usual down the corridor. I found Dudley in the parking lot. He opened the passenger door of the company van for me and I flopped inside, staring forward. The *corps de ballet* girls came quickly across the parking lot, full of energy and purpose, and climbed in through the sliding door chattering like chickadees.

"Well then," he said, with a sideways glance to me. "Off we go."

* * *

The ring on the other end of the phone sounded hollow and distant. I wished it would ring on and on, unheard on the other end, in that other life, back home.

"Hello?" Mother sounded breathless. A bit panicked.

"It's me."

"Couldn't you have called sooner? Are you still in Hollywood?" She was angry.

"Of course. You knew I'd be here 'til Saturday night."

My confidence seemed to defuse her. "Ok. But I thought you would have at least called last night."

"I'm sorry."

"Where are you calling from?"

"The Westwood Theater."

"Who drove you there?"

Such an insignificant question. If she even knew where to begin her questioning, she could have gone on for quite a while. I was relieved to tell the truth. And the truth calmed her.

"Dudley did."

"Is he there with you now?"

"Of course. Do you want to talk to him?"

She was silent for a minute, as if threatening to call my bluff.

"No, I don't suppose I need to talk to him."

The truth, in fact, had made me cheerful.

"Well, happy birthday. I guess we'll celebrate when you get home."

"Okay. I'll be home late tonight, or maybe in the morning."

"Tonight."

"Okay, tonight."

"Anneliese..."

"Yes?"

"We had to take Ma to the hospital last night."

My breath caught. I had been thinking of her last night, just before the crash. Had she been trying to tell me something? Something I'd been too distracted to hear?

"Why?"

"Just some tests. She wasn't feeling right, she said. They're going to keep her overnight. Don't worry too much. Have a good show."

"Should I call there?"

"No, no, I'll be there this evening. I'll give her your love."

"Okay. I love you."

"Love you, too."

The dial tone left an empty chamber full of Ma and the lies I could have told if I'd had to.

* * *

I sat on the edge of the stage, dangling my feet into the orchestra pit, and stared into the empty red seats. They folded in on themselves along slanting aisles. Above, the lighting booth waited and heavy black doors at the edges stood like sentinels in the quiet.

Hollow footsteps crossed the stage behind me. I did not turn to see who they belonged to. I thought of Ma and traveled in my memory to her living room. I was eight years old, lying on her green shag carpet on a lazy afternoon, staring at the ceiling. Pop sat in his recliner with a thick tattered volume of Shelley poems, the one he won at church as a child for his recitations in Penzance. Ma sat on the green velour couch, crochet hook flying, while long delicate laces emerged from the ends. She had tried, once, to teach me but we had both become frustrated with my left-handedness.

"Someday, Leesie, you will have a baby," she said. "Your baby will never know me. But that baby will have a blanket and some booties and they will be from Ma."

"Why won't my baby know you?"

"Oh, I'll be long gone by then."

I had soaked those words into my bones, unable to touch the sadness that lingered over my heart. Lying on the floor, staring up, I had imagined my soul leaving my body. I watched it rise to her ceiling and penetrate the white popcorn coating. I imagined offering my soul to God. I let it go completely and felt void of all emotion. No soul inside me. Then, just to be safe, I watched it come back down and enter my chest. I still felt empty and wondered whether I had lost something on that journey. Something God still held. That was okay, I thought.

Ma talked about dying as if she didn't mind it a bit.

"I just want to see the old country again before I go," she told me once, "but Pop can't travel so I'll just have to wait 'til *he* goes." It was a matter-of-fact statement. She was not disturbed by death, and so neither was I.

I decided I would tell my baby all about Ma, if I ever had one. I would tell everything I could remember by then. I couldn't imagine a worse thing than to be a child and not have Ma to visit. To never hear her soprano voice over the phone when I called her. To never sit beside her with my arm linked under hers and feel her soft movements as she crocheted. To never eat her biscuits at the kitchen table while she showed me again how she could not draw. Or walk to the store alongside her, over the railroad tracks, while the mission bells rang, swift and small steps not hard to keep up with.

From his tilted black chair, Pop began to read aloud from Shelley. His voice was low and airy, his cadence like a metronome. He began without introduction or advice.

Like the ghost of a dear friend dead
Is Time long past.
A tone which is now forever fled,
A hope which is now forever past,
A love so sweet it could not last,
Was Time long past.
There were sweet dreams in the night
Of Time long past:
And, was it sadness or delight,
Each day a shadow onward cast.

He let the silence ride for a moment then looked at me. "Do you like Shelley, Leesie? That's what I just read to you." Ma's needles flew without interruption. "I used to know it all by heart," he said.

"It's pretty. Kind of sad," I told him, still staring at the ceiling.

"Does Mom ever read poetry to you?"

"She reads *A Child's Garden of Verses.*"

"Stevenson," he said. "Your Mom likes him."

"My dad likes Edgar Allen Poe," I told him. "He read about the Raven to Ingrid and me one night when Mother was out." I didn't tell him that we didn't like it. That it frightened us. That we felt he scared us on purpose.

"Maybe someday Leesie will write her own poetry," said Ma.

My eyes clouded and blurred at the memory, and I stared harder at the folded red seats hoping to find my way back to the theater and the promised reverie of the evening. Strong hands gripped my shoulders and I turned to see Christopher.

"Mind if I sit, Sweetie?"

"Hi, Christopher."

"Feeling ready?"

"Absolutely."

"We're going to be good together. Everything is tight." He was quiet for a moment, then continued, "You've got Rebecca a bit freaked out, you know."

How much had she told him? Did every detail escape those lips that landed on mine in the aqua room? And did she say to him, as she said to me, that I should not make more of this than it was?

"Freaked out how?"

"You know Ricky and I, we both want the same things," he continued. "We like to go out, we like to dance, we like to cook, we like to flirt, get high. We're just happy with each other."

He draped his arm across my shoulders.

"But Rebecca, she doesn't know what she wants. You think you know what you want, but you're too young to know that, really."

There was that blasted reference to my youth. I felt rebellious. I wanted to show Christopher and Ricky and Rebecca that I would live by the same rules they did. If not with them, then alone, or maybe not so alone. Then what would she think? Jealousy might go both ways. If I had disturbed her, as Christopher implied, how much more could she be disturbed?

"Thanks for the advice."

I continued my stare-fight with the empty theater. Tears blurred my eyes. They were the type that seep out of confusion and consternation. The type a child might try to hide, as she grew too old for the breakdown that was swelling just behind her heart.

"How about trying the *tour jeté* lift with me."

I blinked and looked away quickly to swipe my eyes with the back of my hand.

"I'm not warmed up," I said, making my voice as I-don't-care as possible.

"Nor am I. We won't kill each other."

He stood and offered me his hand, which I took, as he helped me to my feet and led me center stage.

Without music then, in the quiet, cavernous theater. We retreated from each other two of my body lengths, still facing. Our eyes came together in the space between. Fallen away were Rebecca and Ricky. Existing in the moment was the old black-boarded stage, the outstretched hand awaiting, the muscle behind it, the kinetic energy about to unleash from my stillness.

Like a slingshot I let go and covered space, my right hand to his right hand, my jump to his shoulder, assisted by a quick thrust, my hip bones landing just to the right of his neck, the bend of my back to the rafters to hold still, the solid grip at my waist, and then the twist to cover his body, a slow descent that melted us together, and the soft-tipped landing.

A single strong hand steadied my hip bone as I held my position until it was solid. He let go and left me atop the space of a silver dollar, unmoving for a moment, then replaced his grip to drag me off balance and flip me to face him, stage hand to my shoulder. *The Lovers.* I remembered Wesley in the studio, laughing about a gay man partnering me for such a romantic *pas de deux.* But it never matters; those who dance together are lovers.

Chapter 6

When we were younger, maybe 10 and 11, Ingrid and I were packed into the back of the beige Rambler with pesky little Katrine. We were on another long road trip and we were hot. But we were not at liberty to ask for things because we were ornamental after all, seen and not heard in the back seat. Side by side and thirsty, and perhaps desperately needing to use a bathroom, no matter the length of the trip, Ingrid and I would not have said so. Only Katrine would open her mouth now and then and ask for a gas station stop or a drink. But the disgusted and impatient wrath she received from our father kept Ingrid and me sure that we had been right to keep still.

On that hot day, we passed a bright yellow and red *McDonald's exit ahead* billboard. I looked at Ingrid. She was staring out the opposite window with the faraway look that sees only blur going by. We had been on the road nearly two hours and I could feel the sparkle of Coca-Cola on my tongue. If only I had the guts to ask for it. I didn't. Anything wet would do, really. I longed for it.

Hot desert wind blew back from my father's open window sending his sweet Captain Black pipe smoke with it. I wondered if Ingrid would be braver, but she had not noticed the sign. I focused on her mind perched next to mine and wondered if I could get inside it. I began to invade her with my thoughts, out through the open vent from which I felt my daydreams come. Through this portal, which opens just before sleep, sending me all manner of strange thoughts, I now sent pictures of Coca-

Cola to Ingrid and delicately recreated the sensations of wet and fizzy sweetness on my thirsty tongue to hers. It was really very quick and simple.

"Could we stop for a Coke?" Ingrid said, within seconds. She looked startled at her own words. Her expression said she wished she could retract them. I held my breath waiting for our father to yell. Wide-eyed, I wondered if she had really heard my thoughts, received my pictures. To our surprise, our father did not yell. Perhaps he was as shocked as I that she found the guts to ask. He sighed and consented. Ingrid looked at me and we exchanged a relieved smile.

Katrine, who was five, began to chime in.

"Me too, do I get a Coke, too?" she asked frantically and loudly.

"Of course," said Mother.

Katrine bounced in her seat in anticipation. I leaned close to Ingrid.

"I told you to say it," I said quietly.

"What?"

"About the Coke. I was too scared to ask so I told you in my head to say it."

She looked at me but not skeptically. Although she was a practical girl, she too had grown up with Ma and was used to the stranger side of the family.

"You did?" she frowned. "Try it again."

"I don't know if I can," I said, "I think I have to want it really badly."

"Hmm."

"And I think you have to be sort of not thinking of anything like you were. Just staring out the window."

"What are you talking about?" asked Mother, turning around in her seat to see us.

I thought I had been quiet. I thought that Katrine's voice permeated everyone's ability to think as she chanted the McDonald's jingle. But mothers are like that. They can home in on the important details and break you out of hiding even when you think you've covered your trail. At least mine could.

"Nothing," I said.

"We're just talking about Coke and how we're thirsty," Ingrid said, rather quietly so as not to incite my father and redirect his attention from the coming exit. It wasn't a lie, entirely. Ingrid was not a fibber but Mother knew a tone of secrecy passed between sisters when she heard it, even if she hadn't made out the words. She let it go and turned back around.

Ingrid looked thoughtfully out the window again while Katrine continued her bouncing. Perhaps such small experiences, which continued throughout the following years, led to the reception at the front door when I came home from the studio on a summer evening. As soon as I opened the door Ingrid took my wrist and led me through the kitchen.

"You have to come," she said, her voice excited. "There's a baby hawk in the garage. We've been trying for hours to get him out but he won't go to the door. It's wide open but he just keeps banging himself at the window."

When we opened the pantry door that led to the garage I found my parents shooing a big brown and black spotted bird with a pillowcase toward the garage door. The frightened hawk only circled and perched in the rafters. Long static dust particles floated in the air interrupted by billowing pillowcases and beating wings. The harsh evening sun coming sideways through the dirty window illuminated the dust into sunbeams. The hawk peered down furiously.

"Do something," Ingrid said to me.

Though I knew what she was asking, we would not have discussed it. My father looked at me with raised eyebrows but even he did not ask questions.

"Well," he said, "she always has been a little witchy." It was not an unkind sentiment. More of a go-figure comment. Something he didn't quite want to understand. He went into the house, letting the door slam.

"You want to try?" said Mother, "We haven't had any luck."

"Yeah," I said, "I'll try."

I conjured the tingle that travelled over my skin like electricity. This was something I was good for here at home. An identity that had begun to form when I was little. When I would say to my mother, "Was that the phone?" and it would ring then. But it hadn't rung before, my mother was sure of it. She would knit her brow and answer it. Or Ingrid and I would sit on her bed and I would startle because a poster had fallen from her wall. Only it hadn't yet. I would look around behind me and ask her what fell. Then it would let go. None of us ever imagined I had caused the things to happen. Only felt them a split second early. What else it might mean we could only guess.

"It runs in the family," my mother had said sharply when I asked her about it, "it's not special." After that I let the subject drop. It seemed to make her nervous.

Mother followed my father into the house, leaving me to the trapped hawk. She didn't let the door slam. Ingrid remained quietly near the door. I sat down on the dirty floor and began to occupy the front of my brain, to keep the portal open. From there, I would try to find the hawk's portal and send it pictures the way I had sent Coke images to Ingrid years ago but I was not at all sure it would work the same way. After a few seconds I became aware of Ingrid watching.

"I think you have to go, too," I told her, "or I won't be able to do it."

She slipped into the house. I began to count in my head. Then I switched to ABC's and felt the channel begin to relax and open up. I stole a quick glance at the bird while keeping my mind relaxed in back, occupied in front, running always numbers, letters and feeling like a tightrope walker with a balancing stick.

I hadn't intended to make eye contact and looked away quickly. Wild and frightened, it blinked. I closed my eyes and began to send it pictures. First, an image of the open garage door. Then the rafter on which the little hawk perched. And finally, I sent a picture of the hawk itself, turning and leaving its perch, flying through the open door. It needed details. And simplicity.

That quickly, I heard the rustle of wings and opened my eyes just in time to see him fly out the door. He landed on a street light across the road. I watched him for a minute then pulled the garage door down to keep him from repeating his mistake. When I went into the house through the garage, my family had returned to dinner preparations in the kitchen.

"He's out," I said casually, still feeling the tingle all over and my heart beating quickly.

"Must have been after a mouse in there," said my father.

Chapter 7

Sixteen is a lovely year for tears. They don't mean enough to send you tumbling over the edge. Just enough to explore the edges of tolerance. Just enough to understand that love can take us spinning if we are not careful and lose control. At sixteen, I gave tears to a woman who was still darning the last hem into the tulle of my skirt.

Her hands moved in and out and she was careful not to look at me, her eyes never leaving the needle, which she worked as if it were the only worthy purpose. A heavy door clunked closed towards the back of the theater. A thin man of maybe fifty with red wavy hair, a little too long for his age, stood looking at the stage, arms folded across his chest.

Rebecca and I glanced from where we stood on stage but he did not speak so we returned to our alterations. Dudley came from backstage and hailed the man.

"Good morning, Étienne. I thought you might not make it today." Dudley's voice reached to the back of the theater. He sounded stiff and formal. Could it be that this man intimidated Dudley? I couldn't imagine Dudley lowering his stiff chin for anyone.

"Wouldn't miss seeing a new generation of your dancers, sir," the man said, casually.

Dudley hurried down the steps and up the ramp to meet him. I did not like that the man wouldn't move to meet him halfway. It seemed to me courtesy would have dictated that he do more than stand there and let the older man come to him. Now I looked down at Rebecca and she exchanged a disapproving glance with me.

The man's jeans were overly tight and dark washed. His spotless white T-shirt fit him snugly and his hair was sprayed into a shape that must have taken someone an hour to perfect. He and Dudley talked as they walked down the ramp and up the stage steps. The man called Étienne stopped in front of me and watched as Dudley spoke to him of our run at the Westwood.

Étienne didn't speak, only regarded me as if I stood there for his enjoyment. His eyes wandered up and down my body as he listened, never looking at Dudley for a second. Rebecca watched him suspiciously. I felt like a specimen. He made my skin crawl.

"And who is this one?" Étienne asked when Dudley's update wound down.

"This is my Anneliese. She will dance the *pas de deux* with Christopher tonight. She's quite easy to watch," Dudley offered. He sounded proud but reserved. Perhaps protective.

"I can see that."

Dudley looked momentarily uncomfortable and added, "...On the stage. Let me introduce you to Christopher," he said quickly and led him backstage as if trying to avoid any further words from the man. They disappeared with a clump of wooden footsteps.

"There's someone you might want to stay away from," said Rebecca. The first words she'd spoken to me since she'd come into the theater that morning. I was still feeling raw.

"If I didn't?" I said.

"You'd be an idiot, now turn a little more to your right."

I shuffled. And thought. Rebecca hadn't liked the man's attention falling on me. Was she used to having the attention herself? Or was there something else?

"You keep your mind on tonight," she said, pulling an authoritative tone with me that she felt accompanied her years.

* * *

57

As the theater lights fell that night, I was not feeling shivers of anticipation. Instead, I was something wild on the prowl. I lurked in the wings taking in the music of the prelude. There was time. Many long minutes of choreography would move about the stage before my entrance. At the gentle crescendo, the heavy curtains parted and bright washes of hot light fell on the dark stage and upon a chorus of lanky young ballerinas in white tulle. Small crystals glued to their foreheads caught the light now and then, giving the audience a wonderful, fiery effect.

It was strange how the sweat, shuffle, slump, sometimes even disgrace of studio class and tearful rehearsals could result in something so delicately flawless and graceful. I thought of how the audience saw them there as if it were all so natural. For instance, they couldn't know that Theresa was anorexic, or that Bridget sprained her toe last night and had sworn like a construction worker for a half-hour. How about the fight between the two who had not been chosen for the featured duet? An ugly scene to be sure. How would people, cloistered safely in theater seats, see them if they knew the girls behind the dance? What if they knew me? I preferred the anonymity of the stage.

"So, you are Anneliese," whispered Étienne, appearing behind me and standing too close.

"I am. Who are you?"

"Who am I? Dudley didn't tell you?" He was incredulous.

"No, he didn't." I tried my best to sound disinterested.

"I own the *Triple O* salon in Westwood. I'm sure you've seen my commercials on TV? The magazine ads?" He was far too pleased with himself.

"No." I lied. He did not react.

"Dudley and I are old friends. He promised to lend me a few ballerinas for a commercial I'm filming for my salon. I'll pay him well and it will give your company the boost I hear that it needs." He winked.

I wondered what he held over Dudley's head. Or was it really just the promise of money, always in short supply.

"Well, there you have them on stage," I told him, "Ballerinas. Theresa has lovely hair. And Bridget is an accomplished dancer."

"I was thinking more along the lines of... you. What does your hair look like when it's down?"

"It's long."

His eyes began to travel again. I turned my back to him and watched the *corps de ballet*. Jade and Dudley appeared at the headphones, communicating with the lighting booth across the stage. I excused myself to talk with them, skittering quickly and quietly behind the backdrop curtain.

"Jade, why aren't you in the audience?" I knew I sounded childish. "I thought you would be watching tonight. Rebecca saved you a seat!"

"Too much to do here," she said, handing a headset to Dudley. She scurried backstage. I was disappointed. I wanted her to see it front-and-center to prove to her that she had perfected this piece on me. I wanted to give it back to her now, ten weeks from the day she handed it to me. I ran after her.

"Jade!" She turned, looking stressed out.

"What?"

"Would you please go to the audience for the *pas de deux*? I want you to see it." She softened.

"I'll try. I know you can do it. It's going to be fine."

I wanted to tell her it would be more than fine. She hurried off and I returned to the wings with my heart beating a little faster. I didn't often use such a familiar tone with her. Or ever a pleading one. But why wonder about that? I'd been peeled open that morning. I had not replaced the usual thick skin we all wrapped around ourselves at the studio; the skin that could rebound from insult, humiliation, fatigue and failure. I returned to my wing, no longer a wild thing.

"You'll never guess who's in the audience." Rebecca was there in the dark.

"Bec, go and sit out there!" I'd had it with everyone not sitting where I wanted them to. I might have stamped my feet.

"Will you relax? I'm going at the intermission. I had to tell you."

"Alright, who?"

"It's your dad." I froze.

"Are you sure? They weren't going to come all the way here. They saw the *pas de deux* back at the studio performance."

"He said he wanted to see it again and he was close to town anyway."

"You talked to him? He recognized you?"

"He did."

I couldn't imagine the two of them conversing. I liked my two lives separate.

"What else did he say?" I really couldn't imagine him here, tonight, when I was Anneliese-the-ballerina. Not Anneliese, Victor's daughter, quiet and reserved. Seen and not heard. Speaking when spoken to. I felt slightly invaded. But I relaxed. At least he wanted to come. At least he was sitting.

Chapter 8

No longer a dancer on the stage, I was Christopher's lover for eight whole minutes, and he was mine. Entering from opposite wings our eyes had already become, for each other, someone else's eyes. We stirred in the dim stage wings waiting for the violins. Upon our cue, I met this lover with hesitant steps that found ground and stillness for a moment, and then attacked. I bent to his strength with the solid lines that took shape in my body. I felt the distress of lost love in his ribcage. He sucked the last longing breath from my lungs. Our bodies struck, rebounded, salvaged and completed. His fingers trailed where and when they should trail and my glance fell along the range of my shoulder, wrist and beyond. We knew no one, and nothing else. Not exhibition. Not drama. We were within.

Whoever sat, or did not sit, before me was of no consequence yet. When the applause began, Christopher held my eyes a moment longer, not yet ready to relinquish this depth of enchantment. The energy between us held me rapt as they clapped. A tear fell down his face and so I saved him then. I smiled and turned him to the audience, slipping into acknowledgment. I could see the slight incline he allowed his head. Not his usual arm-in-the-air flair with deep accompanying bow, but instead, just this: his head, chin to chest. Applause continued a few seconds more. Heaven. Christopher. Me.

We stood. Roses came. I handed him the customary single bud with a slide to my knee, eyes downcast in his direction. His hand presented beneath my chin where I placed my fingers as he slid me back to life, and we backed away, backed away, turned and ran upstage.

In the wings I threw my arms around his neck and hugged him. He was Christopher again. The spell fell away. But not the magic. Dudley greeted us at the edge of the wing with the word, "Exquisite." I could not remember, ever before, happiness such as that.

Then I thought of my father in the audience. Embarrassed that he witnessed me in such a state, I hoped he had seen the ballet on the stage. Only the ballet and nothing more. I didn't want questions. Within moments, I would not be allowed space. Within hours, I would not be allowed freedom. Something like panic began low in my stomach and I tried to push it away so as not to muddle the effect of the dance. Christopher kissed my cheek and turned to Ricky, who stood patiently to the side until he was needed. And he was needed. Christopher was right, this morning, when he told me how he and Ricky belonged together. I smiled and left them alone.

In the dressing room I began to gather makeup, shed clothing, and pointe shoes. I felt Rebecca's presence before she said a word. Before I saw her approach in the mirror. I turned into her arms and she wrapped me tightly for an instant, let her lips graze mine, and stepped back. Her face was pained.

"Sit," she said.

She turned me before the dressing mirror and pushed me into a chair. She began to pull pins from my tightly woven hair, her fingers working like a mechanic in a garage. Her face, which I watched in the mirror, held business. She unwound the tight, slicked knot, brushed out glitter and gel and let my hair fall around my shoulders.

"Someday," she said, "some guy's gonna give his two front teeth for you."

"I don't want some guy," I told her.

"What's wrong with men? I love men," she said. Now her fingers pulled through my hair and lay about my collarbones.

I knew about men. Men tried to control. My father was one. And I also knew about men who were like cats. All you had to do was wiggle something pretty in front of them and they followed and pounced with a wild and empty look in their eyes. They groped until they caught and held you. Then you realized you were the only one present with a thought in your head.

"Have you ever been with a man?" she asked.

"Sort of."

"You've kissed one, then, right?"

"Yeah."

"But nothing else."

"Not *nothing* else. Can we talk about this later? My dad's going to come in any second and I won't even be able to say goodbye the way..."

"The way..."

"The way I want to."

"How's that?"

I looked down. She gathered my hair again and let it fall down my back. There was a knock on the open door and my father poked his head around.

"Everyone decent?" he asked. I looked up suddenly and Rebecca backed away.

"Hi, Daddy. I'll meet you in the hallway in five minutes," I said, forcing cheer into my voice. He disappeared down the hall and I pushed the door closed.

"I need your costume," Rebecca said, for she was in charge of such things.

She began releasing hooks and eyes down the back of the tight satin bodice. It felt good to breathe. I threw on black warm-ups, peeled the tights off my toes and folded them up to my ankles so I could slide into sandals, exposing mangled, discolored skin, thick calluses and protruding veins. I was not embarrassed by my feet. They were my trophies. Evidence. Tattoos of pain and hard work.

Robbed of the minutes I would have used to say what I wanted, I picked up my dance bag, flowers, and turned to go.

"You don't understand," Rebecca said, as I left the room. I stopped and looked at her.

"Then make me understand." I took a step back into the room as she took one toward me. Suddenly face to face, she took two handfuls of my hair pulling them forward over my shoulders.

"You don't know what it means to me," she continued, "just to brush your hair."

It was what I needed to hear. Something like pain presented in my throat. I couldn't speak, but anyway, there was nothing to say. I only looked at her eyes where some vague realization was completing itself. I knew, then, I could bear the long drive home in my father's car.

* * *

"I talked to a man in the hallway," my father said as he lit his pipe and steered the car with his knee. We drove sensibly down the 405 freeway in his big silver Mercedes sedan. It was late and the adrenaline of the night had drained from me.

"What man?"

"His name was something French. Real smooth looking guy. Wants to use you in a magazine ad or something. You know anything about that?"

"Not really," I said.

"Now, I don't really like this guy," my father continued, "but it might not be bad experience and I hear he'll pay Dudley pretty well for the use of some dancers."

That was the part that kept bothering me, besides the obvious slime that was Étienne. I was part of a deal Dudley was making and I hadn't exactly been consulted. On the other hand, Rebecca wanted me to stay away from Étienne. That made it interesting.

"Do you want to do the ad?" my father asked.

"I don't know. Maybe."

"Well, what I want you to know is this: I don't want you to be alone with him. Wherever he says you need to be to do the shoot, you don't go there alone. You take one of your buddies with you."

"I will."

"Dudley's a nice old guy but I don't know if he thinks about these things the way a father would."

"He does," I said. What I meant was, I always thought he did. But now I wasn't so sure.

Along the quiet highway, my eyes growing heavy, I replayed the words Rebecca had spoken. Had I understood? Was this what it was like to be in love? To wrap the mind about another, unable to be anywhere else? But perhaps it was only the power that she had just given me: the power to affect her, a woman ten years my senior, who inhabited the adult world I coveted. I wondered about her men. Like flies buzzing around her while she laughed, too loudly, I thought. Men touched her as they wished and she allowed all of it, was happy to be the object of their desire. I didn't quite relate to her response. I flirted only to be sure I could have them if I wanted them. I didn't.

What I wanted, what I thought perhaps I had, was someone who would experience each moment as I did. Someone who knew what it felt like to be a woman in love to the soul, not simply to experience physical desire. After all, my mother had told me long ago that sex without love was meaningless. I could tell she was right as soon as I began to have an effect on the opposite sex. How was it that I had the effect so young? Perhaps they found my adolescence bewitching. That would excuse those who had flirted and found reasons to be close.

All the way home I worked on one question: how could I be with Rebecca? Living at home, I was kept young among the sisters of the house. But when there was a party, when wine was poured, Ingrid and I moved among the adults who soon forgot that children were present. Handed glasses of cabernet or white zinfandel, we were happy and laughing, bewitched by loud music and the presence, in our house, of strangers. From those nights had come my first taste of freedom, my first reasons to leave childhood behind as something to be packed away and forgotten. I wanted to forget. And I wanted Rebecca to forget. I wondered if Ingrid was busy sweeping away her childhood. I thought she probably was.

"Why did you decide to drive up to see the show tonight?" I asked my father. He puffed on his pipe, smoke threading through his black mustache.

"I had to be in the city. I wanted to see it again," he explained, a bit defensively, I thought. But perhaps it had more to do with wanting to witness the crowd with which I was keeping company. Had Mother sent him, not quite comfortable with our quick phone call? Perhaps it was purely an impulse. Somewhere deep inside me, there was a child who liked to be protected. Much louder and more present was a girl who wanted to live her own life.

"You know I prefer the classical dance," he said, changing the subject, "much more than that modern stuff you do sometimes."

Ever the German, I thought. Ever the purist. But I secretly agreed. Another small and interrupting fountain of pain: "Is Mother with Ma tonight, at the hospital?"

His tone changed and his brow sank low. "Yes. Your mother is with her. You can see her tomorrow."

I didn't like his tone but I didn't want to hear more just now.

"I think Ingrid's wishing you'd spend a little more time around the house these days. She has to take care of Katrine a lot while you're gone and Mother's at the hospital. It's not really fair."

"I know. We're done with shows for a while."

In my head I was counting the hours until I returned to the studio. I couldn't talk to Rebecca until then. But I had words for her. I would have to save them up. I would buy a notebook.

"And what about the hair salon guy? Is he going to call you?"

"I really don't know, Daddy." I'd have to consult with Dudley on that. By the time we pulled into the driveway I could barely drag my bag from the back seat and fall through the front door.

"Goodnight. Thanks for coming," I said to him.

I passed Ingrid's room and looked in. She slept soundly, surrounded by posters of Rod Stewart, John Travolta, Don Johnson. Neil Diamond was plastered to her ceiling in black and white and looked down at her in her white curtained bed. I smiled.

* * *

In my own bed, in the dark, my mind wandered to long ago days when life's complications were not of our making. I thought of Ingrid, her academic ambitions, her rock and roll star fantasies. Through the years we had grown up on this street while the months swirled by and the seasons changed, and our hearts changed as well. In my mind I traced the edges of our neighborhood and mapped the changes in our town. The far off baaahs from the sheep in the hills had been replaced by the steady sound of traffic. The memory of one long-ago summer floated down Sycamore Drive and as I fell asleep, I conjured every detail...

Ingrid's long hair flew in the warm Santa Ana wind and her sandaled feet whirled the pedals of her new two-wheel bike in big, smooth circles. She wore a brilliant pinafore, aqua with red ladybugs, made by Ma with needle and thread. For every revolution of her feet, mine made six to keep up, dipping clumsily into driveway channels as she soared over them. We steered to the edge to avoid the hibiscus bushes overtaking the sidewalk. I watched her bike sliding gracefully between the encroaching flowers and the precipice of the curb.

"Maybe I should go get my big bike," I called from my green tricycle behind her.

"Maybe you should!" she yelled back, the hint of triumph in her voice not lost on me.

On the other side of the street a boy whizzed by on a skateboard, propelled by a big brown dog at the end of a leash. I frowned and looked away, embarrassed at having been seen. Then, Ingrid went down. Her shrill scream raked my spine. In the road, the front wheel of her bike still spun as she shook her head violently, smacking at her hair with her palms.

"It's caught!" she screamed. "It can't get it out!"

I abandoned my tricycle and ran to where she knelt in the street. Pebbled black tar made indents in her knees and mixed with the blood from her torn skin. She clutched at her hair while an insistent buzzing swam around her head.

"I hear it, but I don't see it," I told her, circling the wreckage.

She got up, sobbing, ignoring her bloody knees, and darted back to our house. I ran after her. She was still screaming when we burst through the kitchen door. My father was dressed in his yellow garage suit, scrubbing grease from his hands at the sink.

"It's tangled!" she screamed. Believing something was down her back, my father turned and grabbed the neck of her pinafore, splitting it down the seam with one strong chop of his hand. The buzz persisted.

"No, no! In my hair!" she whined. She loved her ladybug pinafore.

By now the bumblebee had stung her face. My father's frantic swatting finally ended its tour of terror and Ingrid stood gasping while he inspected the fuzzy black and yellow bee.

"I didn't bother it," she whimpered, "I was just riding." She wiped her eyes with the back of her hand, but more tears came.

"It must have been attracted to your dress," he told her. He got some ice out of the freezer, wrapped it in a paper towel, and handed it to her.

"Hold this on the sting," he said. "Bumblebees don't leave stingers behind. The swelling will go down soon."

"Our bikes are still out there," I said.

My father left through the garage door to retrieve them while Ingrid and I calmed down.

"Does it hurt?"

"A little."

She was frowning and swallowing something over and over.

"What's in your mouth?"

"My tongue is big." She stuck it out. "And...." Panic began to rise in her eyes again, "I can't breathe right." She sucked at the air. A bright red glow spread over her cheeks and her eyes seemed to disappear in her face. My father came back through the garage door, wiping his hands on a shop rag.

"How does it f—" he stopped and went to her, lifting her onto a counter stool. "Open your eyes," he commanded.

"I can't," she whispered.

"Gwendolyn!" he called, then turned to me, "get your mother, she's in the yard."

I ran out the back door and found Mother surrounded by small purple flowers in little black plastic trays. She hacked at the hard clay with a spade under the mulberry tree.

"Ingrid was stung by a bee," I called to her, "she's all puffy!" Mother dropped her shovel and followed me into the house. In the kitchen she took one look at Ingrid and went to the phone.

"I'll drive her myself," my father said, gathering Ingrid up in his arms. Her head lolled, and she righted it enough to tilt it onto his shoulder. Mother grabbed my hand and we followed out the door.

Late that night we lay in our single beds in the room we shared at the end of the hall. We were propped on our elbows whispering in the dark like it was any other night.

"What did they do at the hospital?"

"They gave me a shot in my leg."

"Did it hurt?"

"I don't remember. Not really." She held her shaggy stuffed dog, Precious, under one arm. I searched for my purple rabbit under the covers, found him, and collapsed on my pillow.

"I can't get stung again, though," she said, "or it will be worse."

"Why will it be worse? What will happen?"

"I don't know. But the doctor said I could die from bee stings because I'm allergic."

I had been stung once. It was on Easter the year before. I had picked up a pink and blue egg in the tall, dewy grass, disturbing the honeybee who thought it was a flower. The sting hurt a lot and itched for a while but then was gone.

"Are you scared?" I asked.

"Not really," she said.

She hugged Precious and sandwiched him between her head and the pillow. I put my head down, too, and closed my eyes, scared for her.

Chapter 9

It was summer now and we did not rush off to school together as we'd done all year. I went to Ingrid's room, pushed aside the white, filmy curtains surrounding her bed and jumped in. She rolled the other way.

"Wake up!"

"It's summer. Go back to bed," she groaned, half asleep.

"Come on, Ingie, get up!" I suddenly felt as if I hadn't seen her in ages, my original playmate, my scholastic cheerleader. I wanted her to wake up so we could gossip and giggle like we had before I had become so embedded in my other world. She groaned and stirred.

"Oh, you're back," she said, finding consciousness. "Ma is in the hospital."

"I know. We should go today." Ingrid had her driver's license and Daddy's old car.

"Yeah, okay. But we have Katrine until Mother gets home. That is, actually, you have Katrine. I had to play with her yesterday. Three hours of Barbies."

"I know."

She sat up, swollen around the eyes, and stared out the window. She had probably been up until midnight, watching reruns of Clint Eastwood movies.

"What did you do last night?"

"Nothing. Watched TV after I put Katrine to bed." Yep.

"I'll make you some tea," I offered.

"That would be good."

When Mother came home, Ingrid and I were sipping tea while Katrine colored in her Barbie coloring book at the kitchen table. Mother's eyes were tired.

"You two can go ahead to the hospital," she said to Ingrid and me.

"Can't I come?" said Katrine.

Ingrid and I exchanged glances, preferring to have some time together to talk without fear of Katrine announcing everything we said to the world, namely our parents.

"Take her with you," Mother said.

"What have the doctors been saying?" Ingrid asked.

"They're still unsure. It will take a week or so to get tests back and then we'll see. They'll release her tonight. Daddy and I will pick her up and take her home to Pop."

* * *

Ingrid's spike-heeled shoes clicked down the hospital halls as we left Ma's room. We were quiet. Nothing scary had been told to us but somehow, we expected it might come. Ma's cheery mood had been a little unnerving. Like a secret.

"Can I sit in the front?" Katrine asked when we got back to the car.

"No," we both said.

Ingrid put on the radio. And turned it off again. She let out a heavy breath.

"What do you think?" she asked me.

"What does she think about what?" said Katrine from the back seat.

"Nothing," said Ingrid.

We got off the freeway near Doheny Beach and drove by the railroad tracks. The ocean lay flat and clear blue where it met the sand. A hundred white shorebirds stood still. The train rushed by, blocking our view with its noisy flicker.

I remembered trying to fall asleep one night in Ma's big double bed. I had heard the train whistle all night. I listened as long as I could to the rumbling deep down the tracks. And in the morning, the church bells from the San Juan Capistrano Mission would wake the finches in their bamboo house. They would flutter, beep-beeping about the perches, scratching and ringing the little bell above their swing. And soon after, I would hear Ma's voice admonishing Pop in a harsh whisper for something he had or hadn't done. Then bacon would fry. Biscuits would bake. I would wake up in the happiest place I knew.

At the hospital in San Clemente, Ma had seemed happy. I wondered if it had been only a show she put on for the sake of the children. Ingrid drove down the highway staring forward as if she didn't see the road. I felt the future coming in a way I had never experienced it before. Until I saw Ma in the hospital, tomorrows had always been exciting and promising. Now I had to wait a week to know if I could go back to visiting a small apartment in San Juan Capistrano with black and white finches and church bells and trains. And I was afraid of that week. I didn't want it to come.

A banner hung on the fence near the harbor announcing Crosby, Stills and Nash at a Doheny Anti-Nuclear rally on the weekend.

"Look at that, Ingrid," I said as we sailed past, "CSN at a nuclear rally."

"CSN here?" she said, sounding far away.

"Are you guys going to go to a concert?" asked Katrine.

"Maybe," I told her.

"Can I come?"

"Katrine, you're too young to go to a concert," Ingrid told her.

"You guys always treat me like a little kid," said Katrine. She folded her arms over her chest and pouted. We drove down Pacific Coast Highway, passed the harbor and the road that led to our high school, toward home.

"Maybe it's not that bad," Ingrid said, finally.

"Maybe," I said. "She didn't seem too sick. It's just weird. She's always been so healthy."

"Let's try not to worry before we have to."

"Is Ma going to die?" asked Katrine. Ingrid and I exchanged glances.

"Everyone dies sooner or later, Katrine," I told her. She was quiet. Ingrid gave me a sarcastic nice-going look. I shrugged back at her.

"Ma didn't look like she was going to die to me," Ingrid told her.

Back home, I disappeared into my room and closed the door. I found an old school notebook with some blank paper left inside. I couldn't think any more about Ma. I was beginning to confuse every pure emotion I had felt in the last two days with every new fear. Words that passed between Rebecca and me haunted my thoughts even in the hospital hallways.

I had to think about Rebecca. It wouldn't wait any longer. And I had to talk about Rebecca. But there was no one to tell. So, I wrote about her. I wrote for her. At an old dark wooden desk that squeaked from the pressure of my pen.

Words leaked from me like tears and sweat. I did not think or hesitate but poured onto paper as fast as they screamed in my head. Each letter on the page satisfied me. I formed them and scribed them. I loved the ink and the flow. Here was white that was silently bleeding black from under my pen. It was almost, I thought, like making love must be. The release was like that, or so I had heard.

There was a knock on my door. The interruption was intolerable. My dad poked his head in.

"What are you doing?"

"Writing," I said. I did not mask my annoyance.

"Excuse me!" he said, "Your mother needs you and Ingrid to make dinner and take care of Katrine while we pick up Ma. I think Ingrid's done her fair share these weeks, don't you?"

"Alright. Just a minute." I was definitely not done.

"Now," he said.

I knew better than to cross that tone. That night, Katrine crept into my room.

"Anneliese," she whispered. I wasn't sleeping either. "Does everyone really die sooner or later?" I was amazed that she had arrived at ten years of age without ever digesting this fact.

"Of course," I said. "It's just natural. You know, like birth."

"Can I sleep in here?" I scooted over in my single bed and she climbed in.

"Why do they die?"

"The body stops working I guess. Like an old clock or a car."

"Daddy always says if you take care of a car, it will run forever."

"Well, if you take care of your body it will run for a longer time. But I don't think he truly meant *forever* anyway. And then there's illness," I said, "Sickness. And then... some things just happen."

I thought of Ma sitting up in the hospital bed. I thought of her scurrying across the bridge and the railroad tracks and of everyone who knew her at the stores she visited. Katrine read my thoughts.

"Ma takes care of her body. She walks to the store every day."

"I know."

"Can it even happen to kids?" she asked.

I wished for the liberty to lie to her. But I decided she was too old for fairy tales.

"Even to kids," I said quietly. I could feel fear building in her.

"But not usually," I added, "it's very rare that serious sickness happens to kids."

In the darkness, her breath gasped now and then. I knew she was crying. I didn't have words for her. I waited until her breathing relaxed and she slept.

Later in Katrine's life, she would know a boy and she would love him. She would trail him at school and hope he would notice her. And one day she would have to visit him in the hospital, sick with leukemia. He would tell her that he did not believe in God and that she would have to let him go. Then he would go away from her, forever, but she would hold onto him for the rest of her life.

I crept out of bed to see if Mother and Daddy had come home. I found Mother at the kitchen table with a glass of scotch on ice. I heard my dad snoring from down the hall. Mother's eyes were red.

"Don't worry yet," I told her, sitting next to her and hoping Ingrid's advice would distract her.

"I know," she said, "I just don't know what I'd do without her." She put her head down on her arm and began to cry.

"I don't either," I told her. My own tears fell then, onto the table, dripping steadily. I covered her hands with mine.

"It might be fine," I said after a while. "A stomach ulcer maybe."

"I know. I have never given much thought to losing her. I've never lost anyone I loved." I hadn't either.

"Thank you for your help with Katrine," she said, muffled. "Has she been a pain?"

I suddenly felt very guilty.

"She's been pretty good, but it was mostly Ingrid. I've been away a lot."

"You have, actually. I've missed you. Ingrid's missed you, too."

I was torn. I couldn't wait until class, still two nights away. But I promised myself I would be there for Mother until then. That I would try not to think of the studio. That I would ride bikes with Katrine and stay up late with Ingrid. And I would go to see Ma in the morning.

"Why don't you go to bed now, Anneliese?"

"Are you going to go to bed?"

She reached across the table, picked up my father's corncob pipe, and looked at it for a while.

"Not quite yet," she said.

"You really should," I told her.

She put the end of the pipe in her teeth. She looked silly. I smiled.

"Have you ever smoked?" she asked me.

"Once or twice." It didn't seem at all necessary to lie. There were much bigger things at hand.

"Have you ever smoked?" I asked her.

"I tried it once when I was 19. I just coughed," she admitted.

"I didn't much like it either," I told her.

"You tried it at the studio, I imagine?"

It was the truth. But I knew it would further color her opinion of the studio and the company I was keeping.

"No," I lied then to protect my other life, "Hannah and I tried it once." My mother loved my childhood friend. I figured she was a safe alibi.

"Where did you get the cigarettes?"

"From a machine."

"Figures she would try something like that," said my mother, smiling and instantly forgiving both of us. "I'm glad you didn't like it."

"I'm glad you didn't like it either," I told her. I got up and hugged her and went to bed.

From my bedroom, I heard the door of the liquor cabinet open again. Liquid gurgled into her glass. That was a lot of scotch, I thought, having felt its effects once. But she needed it, I supposed.

* * *

Katrine was full of energy in the morning.

"Will you do something with me?" she asked.

I glanced to my desk. What I wanted to do was write. I thought of Mother last night, the pipe in her teeth.

"Okay, what?"

"Ride bikes?"

"Okay."

I hadn't meant to go all the way to San Juan, but once we were on Emerald Bay Parkway, we kept on going. The same railroad tracks that ran behind Ma's house reached into our town as well. We heaved our bikes over a chain link fence and skidded with them down a dirt embankment to the tracks. Alongside of them ran a cement wash where we peddled, unthinking, toward San Juan Capistrano. It was as if something pulled us along and we did not question it. I thought for a moment of what I had told Mother as I went out the front door. "I'm going to ride with Katrine," I had yelled, giving no time or destination. Sometimes, Katrine and I would be out for hours. I would call her from Ma's house.

The ride south to San Juan took us two hours. The day was warm and dusty. Katrine began to fade behind me.

"Come on, keep up!" I yelled to her.

"I'm trying but you're going too fast!" I slowed a bit until she rode beside me.

"We're almost to Ma's house, aren't we?" she said.

"We might as well go all the way there," I told her.

She smiled. Seeing Ma was just what Katrine needed. It was just what I needed.

Where the wash met the old part of San Juan, we crossed the rocks at its base and struggled up the other side. Another chain-link fence. We heaved our bikes again, climbed over and stood across the street looking at her front steps. Katrine hesitated. She was frowning.

"What's the matter?" I asked her.

"I'm afraid to go in."

"What do you think will happen?"

"Can someone catch what's wrong with her?"

"I don't think so, Katrine."

"I want you to be sure."

"Okay then, I'm sure. Come on."

We crossed the street and went up the steps leaving our bikes on the sidewalk below. We knocked lightly on the screen. The door was open to let in whatever summer breeze might blow through. The bees hummed over our heads in the red bottlebrushes. We peered through the screen.

Ma came from her bedroom a little more slowly, I thought, than usual.

"Oh!" She was startled and clearly angry with us. "I just spoke with your mother. She thinks you're out riding your bikes!"

"We were, Ma," I said, "they're down there!" I looked to the sidewalk. She opened the screen and ushered us inside.

"You get on the phone and call your mother, right now!" Katrine and I were disappointed with the reception.

"Who's there, Flos?" said Poppa, from the hall.

"It's the kids!" she yelled.

"I was going to call her as soon as we got here, Ma, we just got on our bikes and kept going and figured we'd come all the way."

"All by yourselves?" She was frenzied and I was feeling a little miffed at her.

"Ma, I'm sixteen years old. It's not that big a deal."

"Oh, I suppose. But I worry so about you all. Don't go doing that anymore. And call your mom."

I sighed audibly and picked up the phone. Even Ma wanted to keep me in childhood. I explained our ride to Mother who wasn't concerned.

"Katrine rode all that way?"

"She's fine."

"Thanks for entertaining her today. I didn't really have the energy. Sometimes she takes a lot out of you."

"I know," I laughed. "What's Ingrid doing?"

"Sleeping in."

"Okay. We'll be home before dark."

"Leave by 2:00, no later."

"We will."

"You see," I said to Ma, "not a big deal."

"I forget you're grown-up," she said. "I'm sorry."

Chapter 10

Ma knew that in the old country, you didn't always speak your mind. She knew that if you relied on God you could get your message across. And sometimes God would come to you in ways you didn't expect. Sometimes, mysteries were revealed in the natural and the unexpected. She taught me to look for God in the smallest places and in the faces of the old.

I had watched her gaze into her teacup waiting to discover answers to her questions. She never discussed what was revealed to her. But she always seemed satisfied. Sometimes I sat next to her quietly and felt the heat and peace that mingled and played about her. I felt her blood inside me, passed down through Mother. But Mother was not quite like us. Ma and I were not what people would call practical. We knew that there was more to life than logic and reason. We had been shown. I leaned against her at the kitchen table and let my eyes fall into the teacup. Little black and shiny leaves lay in a wet mound. But I did not have a question then.

Now I wondered what the leaves would say if I gave them Rebecca. I wondered what Ma would say, but I dared not ask. I would have to find my answers the way Ma did. Perhaps not leaves, but something else.

* * *

On a late summer night, Ingrid and I followed our school friends down the cliffs at Monarch Bay. The rope was cold, wet, and frayed in places. Waves splashed thirty feet below us. But when you're fifteen and free for a night, danger doesn't present quite the same way as when you are watching for it. I descended unthinking, bouncing off the rocks and red dirt that tumbled from beneath my bare feet and hit the sand soundlessly somewhere below.

Almost to the beach, I looked up and saw Ingrid's smiling face moon over the edge of the cliff. She yelled to me to hurry. I looked down and decided to drop the last five feet. I let go and puffed into the cold dry sand. Ingrid took the rope and swung her legs over the ice-plant edge of the cliff. A small group of boys and girls followed.

We were not at the beach to create mischief. We were not there to make noise or play loud music. We had blankets to sit on. We had talk and each other. And a little later, a simple beauty to remember forever.

Teachers were discussed. And chemistry homework. Perhaps a crush was admitted and a back rub given when the hour was late enough. I stared out at the steady waves of the Pacific. They were breaking small and even. Moonlight sparkled. It would be an hour or so before the grunion would run and we would stand among their silvery bodies and watch the frantic burrowing about our feet.

I left the blanket, where a boy sat with his back leaning against my sister's and walked to the edge of the water. Small waves left a foam edge a moment before disappearing. Like milk spilled on velvet. The moon was full. I sat back on the damp sand and began sculpting it into a creature, just out of the water's reach.

Thoughts of Rebecca seeped up on the tide. I made a deal with the sea. I dug a small trench around my sandy seahorse. If the waves fill the trench before the seahorse is complete, I will know that she loves me. I patiently sculpted the tail that curved tightly at the end like a nautilus. My brain was open somewhere in its most primitive territories. It was a place where thoughts were not created, where logic did not interrupt. It was a place where something from beyond flowed in to tell me things. It was the same place Ma's tea-leaf answers entered her heart.

Ignorant of psychology or physiology, I had discovered that if I entertained the front of my brain with nonsense and automatic responses, I could open up the part that could hear like Ma could hear. So, with my hands I made the seahorse. And with the open space that waited to fill with answers and with water, I listened from a deeper place. Expectations and knowledge of tides and rhythms had no place in the moment. The water filled the trench as I sifted pectoral fins onto the sea horse's reliefed side. And I was satisfied with that. The answer gave me peace. I stood up and brushed wet, sandy hands against my jeans.

Up on the beach, Ingrid sat unmoving. The lights from the parking lot, high above the shore, made a yellow glow in the fog that had begun to settle along the coast. The boy with Ingrid looked at his watch and whispered to her. I started back to the blanket to join them, aware of the cool sand giving trenches with my steps. It was the slow way you walk when you're dreaming and taking much longer than you should to reach your destination. But unlike such a frantic dream, I did not hurry.

"About fifteen minutes," said the boy. He stood and pulled Ingrid to her feet. She smiled at me. Others lounging on blankets took the cue and stood and we walked back to the waves. Jeans were rolled up to knees, sweatshirts were tied about waists. Hands were held. Or not. There was little talk as we waded out ten feet in the shallow, gentle waves. We stared into the lacy water. The Pacific was not shockingly cold, as it sometimes is, and we were quickly comfortable with the light splashes that reached our shins.

In the moonlight we saw them as the waves retreated, bounding with frenetic energy, stranded on the dark wet sand. Silvery fish scattered everywhere, whipping their bodies in a frenzy to burrow into holes and lay the eggs that would hide in the sand until the next high tide.

With each wave, the gasping grunion would ride the current back into the ocean and disappear. Another surge of water and another thousand sparkling bodies. Another wave and joy and happiness in the rivulets that surrounded our ankles.

That night I slept a dreamless and perfect sleep.

Chapter 11

With no one to drive me to class Thursday evening, I rode my silver and blue ten speed to the studio. I set out down the parkway, pumping up a long gradual hill and coasting down the other side. Rolling wheat-covered hills were dotted with purple thistles on either side of me. It was a difficult trek to make by bicycle but the allure of the destination pulled me onward easily as traffic zoomed by.

I would be an hour early for class but I would have time to sit in Dudley's office on the old brown sofa and talk to him while he shuffled class rosters or did the accounting. I would have time to go into the studio, alone, and take on whatever had eluded me in the previous class. I could add another rotation to my *pirouette*. I could jump higher, or achieve more *fouettés*, whipping continuously around, until there was no need to stop. And then of course I could casually walk through the adjoining door to Ricky's studio and from there, enter the sewing room where Rebecca would be at work on a costume or talking on the phone. All the way down the parkway I thought of that meeting. The first conversation since the night in Westwood. Would we talk about it? What if she pretended it never happened?

I had my notebook in my dance bag, which I had slung precariously over my shoulder. Every time I engaged the brakes on my bike it flung forward down to my wrist. I might have been annoyed at the indignation of having to ride my bike to class, but when, one by one, my usual ride possibilities begged off for more pressing engagements, I became immediately resourceful. There was no way in the world I would miss class. Couldn't remember it ever happening, actually. In the notebook were the words I had scribbled. Could I ever bring myself to show them to her? I imagined leaving the notebook on her desk and slipping out while she talked on the phone. I imagined her running to meet me in the parking lot, professing a similar inability to think of anyone or anything else. Though I would have preferred it, that was the least likely scenario. It was true what Christopher said: Rebecca didn't know what she wanted. I couldn't imagine her without her entourage of men and high-energy friends flitting in and out at all hours.

I rode into the industrial complex to the very back wing of buildings, then back further, to the parking lot, and leaned my bike against the chain link fence. Large windows surrounding the office of the studio didn't allow much discretion as I walked to the front door. My heart leapt into my throat when I saw Rebecca. I suddenly had no words and no explanation for what had passed between us despite what I had set to paper. She did not look up and I passed her office quickly and went to Dudley's desk.

"What on earth were you doing riding your bike down here? You might have been killed on the parkway," said Dudley. Well, so much for discretion.

"I didn't have a ride," I said. He removed small gold spectacles and looked at me.

"Well, why didn't you bloody call me? I would have picked you up and brought you back down; you live 5 minutes from here by car!"

"I didn't want to bother you, Dudley."

"If it ever happens again..."

"I'll give you a call."

I flopped on the beloved couch and inhaled the smoky atmosphere. Papers shuffled. No music lilted from the empty studios. It was strangely quiet before class. I was at peace and I was at home. Years of my childhood had passed in this space. In some ways it had become more home than my own house, my own family. It was a refuge I craved.

I could see into the front window of the sewing room from where I sat. I suppose I had been gazing for some time.

"You've been spending a lot of time with Rebecca lately," Dudley said, breaking the silence. I sat stone still.

"No more than usual."

"I think a little more than usual. You used to spend time with Hannah and Wesley and your friends here at the studio. Friends your age. What's got your attention? You aren't developing a taste for their marijuana, are you?" Is that what he thought went on in there?

"Of course not, Dudley, smoking makes me cough. And besides, you smoke."

"That's very different and you're changing the subject."

"Not that different."

"I wouldn't recommend you trying anything else they might offer you."

He did know. He wasn't blind after all. I looked at the black and white photographs on the wall of Dudley's younger days in the theater. There he was partnering a girl in a white gown, and there he was in a close-up monochrome headshot, perhaps a man of 25. He was handsome, angular. Not round, as now. The pictures reminded me of Étienne.

"Dudley?"

"Hmm?" His pen scratched at paper in front of him on the desk.

"Who is that Étienne guy, anyway?"

"Well, he is a very old friend, I suppose."

"And he's going to pay you to use us in his ads?"

"Well he's not going to pay me, you see, dear, he's going to donate money to the company. So, we can keep up our performances at places like the Westwood. I did so enjoy staging our company at the Westwood!"

"It was wonderful. But..."

"You do want to be involved, don't you?"

"I've never done an ad before."

"He'd like to use you."

"He told me."

Dudley looked a little concerned. "When did he tell you?"

"Backstage."

"I asked him to let me do the arranging." Dudley's eyebrows knitted together.

"Who else will be in it?" I asked.

"Well, he wants to shoot a commercial. But he wants you for print work. Magazine ads."

"Why me?"

"Your hair, I would imagine." My hair was long and thick and almost black.

"He'll be by this evening to work out details with me while you're in class. If you'd rather not be involved, tell me now and I'll arrange for someone else..."

"No, I'll do it."

"Good. It will make him happy. And don't worry. He's harmless, really." Dudley didn't sound sure.

Through the window I could see Rebecca had hung up the phone. I walked into the studio and sat to put on my pointe shoes. I had decided on black tonight. For my fourteenth birthday, Hannah's family had bought two pairs of pointe shoes for me, an extravagant gift. One pair was dyed a beautiful, deep purple and the other, crimson red. I also had several pairs in traditional pink, but the black ones were my favorites. I wound thick ribbons around my ankles and tested the hard pointe against the wooden floor. A bit slippery. I dipped the tips in the pile of sticky, white resin Jade had dumped on the floor by the door. It squeaked momentarily and then I attacked it moving tip to tip and stepped into a *pirouette*. A tight spot on the mirror, I whipped around once, twice, rolled out. Happy with that, I went on through the door to the sewing room.

Rebecca looked up from the tissue costume pattern she was laying out on the floor. She said nothing at first. Nor did I. I waited for the effect of eyes upon eyes to finish a long exchange of questions and fears and regrets and wishes. She swallowed.

"What's happening to us?" I said finally. She sighed and looked down.

"You know this can't happen, Liese. You're sixteen years old. You have no idea what I've been through this weekend."

"Yes, Bec, I do. Do you think I haven't been through it, too?" Another exhale that fluttered the patterns on the floor.

"I talked to Christopher a lot about it this weekend. I hope you don't mind."

"Of course not, I love Christopher."

"He was telling me... he reminded me that you don't even know about men. How can you choose until you've had both?"

"Oh, come on, Bec, do you seriously think Christopher has had both?"

"Good point. But you're not Christopher. You're just a kid." I cringed.

"You should be dating boys and going to movies with your friends. I told you in LA and I meant it, some guy is gonna be so happy to have you. Don't get involved like this."

I felt a storm brewing in my ribs.

"Look at me, Anneliese. I have a business here. Dudley depends on me. I can't even think when you walk in the room."

I wasn't the only one, then, who couldn't think. That was the phrase I chose to hold onto.

"And you know what else?"

"What."

"I'm not a lesbian."

"Why do you have to put a title on it? Why can't we just be... people who care for each other more than friends."

"Because it seems like an unnecessarily difficult life. And if you put your age on top of that... really, what am I going to do? Call your house and have your mom or your dad answer?"

I had no response to that. I knew that suspicion around my house would grow if Rebecca began to call. I knew that it wouldn't be a welcome worry especially now with Ma's illness. But I didn't see how I could walk out of that room and pretend nothing but a simple, casual friendship had passed between us.

"So, we walk away from each other?"

"I'll always be here. We'll always be friends."

There was so much left undone. I felt a frantic ending coming before the beginning was over. Doors were slamming in my mind. I thought of the notebook.

"I wrote to you," I told her.

She looked pained. As if she wished I would stop rubbing salt in an open wound. She put her face in her hands.

"Do you want me to read it?" she asked. "Or were you just getting stuff off your chest?"

"I don't know. No, it's not like that."

"Well, you can leave it for me if you want."

I knew the words on that page by heart. I chanted them as I ripped the page from the notebook in the other room. They replayed as I put the ripped page on the desk behind her. And again, as I left the room without looking at her and got to the barre just as Jade began the music for class.

Jade was a regular gestapo that day. Gone was the woman inhaling lines from the floor of Rebecca's office. Even Christopher was not immune once he passed the studio door. She drove us and we did our best to respond. Our eyes were wide with dedication, excitement, pain, frustration. Protons bounced from every soul and skittered about in the air between us. I could have held Bridget's frustration in my hands, I could have painted a picture of Christopher's elation as he completed the highest *grand jeté* I had ever seen him jump. Jade gave just enough praise. She never let us feel as if we had truly achieved anything. What she sought was always just beyond our reach.

The *révérence* came at the end of every class. The music just following the grand allegro would change suddenly to a soft pianissimo lilt. Jade would stand center, facing the mirror and lead us through a long port de bras, then she would turn to us, slip one pointe shoe behind the other and slide low into a bow. It was customary to clap for a teacher and, when we had been through a class like that one, all of our emotions poured through our applause. She was our queen.

Christopher let a warm, wet arm fall across my shoulders. Our bodies gleamed. He led me toward the dressing room.

"How are you holding up, sweetie?" he asked.

"Christopher..."

Class vanished from my mind in an instant, replaced by that fountain of pain in my ribs.

"That good, huh?"

I wanted to cry to him. I knew also that anything I said would go straight back to Rebecca. That was good and it was not. Christopher's opinion meant a lot to both of us. Perhaps because he seemed to be so in control of his emotions. And because he was the only one who clearly knew of the terrible and beautiful and impossible attraction that had developed between us.

"You need to get away from here for a while, really," he said. I couldn't, in a million years, imagine doing as he suggested.

"I could never leave the studio, Christopher."

"I don't mean forever. I mean just until you and Bec get some perspective. Some space. Go and hang out with your school friends."

"School friends? I only have friends here!" I had raised my voice and we were suddenly aware of the other dancers around us, packing up dance bags, removing shoes, gossiping. Christopher changed to a whisper.

"I don't believe that for a second," he said.

"Then these are the only friends I want!" I felt tears coming. Swallowed.

"Calm down," he said, "I'm not suggesting that we don't love you or don't want you here. You belong here. It will always be your home. I'm only suggesting that with a little time, you might find this whole thing will just blow over and you'll remember it as a silly phase. Lots of people go through crushes."

"This is not a crush," I told him, my voice cracking. I felt too old for crushes. Too far gone for this to be so simple.

"Maybe, maybe not. But I want you to do something for me."

"What?" I sighed.

He pulled me down next to him on the dressing room bench. Most of the dancers headed to the parking lot or flocked around Dudley in the office.

"I want you to go on a date. With a guy. I want you to open your mind and have fun." I looked into his face, eyebrows raised in defiance.

"Did you ever date a girl, Christopher?"

"Well, let me think. Probably when I was in high school I tried it once," he laughed, "and it was disgusting! But you see *I knew.*"

"What makes you think I don't know?" I was whining.

"Your age..." he fluttered his eyelashes at me, knowing he was treading on delicate territory, "and besides, you're obsessed, and that's not healthy for anyone at any age."

"What does Rebecca say?"

"She says she loves you."

The words hit me like a ton of boulders falling from a mountaintop. I gulped.

"But honey, she can't do this. You have to let her go. She could lose her job. Dudley can't have this kind of thing going on around the studio! A woman and an underage girl, for heaven sakes?"

"No one bothers about you and Ricky," I complained. He looked into the distance.

"People expect it from us, honey. And we're both nearing thirty. We're big boys, we can take care of ourselves, make our own decisions..."

"I can make my own decisions!"

"I know you think so. But will you do what I asked? Isn't there a guy at school or even around here, a *straight* guy, you could go have a good time with? Charley? Wesley?"

"I think Wesley's gonna be following in your footsteps, actually."

"You're probably right," Christopher laughed, "Bad example. But tell me you will do it. And take off a week."

"I can't. I'm doing some work for Dudley's friend, Étienne."

A peculiar look spread across his face. "Oh no," he said. "You're kidding."

"Why?"

"Oh, I did some stuff for him once. Guy's a real winner. Watch yourself with him. If he tries anything, you run away, fast!" He was laughing. He couldn't be that bad. Christopher had lived through the experience.

"Think about what I said. Even if you work with Étienne. You don't need to be here. I'll talk to Dudley and Jaybird."

"Oh God, Christopher, they can't know!"

"Well, dear, I don't think Jade would be terribly surprised. But I wasn't going to tell them about Rebecca. Just that you maybe need a little space. Isn't your grandmother ill?"

"We're not sure." There was another world!

"Well, there you go."

The idea had begun to settle, torturously, in my brain. But not for the reasons Christopher hoped. How badly would she miss me, I wondered? Dudley poked his head around the corner of the dressing room.

"Étienne would like to talk to you for a minute," he said. I felt a little bolt of fear but Christopher elbowed me in the ribs.

"Look alive, here comes the dead wagon," he said.

No more avoiding it, I thought. I got up and went into Dudley's office. Étienne sat on the sofa. Dudley remained behind his desk.

"Have a seat, Anneliese," said Étienne. He patted the sofa next to him. He actually wanted me to sit down right next to him. I looked at Dudley, who gave me a subtle nod. I had to keep from curling my lip in disgust. I didn't want to sit so close to this overly smooth, almost pretty, man. I preferred to stand. But I was Dudley's puppet. I approached the couch shyly and sat as far away from him as I could, then twisted toward him so my knee was between us.

"I'd like to take a few pictures of you, Anneliese. Would that be okay?" He spoke to me like a small child.

"I guess so."

"Would you take your hair down for me?"

I looked at Dudley, but he abandoned me, peering into the paper shuffle on his desk. I was taught to do as I was told by my elders. I didn't argue and removed a dozen pins from my hair until it fell down to my waist.

"Lovely," said Étienne. He reached out. I backed up. Out of the corner of my eye I saw Jaybird and Rebecca leave the sewing room and come to the office door. Thank God for the interruption.

"Hey, what's going on?" said Rebecca, just her usual entrance.

"Rebecca, you remember Étienne from Westwood?" said Dudley, "He's here to meet some of our ballerinas."

"Well, I see one," she said.

"We have plenty," said Jaybird. She was smirking. She made a point of continuing into the studio with Rebecca, talking incessantly so Rebecca couldn't get a word in but was compelled to follow. She glanced back once and disappeared. I couldn't tell from her expression whether she had read the words I left on her desk on a torn piece of notebook paper.

I couldn't tell what was in that glance at all. It was quick. And when she was gone from the room I felt more exposed than ever.

"Étienne thought we could do a studio shoot sometime next week up in his area near Los Angeles."

"Who else will be there?" I asked, thinking of my father's warning. For once I was sure he was right.

"Just you, this time," said Étienne, "I won't be using you for the commercial. Only the print work."

"Will you be there, Dudley?"

"I'll try, yes, I think I'll be in and out. I have other people to see in the city."

I was quiet, trying to think of how to say what I needed to say without sounding like a child. Without proclaiming, "My dad says...." If I was so restricted as to make demands on behalf of my father, then perhaps they wouldn't bother using me at all.

"Will Rebecca be working on the costumes?"

"Oh, I don't think I'll need your seamstress. I have a clothing designer who wants to get in on the gig. Promote his line."

Quiet again. I decided this wasn't the time to bring it up. I would talk to Dudley alone about my father's condition.

"Lend me your eyes a minute, Dudley?" said Jaybird, hurrying into the office, "I want your opinion on the new choreography."

"Are we through?" he said to Étienne.

"For the moment, I suppose we are."

I truly did not like the sound of his voice. There was something conniving around the edges. Something unsafe. Perhaps it was just what Christopher had said, and my father's suspicion, giving me chills.

Dudley followed Jade into the studio. She was working on a piece of choreography for Étienne's commercial. Her simple request left me alone with Étienne and I felt she had somehow done it on purpose. Ma had a saying, "You made your bed, now you lie in it." That was the sentiment in Jaybird's sideways glance as she took Dudley from me.

"So," Étienne turned back to me. Had I been thinking, I would have followed on Dudley's heels. But I had not exactly been bidden to the next room, and anyway, it was too late.

"How about we take a walk outside?" he said, "you're done with class, right?"

"Right," I said.

He got up and held the door open for me. It was dark. I remembered my ten-speed parked against the fence in the back lot. I began thinking of calling home for a ride. I hadn't even told anyone how I'd gotten to the studio. I didn't want to ride home in the dark.

"I'm so glad you've agreed to work with me," he said as we walked toward the chain-link fence.

"It's for a good cause," I said, staring into the darkening hills of mustard weed.

"Indeed." He leaned against the fence under a street lamp, "You know there's something else you can do for me, if you have a mind to." One corner of his slight smile curled toward an ear so that his copper beard listed. I played along. Was it only curiosity to see what would come next? Was I flirting? I didn't think so. I wanted to know the enemy. He had other things up his sleeve, I knew that. My father knew it. Rebecca probably knew it. And Dudley was blind to all but the money. Poor Dudley. It emasculated him.

"If I have a mind to?" My eyes met his for the first time that night.

"I would need you to be somewhat discreet, as you are a, shall we say, minor?"

"I see."

"You would make a bit of money yourself," he continued.

"I'm listening."

"I have another business," he said, keeping his squinty eye glued to mine, "I sell fur and jewelry... as well as style."

"I didn't know."

"I'd like you to model for that business," one eyebrow slid above the other, "but *au naturale*. Just a bit of fur in the right places." My heart began to beat hard. A nervous habit, my hand ran compulsively through my hair, twisting. "You don't have to let me know now," he said, "but keep this conversation between us, won't you?"

"Okay." I occupied my shaking hands by picking at the final flakes of black nail polish. "That's it then?"

Light shone from behind the office and flickered on in the sewing room. I turned from him and walked toward it like a beacon. I would call home for a ride, I thought. I would leave my bike. Something told me I needed to get out of there. Étienne followed behind. I couldn't pick up the office phone and call home in front of him. He would offer me a ride.

I went through the office into the studio. Jade, Dudley, and Rebecca stood around the stereo talking. Rebecca's eyes locked on mine, unsmiling, and looked back down. A chill went down my spine.

"Dudley," I said, quietly, "are you leaving soon?"

"About a half hour," he said.

"Would you drive me home?"

"Don't look at me," said Rebecca. She turned and abruptly left the room. I watched her, wounded.

"Of course, dear, let me finish up here. Bring your bike inside. You can take it home tomorrow."

I was still looking at the empty doorway. Jade shot me a warning look. Did Rebecca talk to her, too? I went through the jazz studio to the sewing room. Rebecca was sitting at her desk in the dark. The glow of the street lamps filtered in enough to light her face, her gold hair, like an aura. She had the phone in her hand but put it down when I came in.

"What was that about?" I asked, crossing the room only half way.

A blue laser cocktail of anger, worry, and pain shot back at me.

"I'm not going to play this game with you, Anneliese."

"I didn't ask you for a ride."

"I told you to stay away from him."

"Dudley wants me to work with him. Should I refuse? It's for the studio."

"That's not what I mean and I think you know that."

"Just tell me what you mean. I thought you weren't playing games." I resented feeling defensive. She didn't have any right to tell me what to do. I already had an overprotective family.

"I'm talking about Étienne." For once Rebecca was not distracted by phone calls, costumes, patterns.

That's the thing about secrets. It's not quite like lying. People have to earn the truth, don't they? Sometimes it's best only to reveal the necessary ingredients. The rest will come in small doses. Or it won't.

Rebecca stood behind her desk. I remained paralyzed in the center of the room, letting her decide the next move. Each step she took toward me set ions to a frenzy: a storm front moving through the desert. She took my hand and led me to the plate glass window. We could see the chain-link fence where I stood with Étienne minutes before.

"I mean you, standing there, still dressed like that, in the dark with him. Your hand in your hair. It drives me crazy. Who knows what it does to him. All at the same time I feel like I have to protect you, I have to rescue you," She looked down. "...and I want you. This isn't right. You have to get out of here."

She flopped back into the chair, drew her knees to her chest, and put her head down, wrapped up like a cat. I wanted to touch her. But not like everyone else who put hands on her. I understood that I caused her tears. Just not exactly why.

"It's just a habit, Bec," I whispered, laying my hand on top of her head.

"Flirting with men like that slime is a habit?" She did not look up.

"No, I mean my hands in my hair, standing like that, and I had just come from class, I hadn't had a chance to change."

"You couldn't throw on sweats before you went outside?"

"I didn't think about it."

"Well, you better start thinking about things like that if you're going to go walking around at night with men like him!"

How long had she watched me by the fence with Étienne?

"He wants me to do a photo shoot, Bec. In LA. Dudley won't be there the entire time." I considered coming out with the whole story. But she would have burst into the studio and choked him. I didn't want her to explode. I wanted the whole thing to dissipate over time. And I didn't want to mess up Dudley's plans over something Étienne might claim was a lie. What proof did I have of the things he said? Étienne was just a hairdresser, after all. He and Dudley had worked together. Dudley trusted him.

"Anneliese, you shouldn't do this."

"I already agreed. What would I say?"

"I don't know what you'd say now. You should have said no when you had the chance." She was beginning to thaw but she was still angry.

"Would you go with me to LA?" I asked.

She let out a long breath. "Why do I feel like I have to protect you?"

"Because no one else is?"

"You don't understand the effect you have on people."

She was wrong. I understood that there was something about me that provoked a response other sixteen-year-olds dreamed of. But the danger of this completely eluded me.

"Please?"

She let her eyes blaze into me a little longer and sniffed. Was she crying?

"I'll go," she said. "Dudley won't understand why. And Étienne will think I'm trying for a job. You couldn't pay me to work for him."

"We could tell Dudley we don't trust Étienne."

"No," she sighed.

For all of the wisdom that accompanied Dudley's age, he was naïve about the modern world. Charmingly so. We liked him that way. All he wanted was his troupe of dancers and a place to nurture their love of ballet. We would keep him out of the ugliness if we could.

Chapter 12

My dream, that night, was the flying kind, swift and low to the ground. Verdant plains passed below me so fast they were a blur. A gully gave way in the flat lands and I flew over it at an exhilarating speed. I melted through an ancient masonry bridge that spanned a bright green channel with a small brook trickling through it. I was not alone.

Over the cliff of vibrant moors, the Atlantic crashed violently, sending up white spray forever. I veered away in flight from the intoxicating scent of the sea, aware that I was looking for something. Something Ma was trying to show me. I was aware of her there, our spirits blended as we raced, land spinning out of sight beneath us. My joy was immense.

We hovered finally, circling over flat stones embedded in the wet grass. Names were etched deep in the crumbling grey stone. Ma was willing me to look but I could not slow my speed to make out the names. I felt her strong pulse in my ribs like a giant bird flapping its wings and sending off great gusts of energy. The question of the stones was answered quickly. These were the graves of my family in Cornwall, generations gone.

I woke, breathing hard, and looked around my room. The stillness was startling after the glorious speed of flight. My ears rang with silence. Thin rice-paper blinds covered the window, weakly blocking the morning sun. My desk sat like a monument at the foot of my bed, sacred only to me. The blue cabinet in the corner held the small crystal animals my father brought home from Austria. How temporary they seemed. And meaningless. They had sparkled rainbows for me when I was very young. When I first appreciated the sharp edges of the small chick, its facets had sent spectral light across the room. From his next trip to Austria had come a rabbit, and the next, a cat. There had been a turtle once, broken by Katrine in a curious trespass. I had coveted these once. Now they sat in the light of my dream as the simplest of objects.

My eyes wandered down the blue cabinet shelves to the double doors at the base that once opened with a church key now long gone. The cabinet had belonged to my mother and she had kept the key for years in the back of a dresser drawer. Ingrid and I had been fascinated years ago, but never peeked. Now in my room, the double doors required a butter knife shoved sideways between them, that when flattened out, would pry the doors open suddenly and swing them wide with force. Always, when I opened them, I was greeted with the scent of old pine and shellac mixed with yellowed paper.

Among old letters and documents my mother never removed, I had wedged a wicker basket that held matchbooks from every country I could think of. My father's profession had taken him from camels in Egypt back to the North Sea from which he had come. From New Zealand to Singapore. He brought home the matches he had swiped while traveling these places to light his corncob pipe of Captain Black tobacco.

I imagined him skirting the hostess counter of a fine restaurant, reaching into a basket like the one I kept, full of matchbooks. He would reach in as an afterthought as he raced for the taxi waiting at the curb. He would be dressed in a business suit and the matches would be thrust into his pocket for later when he would sit with a martini in a crowded airport business club. He would strike one there and dip the flame into the bowl of his pipe as he sucked, releasing small puffs of smoke through the side of his lips, the plastic black stem clamped in his teeth.

When he came home, the matchbox would be deposited in a junk drawer in the kitchen. I would rescue it then, especially if the matches were wooden. Especially if I didn't recognize the language written there and especially if the box was shiny black with a painting on the cover in bright contrasting color: a phoenix or a nude woman with long flowing hair. Amsterdam. Beijing. Thailand. Places I would never see but could touch in miniature through my father's smoke.

I got out of bed and peeked into Ingrid's room. She slept heavily behind translucent white bed curtains. In the summer she often slept until 11:00 a.m. and even then, only woke because I jumped on her bed until she gave up her bond with the pillow and had tea with me. I went into the kitchen. The whole house was silent save the heavy breathing of sleepers. The phone hung on the kitchen wall like an invitation. Would Ma be up yet? She often didn't sleep well at night and sat for hours at her kitchen table playing solitaire. If I called her, could we talk about the old country? Had she somehow shared that dream with me? Would she remember it, if I asked? And yet, to verbalize the dream might be to somehow destroy it. Turn it to mist and cause it to leave me like a ghost giving up.

I went instead to the living room and sat on the couch facing the French doors. Through the deep green leaves of the drooping mulberry tree I looked out sleepily over Saddleback Mountain and thought about how very far we had come, Ma and I.

* * *

It was late September when Rebecca drove us back to Westwood on a day that felt like a dusty furnace. Dudley had promised to pop in and check on our progress, but he was happy with plans of researching theaters for our next Los Angeles production. Rebecca was stiff on the hour drive north and I wished I could penetrate thoughts that were not being offered. I studied her profile as she gazed at the road but could only read a faraway disorganization in her eyes.

Mother had not been comfortable with this trip. She had asked a hundred questions but could not find a suitable reason to forbid my participation. When it came to the bare bones of her confusion, the one question that seemed to trouble her was "Why you, Anneliese?"

I could have answered her with what I knew was the truth. Étienne couldn't keep his eyes off me. He was probably hoping to get me alone somewhere during the shoot, in an empty parking lot, an after-business-hours hair salon, or something equally dubious and clandestine. But my father assured her that he had instructed me not to be alone with the man and that I would have a "buddy" with me.

"And who would that be?" Mother wanted to know, when I had broken the sudden news of the photo-shoot. Her tone triggered a sweat all over my body.

"Rebecca said she'd go with me." I knew I sounded small.

"Isn't that a little like putting the fox in charge of the henhouse?"

"Jeez, Mother!" I said, trying to sound exasperated to hide my nerves.

"Don't *Jeez, Mother* me," she said.

"Your mother has a point," my father had said. "We don't really know that much about Rebecca."

"It's what I know about her that bothers me," said Mother. There was a shake to her voice that made me feel like crying.

"And what is it that you know about her?" I was suddenly defensive, protective.

"I don't like how much time you spend with that woman. I don't like how often she comes up in your simplest conversation."

"I see her often! She works at the studio. I see a lot of people often." I argued.

"There's something about Rebecca," she said

"Will you be home the same day you go to Westwood?" my father asked, trying to find a truce in all this.

"Yes!" I sounded just like the teenager I was, rather than the free roaming, free-thinking adult that I wanted to be. I resented them for it.

"I think it will be okay, Gwendolyn," my father said.

My mother looked into my eyes with a frigid mixture of suspicion and malice, then turned her back and walked down the hall to her bedroom, leaving an empty, icy wake. It took me a few minutes to recover from the void she left by removing herself in that manner. My father and I looked after her.

"I want you back here by midnight," he said, eyes still in the hallway. "If you're going to be any later, I expect a phone call."

"I will," I said.

A car honked in the driveway. Rebecca knew that coming to the front door and ringing the bell would mean facing my parents with a guilty conscience. Like me, she knew something in her eyes, in mine, would give us away.

Perhaps it was this truth that kept Rebecca far away on the trip to Westwood, to Étienne's shoot. The tires thrummed and stillness in the car between us rippled with discord. I decided to try it out on her.

"Is it my parents?"

"Is what your parents?"

"Your quiet."

She reached her hand over to cover mine and squeezed.

"I guess. It's strange to have to hide something I'm feeling. I'm not really used to it."

Inside that capsule of a car, for an hour, she was mine. No phone would interrupt us. No distraction could allow her to run into the next room or call me away to class. A year before, I had loved that car. Now I realized it wasn't the car I loved.

"Me either," I said.

"You're not used to much of anything," she said.

"I guess not."

"Which brings me back to Étienne. This is the last time I'm bailing you out, do you understand? Sometimes I think you enjoy doing this to me."

"Rebecca..." How was I making her angry?

"You know how I feel when I see men drooling after you. Like Christopher told me, you are not my responsibility. You are not my problem." Her words stung.

"I didn't mean to be your problem." I pouted and looked out the window.

"I care for you, Anneliese, you know that."

"And I care for you. Why is that a problem?"

"You still don't see, do you?"

"No, I don't. If two people care for each other it shouldn't ever be a problem to express it."

"I don't see you running to tell your mom about your feelings for me. Can you explain that? Can you see me walking into your house and saying, 'Anneliese and I are going to my house to fool around, we'll see you later'?"

The crudeness of her comment at once repulsed me and fascinated me. I couldn't begin to imagine what it meant. A part of me wanted to find out. I laughed.

"It isn't funny. Did Christopher talk to you about his idea?"

A bolt of something like fear went through me as I remembered Christopher in the studio dressing room suggesting I go away like an unwanted puppy.

"He did."

"And what did you think? Maybe putting some space between us would be a good idea." I began to protest but she cut me off. "You need some time to experience being a kid. To experience boys. And I need to clear my head of this ridiculous attachment."

"I don't want it to go away, Bec." Tears had begun despite holding my breath.

"What am I to you, Anneliese? Have you ever really thought about it?"

"I guess not."

"You have two sisters. You have a mom. A grandma you're crazy about. Why do you want a woman for a lover?"

"Because I understand women. Women understand me. The only man I really know outside my father and grandfather is Dudley. And he's a grandpa too."

"You see, you haven't given men a chance."

Maybe I could become one of those loose girls who slept around with a bunch of guys just to show her she was wrong. I would date six of them at once. I would sleep with all of them. Lose my virginity to some unknown jerk, just to come back and tell her I tried it and now I'm done.

By the time we arrived in Westwood I was drained and battered from the inside out.

"Let's get this over with," Rebecca said.

We walked across a parking lot to a low, wide building of white cinderblock with a black awning. A pink neon sign across the window said "*Triple O.*" I was suddenly gripped with nerves. Perhaps I would be going away, I thought, as I walked through the glass door with bells attached to the handle, but for now, we're still together and we have this day.

We entered to a team of crew workers setting up lights and twisting lenses on cameras. Étienne was lost in conversation with a photographer but he looked at us as we entered.

"Ah, Anneliese, I'm so glad you're here." His eyes shifted to Rebecca. He clearly hadn't expected her. "And this with you is...."

"This is Rebecca," I said, "from the studio."

"And she's here because...."

"Dudley asked me to come with Anneliese and make sure things went smoothly," Rebecca spoke up with easy confidence that no man could break, "And to see if you needed any help."

Étienne frowned. "How very considerate," he said.

Rebecca began immediately to mingle among the crew. Within minutes she had them laughing like old friends. I felt her drifting too far away for comfort as she allowed herself to be shown cameras and equipment. She cracked jokes with the men about who possessed the longest telephoto lens, insinuating a not so subtle connection to their anatomy.

"Well, time is money," Étienne said to no one. And to me he said, "Put this on, Anneliese."

What he handed me was made of lace. And only lace. I scanned the room for Dudley. He was nowhere in sight, but I didn't want to make a scene.

"We're waiting," Étienne said.

The salon was tiled in black and white all the way up the walls. Pink neon tubes stretched across the ceiling. Where the lighting crew scurried, large silver umbrellas shielded bright spotlights.

Étienne explained to the make-up artist that if she did not blacken my lower lashes, I would appear more innocent. That was how he had wanted me, innocent but not so. He would take a child-woman, clothe her scantily, keep her baby face, but the camera would see a seductress.

The dressing room was only a small curtain pulled around a rod. I tried to make my movements slight so as not to attract attention. I wondered what questions Dudley had asked. Or had he preferred not to know the details? I thought of him in his big, white studio. I thought of the honey hollow floors of highly polished, scuffed, pine. The whole place was a testimony to his spirit and his art. It was that spirit I loved and had twirled in, like a salmon upstream for my entire childhood. Perhaps this was the price I was paying for the glory it gave me. I was giving my body like a sacrifice for the magic that was my training, my adolescence, and my identity. In my mind Dudley's gold-rimmed glasses fell down his nose as he peered at me and simply said, "Again."

I took a deep breath and did as I was bid.

"Are you done in there?" Étienne was impatient and cold. "Don't mess up your makeup!"

"I don't think..." I began as I struggled with some way to look decent.

"Is there a problem?"

"Umm, yeah, Étienne, do you see Rebecca around? I could use her help."

"What's she, your handmaid?"

"Would you just ask her to come here?"

I heard him sigh and say something to someone about Rebecca and me. His comment was followed by a snicker from deep in a male throat. Soon heels tapped on the tile floor of the salon.

"Anneliese?" said Rebecca. "What's the problem?" She stood outside the curtain.

"The problem is what he wants me to wear. I thought this was about hairstyles!" I whispered loudly. Rebecca poked her head in. She froze then closed her eyes, shaking her head slowly.

"How do you get yourself into these things?"

I gave her a pleading look.

"What do you want me to do?" she asked.

"Can't you think of something? You know how to talk to them!"

She looked at me covered only in minuscule pieces of white lace. Then she left. Words were exchanged outside the curtain. They were grumbled words. Hushed words. But I heard the word "*child*" and I heard the word "*underage*" and then the word "*pervert.*" Rebecca was holding nothing back. Étienne's comments were not so hushed but they sounded like "*waste of time*" and "*unprofessional*" and "*ridiculous.*" She put her head back into the curtains.

"Get dressed," she said. I didn't ask questions. I hoped to escape quickly and quietly. I hoped that when I emerged there would not be 20 pairs of technical-crew eyes on me.

Dressed again in my blue jeans and black camisole and wishing I had chosen my clothes more conservatively that morning, I peeked out of the curtain. The crew were turned to their equipment, packing up to the barks of Étienne, who was upset with having to pay their minimum hourly fee.

Rebecca gripped my wrist and dragged me through the salon. I felt like a child who had misbehaved and was being removed. In some ways I supposed it was true. Étienne looked up and glared.

"You can tell Dudley our deal is off," he said to Rebecca, disregarding me completely.

"I'll be sure and do that," said Rebecca, casually.

Étienne looked down and shook his head as if he had never worked with such amateurs. I was hoping Rebecca would offer some words of solace as we walked to her car.

"Next time listen to me," was all she said and let my wrist fall. We got in the car without words and she put her head on the steering wheel. I looked out the window at the city. It looked ugly and foreign. I wanted to go home. Rebecca started the engine.

"Dudley's not going to appreciate this. He really needed that money."

"So, you think I should have done the shoot?" I felt at once guilty and used. She looked at me and let the engine idle.

"Not in a million years." She leaned over and kissed me, leaving her lips there long enough for me to shiver.

"Anneliese," she whispered, "what am I gonna do with you?

I rode home in heaven. If she did not want me to fall in love with her, it wasn't working. I wanted to dissect that kiss and spend the next freeway hour planning how to dodge the prying eyes of those who tried to stand in my way. I wanted to own that three seconds in the parking lot of the *Triple O* and replay it as needed. But Rebecca's mind was already beyond it.

"What do you think we should tell Dudley?" she asked.

"I haven't really been thinking of that."

"Well, I have." If she caught my meaning she didn't let on.

"What do you think we should tell him?"

"The truth, I guess. That Étienne is a slime and his money is dirty."

"I don't know what to tell my dad. He'll be so angry he'll want to go to Westwood and get in the guy's face. Étienne will think I told him about the fur and jewelry business."

I stopped suddenly and bit my lip. I hadn't filled her in on that part yet. Étienne's proposition by the fence had lingered in the back of my mind, had prompted me to beg her to accompany me to the shoot, but I hadn't exactly given the details.

"What fur and jewelry business?"

"Well," I managed, "there's something else about Étienne." Rebecca shot me a blue-gray stare. I groaned.

"Remember the day I walked with Étienne outside by the fence? The night you got angry with me?"

"How can I forget? What happened?" she asked, bracing for the worst.

"It's not what happened. It's something he said. I'm a little nervous about telling you because he told me to keep it quiet..."

"You can be pretty sure when someone like him says to keep something quiet you ought to be screaming it across the room."

"Well, I wasn't sure what to do because of this photo thing and Dudley needing the money. But he wanted me to pose nude."

"He told you this before the shoot and you still agreed to do it?" Rebecca looked as if she might blow.

"It wasn't for this shoot, it was for later," I said quickly, "for his other business. A jewelry business." Rebecca shook her head but she was calm.

"You really should have told me this at the time. I seriously doubt he has another business, Anneliese. That was just about getting you alone and undressed. Are you really that stupid?" I swallowed. I guessed I was.

"This guy needs to be reported," she said.

Oh God, no. Then everyone would know how stupid I'd been.

"I wish we didn't need to tell Dudley anything," I said. "I don't want him to be angry with me. And where's he going to get the money to keep us going?"

"We'll think of something and anyway it's not your problem. You should never have been put in that position. We'll talk to Dudley together and tell him the whole thing."

The hills of our town looked inviting even in the darkness. They spoke of home and security. Evening had fallen by the time we were near Long Beach but I hadn't noticed. Now I was getting tired and I would be glad to walk through the front door of my house, if only I didn't have to answer any questions.

"Bec, if I ever had to leave the studio I'd die," I told her in the last mile.

"You're a ballerina, Anneliese. If you didn't dance here, you'd find another studio. And maybe a better one."

"But what would I do without you?" We were driving up my street and I felt the coming separation with each fraction of that mile. I tried to think of all the things I needed to say but my mind went blank. She let my question ride.

I looked for signs of wakefulness in the house as the car pulled into my driveway. Lights were still on and it was well before midnight. So much for sneaking in without questions. Even pleasantries exchanged with my parents would shatter the pictures I hoped to keep clear in my head.

"Where are you headed now?" I asked her, my eyes searching the dark floor of the car for my dance bag.

"Right here," she said and then she was around me wrapped like rose petals. Soft tendrils of seaweed and light and the kind of kiss that can never be left behind, never walked away from. It was a night from which I would never recover even if I never saw her again. Even if I saw her every day after. Her spell held me rapt.

I wanted to remain lost in her but grew nervous of eyes that might be peeking through a curtain to identify the rumble of an engine in the driveway. I clutched at the fingers that were snaked through my hair and pulled back.

"I better go in before they wonder why we're sitting here."

"You better go before I can't let you go," she said.

I opened the front door quietly and heard the TV on in the living room. I peeked around and saw my parents and Ingrid planted on the couch watching something ancient. They were engrossed.

"Hi," I said quietly.

"You're home earlier than I thought," said my father.

My mother stared silently at the TV.

"We didn't do the shoot," I said. I would let them do the asking. My mother spoke up at once.

"What did you do all day if you didn't do the shoot?" Still angry.

"Well, I almost did it. We went there...."

"And...," said my father.

"And Étienne, the guy you met at the Westwood Theater? He wanted me to, um, wear something inappropriate."

My father raised his eyebrows and nodded. His expression said he had expected something like this.

"So, Rebecca told him to forget it," I added quickly, hoping to gain her favor with them.

"Rebecca saves the day," said Mother, flatly.

"Well, I'm glad you left. And I'm a bit pissed off with Dudley for not finding out this sort of thing ahead of time," said my father. "He should have known exactly what you were expected to wear."

"He thought like I did. That it was mostly about hairstyles."

"You can't trust these LA types," my father said, still shaking his head.

"I guess I'll go to bed," I said, glad for the ease of departure. Their eyes were heading back to the movie. I bent over the couch and kissed Ingrid on the cheek.

"G'night, Ingie."

"G'night," Ingrid said quickly. She had not removed her eyes from the black and white romance on the screen.

In my small room with the periwinkle walls I had painted myself, I went to the old pine desk at the end of my bed. My notebook sat as if untouched, but I knew that it had been not only touched but opened. Not only opened but graced with a pen. I knew this because it vibrated and glowed from the desk with energy other than my own. I touched its parchment cover and flipped through the pages. I caught my breath even though I knew it would be true. I could feel Ingrid as if she were an extension of myself. She was present on the page even in the darkness of the room. I flipped on the desk lamp to read but I saw only a line.

"*Ebony has my blood in her veins already*," said the pale blue ink. "*Does she need it on her hands as well?*"

That was all. I thought quickly to the last conversation I had with her. Driving back from Ma's house? Had we talked about Rebecca? What did she know? The words I had spilled in my notebook were vague, named no one. What had I not given her that she needed?

I was moving ahead of my older sister with an unfriendly speed. That evening she had been only a blur as I headed into the world I kept separate from her. My world held every delicious mystery I was demanding to unravel. Ingrid only wanted perfect grades, didn't she? She only wanted to get through school and attend a good college and get married to a nice man and have a few kids, didn't she? I thought of the black and white screen lovers she watched on TV with rapt attention. Maybe she wanted more.

Chapter 13

Steering wheel in one hand, stick shift in the other, I was immediately at home in my dad's old car with Katrine sitting next to me. We took the orange grove road along the same creek where we had ridden our bikes all the way to Ma's house. There was no academic test, no *pirouette* even, in my history that matched the supreme level of pride I took in my driver's license.

The old concrete road was creased with lines of tar every twenty yards or so, causing a rhythmic train-like thrum under the tires. In twenty minutes, I turned into the back-alley driveway of her apartment and Katrine and I knocked on the glass-louvered kitchen door. Ma had her purse tucked under her arm ready to come to Sunday dinner. A World War I veteran, Pop had developed a debilitating case of agoraphobia and would rarely come along on the short trip to our house. She kissed him on the head where he sat in his recliner before following us across the lawn, under brilliant red bottlebrushes swarming with bees, and out of the wooden gate to the car.

"Oh, Leesie!" she said, glancing around for other possible drivers. "You got your license?"

"Yep," I beamed. Katrine climbed into the small backseat of the hatchback and Ma edged herself into the passenger side with some effort. Seconds later she began to cough. When the cough did not subside, I glanced into the rear-view mirror. Katrine was a worrier. I decided not to call attention to my concern.

"I'm going to run back in and get some water," I said, "do you need some, Ma?" She continued to cough, now gasping, failing to draw air into her lungs.

"Go get some water while I stay with her," I said to Katrine. Her eyes grew wide and she shook her head violently as she climbed out of the car on my side. Ma continued to cough.

"Then you stay here with her and I'll get water."

"No!" she shouted, "I'm coming in with you."

"Either get the water or stay with her!"

"I can't! I'm scared!" I had never hated my sister quite so much as I did in that moment.

"I'm going to call an ambulance," I whispered to her.

"Why?" she whispered hysterically. "What's wrong? What's happening?"

Now I had a panicked child and a choking grandmother on my hands. I ran to the house with Katrine trailing on my heels, leaving Ma to cough in the car alone. In the house I filled a glass of water and called the emergency line. Tethered to the wall by the phone cord I shoved the glass at Katrine.

"Take it to her now!"

"I can't. I'm afraid to."

"She's choking. Go!"

"No, I can't!" She collapsed in tears on the floor.

The operator came on the line and confirmed Ma's address. By the time I got to the car with the glass I heard sirens. Ma, her pallor ashen, sat in the front seat with a deep frown across her brow. I handed her the water and she took a small sip. Another 30 seconds and an ambulance pulled into the driveway next to us, followed by the obligatory fire truck.

"Is that for me?" Ma said. "I don't need an ambulance!"

"Just in case, Ma. Let them check you out."

Two paramedics helped her out of the small car and followed us back inside the apartment. Katrine cried quietly on the couch. She was worthless under pressure and I was furious with her.

"I couldn't get my breath," Ma told the man who held a stethoscope to her chest.

"Sounds like a little pneumonia," said the paramedic.

"Pneumonia?" Ma asked, surprised as I was, "but I feel okay, really."

"Well there's a little water on your lungs, ma'am," he said, "best call your doctor and get in to see him soon, okay?"

"Okay. Thank you, Love," she said to the paramedic and dug in her purse to give him money.

"That's quite all right, Mrs. Pearce. You get better soon." The men left out the kitchen door.

"Do you still want to come to dinner?" I asked Ma. She sat on the green velour couch, still frowning and quiet.

"I believe I'll stay home with Pop," she said. "I'll call your mother, you go on back."

"Okay," I said, "Come on, Katrine." She still had tears in her eyes.

Back in the car, I slammed the door hard. Isolated in that space I turned to Katrine in the passenger seat.

"Do you realize how selfish you are?" I attacked her with what Ma would have called piss and vinegar.

"I was afraid!"

"Afraid of what? Helping?"

"I didn't want to be alone with her if she died." Katrine fell into sobs again.

"All you needed to do was hand her some water!"

Our grandfather's phobias had taken root. Soon she would not ride elevators, fly in commercial airplanes or revel in the steam of a blanket-covered sweat lodge on the Hopi Indian Reservation—the stories I would tell you if I had another lifetime. I backed into the alley and drove us home in silence except for the bumping of Orange Grove Road.

* * *

Ma chanted an old army march as we walked across the bridge over San Juan Creek toward the railroad tracks, "*Left, left, I had a good job and I left. First they hired me then they fired me then I got mad and I left, left....*"

I had my arm tucked under hers and I skipped quickly, changing my pace to match hers. Another school year had begun and Ingrid had dropped me at Ma's after school to help with her shopping. Ingrid had already sunk deep into her academic circles, studying literature and preparing for academic decathlon. She was a junior this year and I had turned sixteen in the spring.

Ma's hospital tests had shown a dark spot on her colon. The doctors operated immediately and removed a golf-ball-sized tumor. They were fairly sure they had removed the cancer. Ma had been in the hospital for 2 weeks following. We had been happy when she emerged from sleep, smiling when she saw Ingrid, Katrine, and me gathered around her bed. She showed us the staples dotting her belly with a laugh.

"Does it hurt?" Katrine asked.

"No, not much," she said grinning, "but boy am I hungry! When I get outta here I'm gonna have some of your mother's chili!"

Tubes protruded from her arms and nose but still she smiled. We hugged her carefully around the neck.

Now she was home where we wanted her. Her energy was not what it was, but that was expected. It was a sunny day in October, temperatures still reaching 85 degrees.

Bells rang and the gates at the train track lowered as we approached on the way to the market. We gazed down the tracks looking for the train. It rushed in with a roar and passed in front of us spitting a noisy clatter. Ma grabbed her straw sun hat just before it blew off.

"I love the train," she said as it continued on, fading down the track to the station, "I'd like to ride it down to San Diego and kiss that big Shamu before I go." There was her friendly relationship with death again. 'Before I go' sounded like a vacation to heaven. "Did you ever see Shamu?" she asked me.

"Yes, when I was little."

"I would love to see him!"

"Why don't we go, Ma?"

"I can't leave Pop for that long."

I was frustrated. She couldn't do anything without worrying about him. It was almost as if she was holding back all of life until he died.

"He would be all right for an afternoon!"

"Oh, you know him. Everything has to be just right and I have to do it for him."

I made up my mind that I would drive her there myself.

"Mother could take care of him."

"I just don't know."

We walked into the parking lot of the market where a group of teenage boys were walking in our direction. They turned their heads as they passed.

"Oooh, Leesie, that tall one about undressed you with his eyes!"

"Oh Ma, he did not."

"Almost broke his neck looking back!" she laughed.

I was embarrassed. She was my *grandmother*, for heaven's sake. Grandmas didn't think of those things, did they? Grandmas made biscuits and crocheted baby blankets. But then I thought about her. This was Ma, whose tightly folded copy of "*How Do I Love Thee?*" still harbored safely in her pocketbook after six decades. I relaxed.

"He was kinda cute, Leesie..."

"I guess." I was smiling broadly.

"You have a boyfriend yet?"

"No, too busy." I definitely didn't want to discuss it. I was quiet.

"You take your time, dear," she said.

Ingrid picked me up from Ma's house in the late afternoon when the sun was setting. We took Del Obispo Road all the way to the ocean, where we would turn north along the water toward home.

"How was Ma?" she asked.

"Ma needs to live her life," I said, frowning and thinking of Shamu.

"What are you talking about?"

"She waits to do anything until 'Pop is gone.' I guess she's never thought of the possibility that he might not go first. He's so much older than she is. But you never know." Ingrid was quiet.

We waited for the green light at Pacific Coast Highway looking at Doheny Beach. Suddenly she smiled.

"That was a great concert," she said, remembering our late summer Crosby, Stills and Nash experience at Doheny.

"It was."

We had huddled under blankets in front of a black, hastily built stage. A hurricane had blown up from Mexico and the wind coming from the Pacific was smacking sand in our faces and the faces of the large crowd. Dark clouds gathered quickly. Electronic equipment was set about the stage with purpose. Black tarps covered the top of the scaffolding with more black curtains hanging down.

The audience had gathered early and waited well past the scheduled performance time. It was perhaps an hour before a band member climbed the stage and turned on a microphone.

The rumble in the audience quieted to silence. The man on stage seemed to be having trouble with the sound system.

"No nukes!" shouted a bored fan. The microphone squealed and the man on stage fumbled nervously with cords. The audience took up the chant.

"No nukes! No nukes! No nukes! ..."

Behind the stage and down the strand of beach, the San Onofre Nuclear Power Plant stood ominously generating energy for Orange and San Diego County. It sucked in the ocean water to cool its reactor cores and spit it back out, warm and tainted. We had visions of green fish with 3 eyes and dolphins playing in the warm water with bubbly gray skin. Marijuana smoke hung sweetly in the air. The sky was growing darker. One drop of rain, then two.

"Good evening," said the man at the microphone. The audience cheered. More band members were taking their places on the stage. Floodlights were turned on them.

"We want you to know," the man hesitated, "there's been... a problem." Audience rumble. Rain drops.

"On his way down here to Orange County," the man continued, "David Crosby was arrested for possession of cocaine." A collective intake of breath. More rumble. More drops.

"So, as you can see, he won't be joining us tonight," he continued. The crowd booed.

"But we're going to entertain you anyway, and we're going to be loud. And we're going to tell Southern California Edison where it can put its nuclear power!" The audience recovered from its booing and began to cheer again.

Ingrid and I were new to this scene but we were feeling pretty aligned with the whole thing. We belonged in that crowd. We weren't screamers. We were watchers. Under the blanket we inhaled the sweet drifting smoke and listened to Steven Stills and Graham Nash sing "*Teach Your Children.*" Bic lighters flickered on, frolicked a moment in the wind, and blew out.

Thunder struck, followed quickly by a flash of lightning. The band members exchanged glances and wound their song to a quick ending. A lighting tech walked on stage.

"I'm sorry, folks," he said, taking the microphone from Graham, "it's too dangerous to continue using electric equipment during a storm. We're going to have to pack up."

The audience murmured but did not boo. The rain began to come down in sheets and people were already drifting toward the parking lot in great droves, beach-blankets over their heads.

Ingrid and I ambled among them. Ahead of us, newspaper covering his head, a man yelled, "Rain makes the weeds grow!" Ingrid and I laughed. We loved the rain. We did not cover our heads. We let it drench our hair and turn it to kinky, dark knots. We were walking slowly so as to catch every drop offered to us. Rain was so rare in Southern California we didn't want to miss any of it. We grinned all the way to the car. Sand plastered to our wet skin, we were beginning to feel cold and shaky. We got into the silver Honda hatchback and slammed the doors, laughing.

"So much for that," she had said, still grinning and shivering.

"Can you believe David Crosby was arrested?"

"Of course, I can believe it!" she said.

"But rock and roll guys do that kind of thing all the time without getting caught."

"Maybe they decided to make an example of him," she said.

"Maybe. I love the smell of pot smoke in the rain," I said. She gave me a strange look.

"You don't smoke it, do you? Down at the studio?" She started the engine and threw the car quickly into reverse.

"Of course not. I just like the smell," I paused. Turnabout is fair play, I thought, and asked, "Did you ever try it?" I was shocked by the lack of a quick, forthcoming answer from my academic sister. A small smile teased her mouth. She looked suddenly like a child hiding something behind her back.

"You have, haven't you!" I shouted.

"Just once," she said, "and you can't tell anyone about it."

"Who gave it to you?"

"The guy who took me to his junior prom last year."

"The son of the guy who works at the San Onofre plant?"

"Yep."

"Doesn't that figure!" I giggled but my smile quickly faded. Suddenly I saw a way to talk to Ingrid about Rebecca.

"Actually, I'm not exactly telling the truth." She took her eyes from the road and looked at me with raised eyebrows.

"Once I tried it against my will...." Eyebrows even higher, "Watch the road! You know Rebecca at the studio?"

"Yes..."

"She had just taken a drag one night when we were in Westwood last year, and she kind of, she sort of... blew it into my mouth." There. Out with it.

"How did she do that?" Her eyebrows might have left her face but at least she was looking forward.

"She leaned over and put her mouth over mine and blew in," I said.

"Did it get you high?"

"No, not really." That wasn't the point, I thought. She was quiet for a while. I wondered if she was imagining how this would all work.

"Rebecca's an interesting person, isn't she," said Ingrid.

"She's a lot of fun at the studio. Everyone loves her," I said.

"I've been down there with you a couple times. She doesn't talk to me. She doesn't really like me."

"She doesn't know you. She's one of those types who only hangs out with dancers." That wasn't really true. If they were men, they could be anyone. "Anyway, she thinks you're very studious." She had asked me once why Ingrid was so stuffy. I wasn't going to tell her that.

"Did you tell her I'm not?"

"Sure," I lied, "don't worry about it." I wondered why I hadn't defended Ingrid to Rebecca. Ingrid was studious, sure, but she was also a great sister and friend. A guilty tingle covered my skin.

I wanted Ingrid to like her. This wasn't going well. I had the feeling she resented my closeness to Rebecca. That maybe she didn't like the existence of a part of my life in which she didn't belong and in which she couldn't exist. But Ingrid was my constant companion. How could I continue living with her, going to school in the same car, going out with the same friends, and not explain to her that I wanted to be with Rebecca all the time. I wanted to tell her that Rebecca was in love with me. I wanted to tell her that the feeling was mutual.

"Actually, we spend a lot of time together," I continued.

"You sure spend a lot of time at the studio."

"Does it bother you?"

"Sometimes."

"Maybe you should try taking a jazz class from Ricky or something."

"It's not my thing."

Something in her voice told me I had hurt her. Our collective thoughts were hanging heavy in the car as we drove north on Pacific Coast Highway until we reached Emerald Bay Parkway and headed inland. Rain had slowed to gray drizzle. Our smiles had faded.

That was two months ago. Now we drove the same highway toward home, thinking of Ma, thinking of a new year in high school. I alone thought of Rebecca and wished I could shout her name from the rooftops.

Chapter 14

In the morning I woke to low conversation in the kitchen. Mother's words were thick and short. A sense of dread went through me. Perhaps it was guilt. Or intuition. But I knew they were talking about me. My father was finishing breakfast that Mother set for him every morning. Cereal and tea were laid before him with the right amount of wheat germ sprinkled on his cereal and the right amount of milk in his tea. On any weekday morning he would finish quickly and leave for work, not returning until late at night. I crept out of bed and stood at the edge of the kitchen. Mother looked up.

"You're up early," Mother said looking up from her preparations, "But since you are, we want to talk to you."

"Can this wait until tonight?" said my father.

"I'd rather not," she said to him.

"What is this about?" I asked. I pushed fear back. Tried to sound calm.

"Well, quite simply we want you to take a break from the studio," Mother said, "for a number of reasons."

I was momentarily speechless. I wondered if this was what it felt like to bleed internally. Swallowing hard, I wanted to ask questions. I wanted to tear away pieces of their arguments. I did not want to understand their intentions.

"We know you're a good dancer," said my father, releasing his breath, "and we don't want to stifle you. But we believe you're in over your head with these older people at the studio."

I stared frantically past him, searching for a simple rebuttal that would make it all go away. There was none forthcoming, so he continued. His words were marbles rolling in chaos across the floor. I could not find sense in them. My heart only raced as I grasped at them.

"You've been very moody," Mother said. "You just aren't yourself anymore. You don't smile or joke with your sister…"

"I'm just tired," I tried. But I knew it was weak.

"And I don't think Dudley has your best interests in mind," she continued. "He's a sweet old man but his bottom line is his studio."

"That's not true," I said, though in my heart I knew she was right.

"What matters to me is that you are becoming someone I don't recognize." The anger was creeping back into her voice. But it was tearful anger. It was the shaking voice I remembered from the morning. I hated her like this, so tightly wound she would unravel and fly in all directions if she were pushed any further. But I heard myself trying anyway.

"You can't stop me from dancing!" I tried not to cry or appear weak.

"We would never stop you from dancing," said my father, ever in control, "but we don't want any more of these trips to Los Angeles. We want you to find another studio if you really want to dance…."

"But Dad…" I started. He cut me off, holding up his hand for me to let him finish,

"Or else we want you to take a break. Concentrate on school. Let's see if you can get grades like Ingrid's."

"Let's see if she can dance like me," I muttered, looking at the floor.

"It's not a damned competition," said Mother. "It's about your life. And our lives. We are the ones who have to live with your selfish obsession with ballet, and frankly I'm sick and tired of hearing about Jade and Rebecca and who has what role in the ballet and what theater Dudley's going to get. I really don't give a shit anymore."

By the end of this oration her voice had elevated to a shrill scream. I stared at her. Then at my father. He looked into his tea. There was nowhere to run.

"For how long?" I demanded.

"Let's start with two months," she said.

In the minutes that followed I could only think of how I would get around this new proclamation. I would skip school. Would Ingrid cover for me? She would never go behind my parents' back. What about Hannah? Could I ask her to be my accomplice? She felt replaced by Rebecca, too. My father stood and picked up his keys, his aviation sunglasses, his leather jacket, and headed for the garage. I would not look at Mother. I would not speak to her. If she thought she could control me like this and turn me back into a passive little mouse, she was wrong. There was no more of the old Anneliese she had known. I had changed and she would never, if I could help it, know just how.

I stomped down the hall to my room and slammed the door, not caring about the early hour. I allowed my anger to bleed. I picked up my notebook and screamed on paper. I bled into Christopher who had suggested a separation in the first place. Into Ingrid and her grades and her jealousy. Jaybird for her sarcastic comments and sideways glances, Dudley for his lack of caring, Rebecca for being able to let go.

I expected Mother's knock on the door. I wouldn't answer it. I would brace myself against it. She could go on knocking. Instead the door simply opened and a look of fury spread across her face.

"Never walk away from me when I'm not done talking to you," she said.

"I was done," I said.

I had never spoken to her that way. We were friends, she and Ingrid and I. The pain in Mother's face was a picture of that trio crumbling, becoming lost to her. She began to cry.

"What about Ma?" she said. "What would she think of all this?"

"I haven't talked to her about it," I said.

"No, you wouldn't have. Because you don't even know that she went back into the hospital yesterday afternoon and tomorrow they'll be doing surgery again. You wouldn't know that because those people at the studio are more important to you." She slammed my door.

Guilt and anger settled in at once. Ingrid's head was the next to poke through the door without knocking. She looked tired.

"What's wrong?" she said, "why's everyone yelling?"

"They want me to leave the studio," I told her, tears rolling down my face.

"Maybe it's not such a bad idea," she said with all the practicality of our father. "You need a wider focus."

"You, too?" I said. But the betrayal was not unexpected.

"Anyway, the Jefferson Starship concert is tomorrow. I got us tickets."

A small ray of light. An evening with Ingrid. Our old music. It would be a distraction.

"Okay."

She shut the door.

* * *

A few gold leaves still clung to the sycamore trees in San Juan Capistrano when Ma came home from the hospital. Cold, ocean-borne winds swept them down the streets and across the railroad track. The train whistle sounded far away. The mission bell that chimed on the hour was hollow like a foghorn. Ma was weak and needed full-time care. Mother brought a hospital bed into the small apartment. Poppa hovered in doorways and frowned, leaning on his cane as relatives came and went, bringing food and wine and stories. Celtic folk music played somewhere on a stereo: The Irish Rovers, Barleycorn, signaling the arrival of my cousins.

When Ma was awake, she would struggle to understand where she was. Far-flung daughters travelled to see her and gathered around her bed, fussing over her as if they had always been there. Eyeing them skeptically, I knew she would be happy to know they came, even if it was only to say goodbye. Doctors did what they could, but in the end sent her home with enough morphine to dull to the pain. We measured syringes and practiced injections on oranges. Plastic receptacles collected bodily fluids. We held vigil.

On the wall near her bed hung a black and white photograph of her first daughter, framed in old green wood and draped with a black rosary. Little Gladys, two years old, wore a babushka and beads around her neck. Something was trapped in her chubby hand. A joyful grin lit her face. She stood on the sidewalk in front of her house in that monochrome world, little feet firmly planted in chunky white boots. Ma believed that God had taken her daughter when she confessed to loving Gladys more than Poppa. But I knew it was diphtheria that stole her child. Now, Gladys' soul drew near. I could feel her glowing on the wall behind me as I sat by the high hospital bed-rail, talking quietly to Ma, swimming through the layers of consciousness made opaque by the morphine. A low moan escaped her throat so I took her hand.

Here was death and I knew she was not afraid. I closed my eyes and communed with her, letting the vibrations of Gladys pass through us. After a few minutes, her eyes fluttered open and she concentrated on the ceiling. Then she spoke her first words since coming home.

"I have to go to the john," she said. Startled into reality, I was elated to see her back on the planet for the moment.

"It's okay, Ma, you don't have to get up. They have you hooked to these bags somehow." I spoke to her as if we were discussing plans for dinner, but I alerted my aunts in the next room. My mother's twin sisters had been living a few states away all of my life but I didn't really know them. Some ancient family feud I was not privy to kept them distant. Now they bustled busily into the room.

"I have to go to the bathroom," Ma repeated. This time there was panic in her voice.

"No, you don't, Mom, you just went to the bathroom," said one of the twins. "I took you myself twenty minutes ago." I looked at her, incredulous. Ma had not moved for 24 hours. Why did my aunt lie to her?

"She doesn't even know where she is, there's no need to tell her the truth," the aunt counseled me. I gave her my best single-eyebrow, smartass teenager glare. She didn't know her own mother if she thought Ma could be snowed into doubting her own mind and body. My aunts returned to whatever kept them in the kitchen, satisfied with their deception.

Ma turned her head to me. "Help me get to the bathroom, Leesie. Why won't anyone listen to me?"

"Ma, there's a catheter, and these bags, and you can really just go where you are, it's okay."

Her frown began to morph into something like anger. "Why won't anyone listen to me?" she said again.

"Be comfortable," I told her, "I promise you won't make a mess if you just go." She moaned in pain. I could do nothing but be there so I sat and breathed with her, hoping to God she wasn't thinking me belligerent for refusing to help her get up.

It is the body's will to live. But I think that the spirit has the final say. A shell tortured with pain is not a welcoming place and I knew she would not abide it long. Ma knew her God. And she was ready. Mother came in with a shot of morphine and the agony abated. But I selfishly mourned for that moment of consciousness when she knew I was beside her.

I heard Ingrid at the screen door, Katrine in tow. I looked at Ma sleeping now, breathing low, brow still furrowed. Death was new to me but I wanted it to be graceful and peaceful. I wanted to understand it the way she taught me. I wanted to be her escort, as far as I could take her, to the brink of that realm where we existed together, until the moment her spirit escaped its painful prison. I would witness. I would not leave.

Ingrid appeared in the bedroom door. "You can go now, Liese," she said, "we'll stay for a while."

"No, it's okay, I'm fine."

"Mother wants you to eat something. Ma's not going anywhere tonight. I'll be here if she wakes up."

I looked at Katrine's wide, wet eyes. Lanky and fair, she held tight to Ingrid's arm and pressed her gangly body up against her oldest sister as if she meant to hide from a monster.

"Is Katrine gonna freak out?" I asked Ingrid, "Ma doesn't need any of her break-downs."

"I'm not gonna freak out," Katrine said. She let go of Ingrid, put her hands on her narrow hips, and stood up tall. "I just don't want Ma to die!" Halfway through her defiant sentence she dissolved into sobs. But this time I couldn't blame her. I stood and walked to the door.

"Just cry quietly," I told her. Ingrid tossed me the keys to our dad's old silver hatchback Honda. Maybe I did need a little space.

I passed through the aunts drinking tea and Mother's busy kitchen choreography. I skirted Poppa's questioning, open-mouthed stare and the array of medical equipment staged in the living room. Quietly, on the other side of the screen door, I stared at the little town that I loved. From the top of the steps I could see the bridge over San Juan Creek, the red and white railroad guards, the low roofs of the shops where she walked every day with quick, determined steps. All those people in the shops would miss her. They would know she was gone. She brought light with her everywhere she went and left it glowing in her absence. It was impossible not to smile. I hoped I would be like her when I got old. If I got old.

I started the engine and wondered where to go. Swallowing food didn't seem like an option. With no clear thought, I drove a single mile and found myself at the San Juan Mission. Shoving through the 8-foot tall rusty turnstile, I followed a stone path to the chapel where prayer candles glowed in red glass and a single window spilled a shaft of light into the ancient white plaster sanctuary. Where hands that formed the clay still echoed in the thick, adobe walls, Ma kept a candle lit for Gladys. Tonight, I would light a candle for her. Their flames would live together in the little alcove next to the font. I thought it an ideal place for her to haunt.

From high on the wall a statue of the Virgin Mary looked down at the three of us: Ma, Gladys, and me. I drew a new match from a blue tin box, struck it and added her flame to a red glass. Nothing stirred in the chapel as the fire flared and caught the wick. I tried to remember the 23rd Psalm. Doves cooed in the corridors outside the chapel. Distant bells warned of the approaching train a mile down the road. Words repeated and swirled in my head but they got confused at *he leadeth me down paths...* The Lord's Prayer came more easily. I could see in my memory her lips moving to form its sounds in her sleep.

When I finished, I listened hard for anything the church might want to say. I gazed into the deep altar. Stared into the plaster faces of saints. Breathed in the ancient dust floating in the late afternoon sunlight and left the gods to their will.

* * *

After that day, the hours blended together. We slept little. Cried a lot. We stayed busy and passed each other wordlessly in and out of Ma's small room. The finches, Lancelot and Guinevere, chirped in their bamboo house in the next room. Poppa fed the chickadees and watered the impatiens outside to keep busy, his ninety-four years dragging heavily on his thin frame.

But there was a night, not long before her passing, when I sat again at her bedside and spoke, knowing she did not hear me in the way she had before but hoping my words reached somewhere deeper. I made peace with death but I wasn't going to let it come between Ma and me.

"You'll visit me, won't you, Ma?" I whispered, close to her ear. My grandmother was a powerful spirit. I had no doubt she could transcend whatever force swept her away, for I knew she loved us fiercely and I knew of nothing more powerful than love. "I won't be afraid," I promised. She didn't stir but drew shallow, infrequent breaths that kept her with us by a fragile thread. "Is Gladys there?" I asked her. I wanted to believe in the smile I saw on her lips.

Two days later, Ma left us for whatever received her.

* * *

I slept in my single bed, facing a window that framed Saddleback Mountain and the valley below it. It must have been several hours before dawn when I woke to an electric tremor that ran through my body and seized every muscle, paralyzing me. I could move no more than to open my eyes. The cold nights made the atmosphere thin and transparent. Through the window, headlights sparkled from a car travelling the road that snaked through the hills of my town. My awareness sharpened quickly, feeling static energy all about the room. I stared wide-eyed into the dark.

"Ma," I whispered. She had been gone exactly three days. I tried to move my legs. They were heavy but if I concentrated I could roll out of bed. Leaning on the walls to stand straight, I moved down the hallway to Ingrid's room where she slept heavily. Still vibrating, my knees threatening to buckle, I sat on the floor next to her bed.

"Ingrid," I said quietly. She was out cold.

"Ingrid, wake up." I added no volume but I was not asking. I was insisting. She stirred and squinted. "Ma is here," I announced. Ingrid was not the mystical mooner that I was. Practical and scientific, she mostly followed our father's analytical reasoning. She had the German DNA while I was made entirely of the English side.

"Go back to bed," she said, "you're dreaming." She closed her eyes and turned over.

"I'm not dreaming," I said. Something in the calm way I spoke must have caught her attention. She turned back to me, frowning.

"My whole body feels electric," I told her, presenting myself in front of her eyes. I thought maybe she could see it on me. Like an aura. It felt like an aura.

"What are you talking about?"

"There's crackling all around us. Don't you feel it?"

"I don't feel anything."

I closed my hand around her wrist that lay on the pillow next to her face. Now, her eyes flew open and she propped herself up on one elbow. The window in her room began to bend and rattle as if blown from a strong wind, but the trees outside stood still.

"I feel it," she whispered, recognition spreading across her face.

"It's Ma," I told her. We stayed like that and waited. The energy in the room relaxed.

"We love you, Ma," I said to the air.

In the way a child is unafraid of Santa Claus or angels, I did not fear her ghost in that moment. But as Ingrid began to yawn and nod (could nothing keep that girl from sleep?) I began to evaluate the coming moments. Would she stay here, like this, with us? Did she mean to tell us something or was she saying goodbye? What about tomorrow? Would I always be waiting, listening for her spirit around the corners of my house? My sister must have caught my expression.

"There's nothing to be afraid of," Ingrid said, sleep seeping back into her brain, "she would never hurt us."

"Maybe she needs to say something."

"Maybe."

"Can I sleep with you?"

Ingrid moved as far to the wall as she could and I got in beside her, barely fitting my body into the space that remained. Not since we were small had we shared a bed, hauling covers back and forth and kicking each other's legs out of the way. The moment her head reclaimed the pillow, sleep enveloped her. Wide-awake, I stared into the dark room, through the window to the deep night, feeling how gone someone can be from your life but still remain as energy and light.

"Ma," I whispered, "I know I said I wouldn't be scared. But I am a little. If you need to tell me something, maybe you could tell me in a dream." No more than seconds later I relinquished my consciousness and slept beside Ingrid in the tiny bed.

The dream came clear and quick: I was standing on the sidewalk looking up the cement stairs of the apartment complex to Ma's screen door. These were the same stairs where I had looked out over San Juan Capistrano just a week before—the day I lit a candle at the mission. At the top of the stairs stood my father. He was smiling. Next to him a tall, handsome collie dog sat placidly, white and sable, ears curled at the tips. My father's hand rested on the dog's head. The dog, I was aware even in my dream, was like Shamu. One of those things she had always wanted but put off for another day. The orca, the collie, and a grand piano. She could play by ear. I hoped she had all of those things where she was. Standing alone on the street, I stared at the collie's face. There was something about the eyes that I couldn't figure out. I concentrated. Was the dog wearing glasses? Little silver spectacles sat on its long nose. Those were Ma's glasses. Those were Ma's eyes. And soon, the dog had Ma's face as well. As the collie stood, its body morphed before my eyes, becoming Ma. She was stout and steady but just left of alive. She began to descend the stairs toward me. My father remained at the top, observing passively. I moved to her in my dream, reaching to embrace her but she stopped me.

"Don't hug me," she said, "I'm cold." Her face was troubled, her voice full of worry.

"It doesn't matter, Ma," I told her, reaching for her, "what's wrong?"

"What did they do with me?" she asked. "Don't let them..." she said. I sensed her confusion and fear. Even under the veil of the dream I was conscious that her body was to be cremated. Perhaps even on that very night. I did not say so. Ma had dabbled in Catholicism but she was not actually a real Catholic, was she? Did no one ask her how she wanted her life to end? These were not details I had faced. These were adult issues. I had no answer for her. Ma began to back away from me. Carefully she climbed the stairs and soon she sat beside my father again, furry and serene, staring down. I couldn't help her.

I woke to weak winter sunlight gracing Ingrid's window. A song swam through my thoughts, lilting in Ma's airy soprano. It was the last song I heard her sing. Katrine had been crying over some silly thing and Ma held her close on the old green couch waiting for her to settle down:

"Though your heart may ache a while, never mind. Though your face may lose its smile, never mind. There's sunshine after rain, and gladness follows pain. You'll be happy once again, never mind."

Chapter 15

It's funny how memories bring the past in punches, or wander forlornly, leading to stories half remembered. But if we pay close attention, the forgotten holes can be filled in more often than not.

I remember an Easter phone call on a morning lost to champagne and unprecedented April heat. Lying dazed on my single bed in the late afternoon, Siamese cat on my stomach, I listened to the rumblings of my family still sipping from tall crystal glasses in the kitchen. I almost slept. Almost. Until the phone rang.

I propped myself on one elbow, careful not to disturb Burma Rose, and waited for someone to pick up the kitchen extension. Soon my mother's voice conversed with a disembodied someone and I rested back into my pillow hoping to sleep. Instead her high-pitched, tipsy voice called out for me.

"Annelieeeeeeese, phone is for you." A meaningful pause, and then: "And it's a boy...."

I opened my eyes and tried to still the spinning ceiling. A boy. Wesley? Merrick? Whoever it was, I couldn't imagine why any boy would call me at Easter, when everyone was preparing dinner with their families. I gathered up Burma Rose, who laid back her ears with a scowl, and dragged us both to the end of the hall to pick up the phone in my parents' room.

I dumped the cat on the bed and bent to grab the receiver from a bedside table. My head spun. My father, himself three-sheets-to-the-wind, had hovered over my empty glass with the last of the bottle an hour before, and I hadn't resisted. Now I paid for that, flopping onto the bed, phone to my ear. I lay back on a stack of soft pillows and closed my eyes.

"Hurry and pick up!" yelled my mother from the kitchen. "And don't let him know you're drunk. Maybe he likes good girls!" She couldn't see my eyes roll from down the hall.

"Hello?"

"Is this Anneliese?" said a male voice. I heard the extension click into its cradle in the kitchen.

"Yep." I didn't hide my annoyance.

"There's someone here who wants to talk to you." All at once, I recognized the proper lisp and elegant flow of words. Suddenly sober, I pressed the phone close to my ear and whispered into the receiver, glancing at the bedroom door to check for eavesdroppers.

"Christopher?"

"It's me, indeed," he said. "*You-know-who* would like to talk to you."

"So why are *you* calling me?"

"Seriously, Sweetie? What if your mom answered and it was her on the line?" He didn't wait for my response. "Hold on," he said. My heart began to pound in my ears as I waited for Rebecca's voice to slip through the line.

"Liese...?" she asked more than said, her soft voice melting like chocolate in my ear. Her words slurred slightly, pleasantly.

"Hey," I said.

"Hey. So...Christopher and I are in my shop drinking Jack Daniels."

"On Easter?" Through the white filigrees curtains I could see the sun inching low on the horizon. I hoped the heat would fade with it.

"We didn't know what else to do. My mom's in Bishop, Christopher's family isn't talking to him, and neither of us is attached just now, ya know?" Her words stung. I had tried like hell to attach myself to her. To be everything she wanted. "Anyway," she continued, "we're a little drunk and we got to talking..."

"I'm a little drunk, too," I told her, "we had champagne this morning." I kicked myself for interrupting but I wanted her to see me as an equal. One who was free to over-indulge at will. Just like her.

"Who's all over there?"

"My cousins, my aunt, their friends. A bunch of people." My stomach lurched on unsettled champagne and I fought off nausea, trying to concentrate on Rebecca's words. "What were you and Christopher talking about?"

"I just told him that I... that I want you to know that I...Liese, we..."

At that exact moment, the moment when Rebecca's words were straining to reach me on the other end of the coiled phone line, my mother barged into the room.

"Just look at that sunset!" she raved and flung the light curtain aside. "Anneliese, look!"

I covered the mouthpiece. "I'm on the phone, Mother."

"Well put it down for a minute and come and look."

She meant to disturb me. To make sure that nothing was more important to me than my family. She had been excited for me to talk to a boy but now she meant to sabotage. I wondered what she'd heard. "Hold on," I sighed heavily to Rebecca, "I have to do something." I set the phone on the bed and got up to stand next to my giddy, swaying mother, knowing she would not leave until I humored her.

"The sunset is pink," I said, bored and put out. I walked back to the bed and picked up the phone. "I'm sorry," I said into the receiver.

"Be that way!" shouted my mother as she left the room to join the Easter revelers in the kitchen. But Rebecca was no longer on the line.

"I'm sorry," came Christopher's sweet voice, "she just can't. She loves you, but she can't."

"Christopher, please, put her back on," I said, desperate to recapture the moment. "Why can't she? What does she want to tell me?"

"I can't tell you that."

"What can't you tell me? Christopher, don't do this to me!" The humid air and evening heat became a monsoon in my growing panic.

"You wouldn't understand now, Baby. It's not your fault. Just let her go."

"I can't let her go, Christopher, you know that."

"You can, Anneliese. She is miserable. You are miserable."

"I know she loves me, Christopher. Don't say she doesn't."

"I didn't say that. And it isn't the point."

The kind of tears that flow without sound, without breath, poured from me. I was losing again. The only love I wanted. The only love I would ever need. Three miles away, in a window-lined room full of costumes, Rebecca and Christopher sat together with a phone and a bottle of whiskey in the only place I wanted to be; a place I could never be.

"I'm going to hang up now," said Christopher.

"Why did you even call me?" I sobbed. But the vibrant static that connected me to them through the wire was silent. A black hole opened up. He hadn't heard. She was gone.

Burma Rose made it her duty to fix my troubles. She began kneading my hair, claws contracting at the base of my neck as I cried into my mother's pillow. Her purr, low and insistent, sought to penetrate whatever spell so vexed me. Her need to soothe me intensified until her claws sunk deep into my neck. I reached back to disentangle long paws from my hair, then gathered her into my chest where she curled into a ball. The ponderous heat persisted past nightfall.

* * *

The steep hills of Pacific Crest slope toward the harbor where a bronze statue of a sailor stands as if bracing himself for heavy seas. With his back to the ocean, his hard stare is fixed on the cliffs where the town overlooks the ocean. During a storm, you can watch the waves break over the jetty, tossing the sails of the old brig, *Pioneer*. On calm days, dolphin fins break the surface and hollow barking can be heard for miles from rusting buoys where seals cling, rocking and calling and shoving each other into the harbor.

In this town, along these streets, we learned to drive, went to school, got our first jobs, ditched our classes, held hands in the sand, kissed each other with the thrill of freedom, little debaucheries on our lips.

Our science teachers owned a schooner called the *Orca II*. Year after year it floated, hitched to a wooden dock under a seafood restaurant window, its green paint worn and its tall sails furled. Mr. Simons and Mr. Dunne taught us about sailing and took us beyond the jetty, telling tales of the harbor's founder and how he stood up for the rights of working deckhands. But my favorite part of Pacific Crest lore was that the town had been called "*The only romantic spot on the coast.*"

Merrick's house was high on a bluff, just down the street from our high school where he, too, had sailed on the *Orca II* and camped in the Bay of

Las Animas at the end of senior year. I remember his kitchen, much like mine. The tract houses, all built in the late sixties, offered affordable American dreams. Small plots of land and stucco walls, we all lived like the Bradys with green shag carpets and white tile counters. Our fathers were businessmen or doctors, ever dressed in suits and sipping martinis. Most commuted long distances to the big cities, far from the protected beach hubs to the south, where their children navigated childhood with stay-at-home moms, soccer teams, surf grommets and dial-a-ride.

In the kitchen, Merrick's older sister was baking. She pulled oatmeal cookies from the oven and winked at her brother.

"Z'at what I think it is?" he asked her.

"You guys want some?"

"Absolutely," he grinned, "how much should we eat?"

She glanced at me, sized me up. "Two should be enough," she said, and left us alone. Merrick took two cookies from the plate for himself and two more for me, handing them over as he led me down the hall to his bedroom.

"You like *Yes*?" he asked as he dropped the record down the spindle on the turntable. A diamond-head needle zipped and cracked on vinyl grooves. I hadn't heard of *Yes* but I didn't say so. The style was familiar so I simply said, "Sounds good."

"Take a bite," he said, "but eat slowly."

"Slowly?" I laughed. As I bit I caught a familiar scent and began to understand the look on Merrick's face.

"Wait, don't you get stoned?" he asked.

"Um, well, here and there."

"Have you ever eaten it?"

"No."

"Well, it's a blast, go ahead."

I thought of the giddy, tired feeling of marijuana in my lungs laced with the softness of Rebecca's lips. I did not want to think of her. Or lose my cool with Merrick. I took a bite. *I hope you're happy, Rebecca.*

Merrick came to the single bed in his small room with one window and sat beside me. I stared at the wall, lined with plastic yellow bins crammed with carefully alphabetized record albums, and waited for something to

131

happen. I was beginning to feel annoyed by the high-pitched voices oozing from the record player. I decided I did not like *Yes*.

"You probably need more," he said, sliding his arm behind me. I took another bite. His body next to mine felt foreign and stiff. But he was good-natured and happy to be with me, so I did not move away.

"And this," he said, and leaned his weight into me so I lay back on his bed. He covered my body with his. "Is it your first time for this as well?" It wasn't unexpected. We had come to the moment in that unspoken way friends will decide to go for a walk but end up having lunch instead.

"Yes," I said. I felt the oatmeal cookies dissolving and delivering herbs to my blood.

"The pot will make it hurt less," he said in my ear.

Hurt less? "I'm not your first virgin, then?" I said, hoping to sound cool.

"You are my first virgin."

"But not you...?"

He laughed. "No, not me. I'm an old pro. Just kidding. But I'll go slow. You'll be all right."

When I was little I walked under the pedestrian tunnel to Strands Beach with my mother. Graffiti cluttered the walls and Ingrid and I shouted to hear our voices echo back to us. Over an aqua-sprayed dolphin with white foam edges, in red capital letters, FUCK was emblazoned on the tunnel at an odd angle. I sounded it out, as a six-year-old does. Mother made no effort to stop me.

"What does it mean?" I asked her.

"It's what a man and a woman do to make a baby," she said without hesitation. I frowned.

"Why is it written on the dolphin?" I asked.

"No reason. Just some kid being a smart ass."

"How do they make a baby?"

My mother was clinical and spilled it with all the flair of a Grey's Anatomy chapter.

"But," she added, "we only do that with someone we love very much and only when we are married adults."

And here I was breaking all the rules. So what? Right now, I had my virginity to lose. Loving Merrick was the farthest thing from my mind, but he was more than willing to receive what I volunteered.

Mother neglected to tell me about the pain. How was this a thing to be shared with someone I loved? I was pretty sure I would hate Merrick after this.

"Don't worry about the blood," he said, "It will stop."

There, now. At once a sacrificial lamb and an empty vessel. No longer sacred. I was Rebecca's for the taking.

Staring down at me, he reached over to the nightstand where he had set the rest of a cookie and a bottle of Drambuie liqueur. "Bite," he said, and pressed the crumbling sweet stuff into my mouth. Burning and raw now, I swallowed obediently. "And now this," he said and putting a shot glass to my lips. I swallowed again. "The pain won't last," he said. At that moment, I hated Rebecca, too.

Returning to my body now, for in those moments I had wandered off, choosing not to witness, I took the last of the second cookie off the table, finished it, and downed another shot of sickeningly sweet Drambuie. My eyes fixed on the window. I felt like a block of cement. Moving my gaze took conscious effort. I was beginning to feel more than a little scared.

"Was it just pot that we ate?"

"Pot and oatmeal. Why?"

"I don't know. I don't feel very well."

"Get dressed, let's get some air."

I don't remember how long it took to accomplish that task. Moving as if through molasses we passed Merrick's sister in the kitchen. She looked at us with a simultaneous frown and smile.

"How many did you eat?"

"You told us to take two. We ate two."

"Two each?" she looked at the plate of cookies.

"Well, yeah."

"I meant two for both of you," she laughed and shook her head at Merrick.

Merrick shrugged and looked at me. "Coffee," he said. We drove in his old gold station wagon down the road to the Salty Dog Cafe where he led me across the parking lot and into a Naugahyde booth. He sat across from me and ordered. I looked at him and tried to make sense of the face in front of me—tried to still him into a single being. Despite my efforts he swam into double and triple vision.

"I don't like this at all," I said.

"Don't sweat it, it will wear off. You're just paranoid."

"I can't think," I told him. I was beginning to panic. "I want my brain back."

"I'll take you home," he said.

I don't remember the drive but we parked across from my house while I tried to pull myself together enough to go in the house. Overcoming the obstacle of the front door, I made the announcement that I was ill, passed the T.V. watchers and meal preparers, and went to bed, no longer a virgin.

* * *

Weeks away from the studio turned into months. Writing became a ceremony of regret and catharsis. My notebook waited on my desk in plain view. I left it there, knowing Ingrid was curious. An invitation to a mystery that would unfold for both of us, if she cared to know. One day I opened it to write in my black razor pilot pen and there was her lighter blue ballpoint on the next page. It was the stuff of sisters that couldn't be unraveled by those who were outside. It was about me and her and our childhood and marijuana smoke snaking above our heads in the rain. Dizzy with her words, I wrote back to her and replaced the notebook. Soon, it became our ritual. Neglected thoughts found a place on the pages. Quiet conversations waited patiently to evolve. I found my sister again.

Anneliese: I remember you and me side-by-side, glowing, grinning, singing Pentangle loud and wine-washed, "sisters" etched on our foreheads like some supernatural tattoo. Holding hands as if we were six. How is it that I hardly recognize us? How is it that I've lost you?

Next to her words she taped a photograph of the two of us laughing in the sand.

I wanted her to remember this:

Ingrid: A Cornish wake and sleeplessness and the window shook and she tried to say something else. And Daddy didn't know what to say and Stephen said an Irish prayer and Joyce scattered ashes on Ortega Highway and then you said, "She would never hurt you. She loves you. You are twin souls." How old are you? I'm ancient. How young are you? I'm fetal. Carbon, Hydrogen, Nitrogen, Phosphorous, We are.

Anneliese: I opened your door, so seemingly locked, aching for your poetry books, and found them gone. Where are your books? I needed *The World's Erotic* and *Child's Garden* like hell and instead rummaged through mother's antiques. Found "for Jim and Fred, 1899" scribbled in the cover of brittle pages. Speaking to my fingers like a blind man from the past. Hooking me in the heart. It was saying, "touch me!" so I did. And the books sit beside me now awaiting unfamiliar eyes to complete this satisfaction. They and I need each other.

Ingrid: There are small gestures a mulberry tree can make in a California state where seasons sneak around like married lovers and only those who love them notice.

Anneliese: I come along behind you like the weightless things the air pulls along and people say, "Look, she's flying on the wind! Carried on the wind! Does she wish she had flight of her own?"

And so we went on.

Chapter 16

I stood shivering at the payphone in front of Pacific Crest High School in mid-December. All morning, through English, through Biology, I had thought of Rebecca, replaying that summer afternoon in Westwood. I let my mind expand and fill with the time I had finally put between us. Two months had turned into three. I challenged myself to stay away. With Christopher's coaching and my family's victory in my newly calm presence, I had gained some sort of peace. The anger I felt when Rebecca suggested I experience men had fueled my distance even more.

But on this morning Ingrid and I had seen the fog hanging heavily over the Pacific as we drove to school with the suffocating weight of first loss still riding like a mute passenger between us. The cold air filled me with melancholy and longing and suddenly I could wait no longer. I listened to the phone ring into the glass walls of Rebecca's sewing room next to Dudley's office. I imagined her in the next room having coffee with him as the ringing continued. I imagined her on the floor amassed in tissue patterns, frustrated with a ringing phone. Just as I thought it best to hang up, her voice came through the wires sounding tired and dreamy. Perhaps rushed.

"Hello, this is Rebecca."

Not too much silence. It was now or never. In those seconds, hanging up was still an option.

"Bec?" It came out almost as a whisper.

For a moment she let her own silence pass between us.

"I've missed you," she said finally. I realized I had been holding my breath.

"I'm sorry. I had to stay away."

"I know."

"Christopher said I shouldn't even tell you I was going. That I shouldn't call. It was so hard...at first."

"Yeah, Christopher and I talked, too. He's a good friend. Will you be coming back? Dudley misses you, too."

"I would like to. I want to see you." Moments passed filled with nervous breathing. I squeezed my eyes shut tight. Why did I say that so soon? I needed to play it cool.

Finally: "And don't you want to dance?"

"I haven't stopped dancing." I had cleared space in the garage on many late nights and danced until my toes bled into my pointe shoes, loving the pain of ripped skin because it distracted me from the pain in my heart.

"I'll be at Jade's 6:15 barre on Thursday," I said, having no idea how I would accomplish that. Would I be allowed? Relief spread over me anyway. I would be there.

"Guess I'll see you then," she said.

* * *

Échappé is French for escape. Now we are competing, Jade and I. She is the teacher and I, almost seventeen, am the dissatisfied student. Locked into a tight fifth position, toe to heel, we are bound and ready to spring. Forcing energy down into the floor, searching for the lightest friction against the wood, smooth velocity peaking just as the tips of our pointe shoes halt and lock in a wide open second. *Échappé.* We have escaped. Again. And again. I've counted 64 and my eyes are locked on hers in the mirror, both of us gazing ahead, watching each other for weakness, each waiting for the other to falter, tire. We refuse. We go on. Sweat dripping.

"For God's sake, Anneliese, okay, okay," she finally says. It's not that she can't go on. She is just done. "You win."

The dancers behind me left the barre where they stood witnessing this small war with bemused half-smiles. They gathered damp towels, gym bags, discarded chiffon skirts, and headed through the white wooden barn doors to the dressing room. Tonight, my first night back, we would have our annual studio Christmas party and the dancers would spend the night there in old-fashioned slumber party style. Only this year was different. We were not children anymore.

Jade, slight in her white leotard, blonde hair in the tight French twist, took her half-spent pack of Benson and Hedges from the stereo and wasted no time lighting up. Smoke rose and curled from the cigarette between her long fingers, nails glinting violet. She smiled to herself and lifted a cool gaze to me, leaving a ring of wine lipstick on the white paper of her cigarette.

"Rebecca, Christopher, and I are going to *Mugs Away* tonight," she said. "Don't you kids get into any trouble while we're gone."

Her retaliation against my end-of-class bravado went unheeded. I felt her eyes on my back as I walked to the door without responding. *I wouldn't go to that dive bar even if I were old enough*, I pitched a loud thought in her direction. I knew she would be watching closely to see if time away had cured my obsession with Rebecca.

"Are you staying tonight?" Hannah asked me. During my banishment she had returned to the studio but something about her had changed. Or was it I who was different?

I hopped over a pile of dancers collapsed on the floor. "I am if you are." We were past the age when slumber parties held any appeal. But we knew Dudley trusted us and would make himself scarce if he stayed at all. Through the night the studios would be our domain. A thrilling prospect. A bottle of whiskey waited in the trunk of the silver Honda outside.

"Not only am I staying, but Chase is meeting me here," Hannah grinned. She met Chase at camp over the summer where she worked as a counselor. He was Navajo. Tall and dark. Full lipped. Gorgeous and wild. He was Hannah's rebellion against a childhood full of etiquette and pleasantries.

"You invited Chase to the studio?" I was skeptical and not comfortable with blending worlds. The studio was sacred.

"He'll wait 'til the teachers are all gone."

"If you say so."

If not for Hannah rolling her eyes in the elementary school corridor all those years ago, I wouldn't have stood in that place and time, with the previous ten years wrapped around me like a magician's cloak, allowing me to live two completely different lives. To be two completely different people.

Now, like Ingrid, Hannah felt me fading to the edges of her life. Chase wasn't simply a rebellion, I confess. He was the result of a deal I made with her in the spring. Late one Saturday night we sat side by side on twin beds in her room, skimming the pages of last year's high school yearbook.

"Who, on this page, is still a virgin?" she asked me. This was a game. Talk on campus was tossed about with deliberate carelessness. We were pawns in a competition where the only rule was to lose. In our circle of nerds, we had to fight our way into the crowd and even then, we were likely to remain unseen unless we created a bawdy spectacle.

"There are no virgins on this page," I laughed.

"Even the boys?"

"The girls had to give it to someone." Hannah turned to the "S" section where my goofy, self-conscious freshman smile appeared from under disheveled dark hair.

"How about this one?" she pointed to me.

I bit my lip and looked away. Was she ready for this? Was I?

"Come on, you can tell me..."

"Well, I'm not exactly a virgin. Technically." I wanted her to pounce. She did.

"Oh my god, who have you been with?" The divine excitement of leaving childhood behind at any cost!

"I can't tell you that."

"Why the hell not?"

I got myself into this. But it didn't feel right. "Because you might not understand."

"Why wouldn't I understand? That's nuts." She frowned. This game was losing its attraction. I should not have played. "Is it someone I know?"

"Yes."

"Wesley?!"

"Not Wesley," I laughed.

"Christopher and Ricky are out. That leaves, let's see, Tony, Troy, Dane,... Curtis?"

"Stop. None of them."

"Why won't you tell me? I thought we were friends."

"We are. But I don't want to scare you."

"Now you *are* scaring me."

"You haven't been with anyone yet."

"No."

"When you have been with a guy, I will tell you." It wasn't fair. It was precisely what Rebecca had done to me: *The secrets of the universe will be yours if you sleep with a guy.* She pondered my challenge.

"There were cute guys at camp last year."

I smiled conspiratorially. It isn't that I wanted to hide the truth about Rebecca from Hannah, but the thought that she might recoil from me suddenly became a possibility. Would she question ten years of childhood friendship? Would she wonder if I had ever thought of her that way? I was old enough to fear such leaps of the imagination. I had made them myself. A guy in her life would take away the question of her own tendencies to stray from the norm.

Now in December, under cover of night, we ran to the parking lot and popped the back of my hatchback. Glancing around for cloying adults, Hannah pulled the whiskey bottle out of the tall boot where I had stashed it and slid it under her sweatshirt. Facing the studio windows, I kept my eyes averted from Rebecca's sewing room. She had been out when I had arrived for Jade's class earlier in the evening. Now, I supposed, she was at *Mugs Away* with Jade, Christopher, and Ricky. I did my best to focus on the party and made up my mind not to wait for her.

Inside, half a dozen teenage girls, plus Wesley, tossed off spontaneous choreography before studio mirrors, music loud, crumbling Christmas cookies in their hands. They laughed and traded stage props, parading a mock, gaudy musical. Wesley partnered the dancers, grinning like a mad hatter, halting their spins with dramatic flair.

Hannah and I joined the fray, quickly dropping the bottle behind the trashcan on our way into the room. Dudley waddled after us, chuckling at the antics of his young charges celebrating another long year of study behind them. He gathered a few record albums and his cigarettes from the stereo podium and made for the door again. We traded glances of freedom but he turned back to us as if in second thought. We tensed. "Be good, my loves," he called from the doorway, "I'll be back in the morning."

"Merry Christmas, Dudley!" I yelled after him.

"Merry Christmas!" came his fading reply. We were officially unattended.

After a few minutes, Hannah ran to the parking lot and signaled in the dark. Soon Chase skulked in, his arm draped over her shoulder. Clearly out of place, he sat himself on the floor under the line of barres, taking in the odd spectacle of waiflike girls with energy to spare, contorting their bodies into impossible stretches or bounding and rebounding into the air like a herd of reindeer. Hannah sat beside him. I knew she would not be silly in front of him and I was vaguely sad for her sacrifice. I took my turn pirouetting with Wesley, our token boy for the night, our classical technique deteriorating into vaudeville.

But the reverie was soon broken. "What time is it? Turn that music down, you'll get Dudley in trouble!" Jade's face poked around the door from Ricky's jazz studio. I did not like her tone. At the same time, I knew her arrival back at the studio signaled Rebecca's as well. I hadn't dared to wonder if they would be back this way. My heart began to beat double time but I coached myself to coolness. Besides, who was Jade to come in here throwing around commands? We had held this party every Christmas since long before she had set foot among us two years before.

She stomped into our studio and turned the stereo down. Dancers froze and stared at her, smiles fading. Glancing critically around the room, her eyes fell on Chase and Hannah, now lip-locked in the corner and paying her no mind. She turned her glare on me. Wesley's hands dropped from my waist and he took a step back, eschewing guilt by association.

"I want to speak to you in the next room," she said to me. I didn't stop to wonder why Chase was my fault. Everything was, when it came to Jade. I followed her into the dark studio, folded my arms, thrust my weight into one hip and braced myself for the torrent that was Jaybird. Questioning eyebrow raised in defiance, I would not let her get to me. I met her gaze.

"I hope you know he's not staying here tonight," she said. I hadn't really thought about it. I certainly had no investment in the matter. It was Hannah's business. But I was not one to back down from a challenge.

"Maybe he is," I shot back.

"I beg to differ with you."

"Then beg," I said, and turned to the door just as I felt long nails grab my arm and yank me back.

"What the hell?" I yelled louder than I meant to.

My words brought Christopher lilting to the interior doorway of Rebecca's dimly lit office where they had all gathered after the bar. He fell into a familiar *Jesus Christ Superstar* refrain, *What's the buzz, tell me what's happening, what's the buzz tell me what's happening, what's the buzz tell me what's happening...* he trotted a soft-shoe around the dark studio. I would have loved to reply with the very appropriate, *Why should you want to know, why are you obsessed with fighting?* But the mood wasn't right.

"There's a boy in there with them," Jade told Christopher, still holding fast to my arm.

"A boy, you say?" Christopher peered into the ballet side, full of curious charm.

"Be serious, Christopher, they have no supervision," Jade told him. "Dudley just let them stay here alone." I felt my anger rising. "Tell him to go or I will," she said to me.

"You go ahead," I told her, conscious of Rebecca's failure to jump to my defense. She had to have heard us.

I glanced at Christopher as she called my bluff and presented herself to the party next door.

"Don't look at me, Sweetie, it's your drama," said Christopher, "and yes, Rebecca's in there." He left the way he came, to join her.

When I went back to the ballerinas, Hannah was not sulking as I expected. Instead, her wide eyes and stifled laughter were barely held by a dam that broke the instant she met my eyes. Her infectious laugh filled the room.

"Oh my god," she roared, "did you see that?"

"Where's Chase?"

"In the parking lot for now."

"Christ, what a bitch," I said. But my heart wasn't in it.

The party settled down. We threw blankets and pillows on the floor, played Tchaikovsky's Nutcracker low on the stereo and passed the bottle of whiskey around the room. From where I lay, my head propped on Wesley's prone back, I could see Tiffany's arms dancing the choreography as she stared up at the ceiling, imagining an audience. Wesley, flat out on his belly, drummed the rhythm into the wood floor, his eyes flagging.

Around midnight Hannah leaned in close. "Are they still here?" she whispered. I had been waiting for an excuse to find out. "I'll check," I told her and headed to the dark studio separating me from Rebecca.

Lights still shone from her office as I came upon them, Christopher, Jade, Ricky, and Rebecca, draped on the floor, cocaine in neat lines on a mirror in front of them. Jade was the first to notice me.

"Get back where you belong," she said, her words slurring.

"You guys don't need to stay here," I said, not looking at Rebecca, though I could feel her gaze on me.

"Looks to me," Jade said, "like you girls are in need of supervision." She sniffed hard and squinted through watery eyes.

"What are six teenage girls gonna do alone in a studio?" I asked the room.

Christopher looked up from the mirror and smiled, "You want me to get a book and show you?" The room erupted. Rebecca's distinct laughter felt like betrayal. I glanced at her, hurt, and she held my gaze, apologetically drunk.

I shook my head at him in disgust. "This is ridiculous," I said, "we aren't children."

"In your dreams," said Jade, dismissing me with a scoot-along flip of her long fingers.

Realizing I would get nowhere with my protest, I turned to go. Halfway across the dark studio I felt her behind me.

"Hey," Rebecca whispered.

I froze. I did not turn around. I could hear Tchaikovsky still spinning fairy tales in the next room. I felt her approach more than heard it. One of Rebecca's hands slid into mine, and the other encircled my waist. She pulled me towards her in the dark until we were connected, tessellated, my back to her front. "I'm sorry," she whispered into my hair. My breath caught in my throat and I tipped my head back against her shoulder. She pressed her lips into my neck. I felt tears crease at the corner of my eyes.

"Bec," I turned around to see the face I loved. Unruly blonde hair curled to her shoulders. In the dark, her blue-grey eyes were mystical, unearthly. Soft, pure of line, Rebecca's body was not thin and bony, like a dancer. She was carefree. And careless. And I was lost in her.

"I am impossible, I know it," she said. I bent my forehead against hers, still unable to speak for fear of sobbing. "I love you," she said, and pressed her lips to mine. "You destructive..." she kissed me again, "messed up, ..." and again, "angel..." she backed me to the mirrored wall, letting her hands fall over my shoulders, my hips. "Oh god, I drank too much," she said. "Sit with me." I didn't wonder, then, how I was destructive. Or messed up. But I wanted to be her angel.

"I missed you, Rebecca." I leaned against her, watching our fingers lace. Sixty days away dissolved into meaningless wasted time.

"I missed you, Liese, but I tried so hard not to. This makes no sense." She gathered my hair in her hands, wrapping it around her wrist.

"In just a little more than a year I'll be eighteen."

"Then you will live with me." Rebecca's condo was halfway between Ma's house and mine. I had been there once. I remembered a large, floppy black Labrador bounding to the gate and a fluffy Siamese sitting serenely in her window.

"Are you asking me or telling me?" I truly didn't care which but I had my back up against any command. Even from Rebecca.

Her eyes closed tight in frustration. "Everything is not a fight, Liese."

"I'm just tired of being told where to go and what to do and who to see."

"You think that's going to get easier, being with me? You think anyone will just let us be?"

"I don't know. I'm willing to find out."

"I was at the bar one night with Christopher when you were gone. There was a guy playing a guitar. He sang a song about you."

"A song about me? What song?"

"Sad Lisa, you know? By Cat Stevens."

"That's my anthem."

"I thought about you all night. And you called the next day. I heard about your Grandmother. I know you loved her very much. I'm sorry." She put an arm around my shoulders.

"She knew about you, you know?"

"You told her about me?" Rebecca sobered up quickly.

"No. She just knew." I wanted to believe it. Ma grew up in the twenties. The time of Gertrude Stein, Radcliffe Hall.... Ma was no blushing violet. She would have accepted Rebecca.

"Come to West Beach with me tomorrow. I have to pick up some tulle near town. It's a Saturday. Don't you and Hannah have *somewhere to be?*" she nudged me in the ribs with her elbow.

"As a matter of fact we do," I said, and leaned in to press my lips against hers, the gentle pressure leaving me lightheaded and shaking. Our eyes were still closed when a shadow fell across the light in the doorway to Rebecca's shop.

Christopher's backlit silhouette appeared. We looked up. His nervously awkward stance sought desperately to communicate something to us.

"What is it?" said Rebecca. Christopher's frantic whisper replied, "It's Anneliese's dad!"

Seconds later my father appeared from behind him, car keys dangling from one hand, pipe in the other, tobacco smoke still wafting in the December cool of the empty studio.

"Come on out of there," he demanded.

"What are you doing here?" I tried to shift subtly away from Rebecca — to put acceptable space between us.

"I got a call from Jade," he said. So, Jaybird was every bit the devious raptor I knew she was, privy to my strict upbringing and a shameless flirt whenever my father was about. Around the time she had come to teach at our studio, he had developed a habit of picking me up at night sporting a flask of whiskey with four shot glasses, spreading liquid joy and making Jade, and even Rebecca, feel like the most beautiful women he had ever seen. She knew he would jump at her command. She knew he would believe anything she told him.

"Sounds to me like you got yourself into a mess again," he said. "Didn't waste any time, did you? If I'm going to be pulled from my bed in the middle of the night because of my daughter's behavior, I'm not leaving alone. Let's go." He sounded more exhausted than angry. I didn't need another scene. I got up and followed him, not bothering to alert the others to my sudden departure. It was Hannah's fault anyway. I realized I was irritated with her for bringing Chase to the party. And furious with Jade's power-play. Rebecca sat still and did not acknowledge him or speak up for me. How could she? I wondered if she felt the sting of Jade's actions as much as I did. After all, she put Rebecca at risk, too. Was she jealous? Did she love Rebecca, too? Or did she just hate me?

I got in my father's car and sat silently awaiting a tirade, a third-degree, an all-out "what-has-gotten-into-you-I-thought-we-were-through-with-this" lecture. He got in on the driver's side and closed the door.

"What about the Honda?" I asked.

"You can get it tomorrow." He was silent for a few minutes as we drove out of the industrial complex in the dark.

"I want to know what you were doing in there with Rebecca with the lights off," he said.

"Talking."

"In the dark?"

"In the dark."

"There's more to it than that. What is so important that you have to talk alone in the dark? Why weren't you at the Christmas party with your friends?"

My thoughts darted, wove, conceived, defended, as the pause in conversation dilated and stretched beyond acceptability. I decided that he must be fed controversy for his trouble. But not the real controversy. I threw up a smoke screen.

"Hannah brought Chase to the party," I said.

"And..."

"Jade didn't think we should have a boy in there with us unchaperoned."

"I would agree with that. What's that got to do with you and Rebecca in a dark room?"

"Well, Jade and I got in a fight."

"So I heard."

"Why do you flirt with her? She's a bitch," I said.

"I don't flirt with her and this isn't about me," he said, then added, "She's an attractive woman. Don't change the subject. I want to know what you were doing."

"I told you, we were talking."

"What is the subject of this clandestine 'talk' you were having?" I decided my best play was to let him believe he had won. Confess to dark deeds I never committed.

"Why do I have to tell you?"

"Because I'm your father." This would have never worked on me if the truth were at stake. I let the deception play out.

"Okay," I sighed in mock defeat. "There's a boy at school. I like him a lot. Rebecca is the person I talk to about guys. She gives good advice. I can't ask Mother or you."

He was quiet, mulling this over. A long minute seemed to gain mass and shout in the silence. If he believed me or not, he didn't let on. Finally, he spoke.

"When I walked in, you were in her lap or she was in yours, and it was too close for my comfort. If your mother had caught you, there would have been hell to pay."

So. My ruse had likely failed. But he let it drop. Grateful for the quiet on the quick drive home and not at all sorry to leave the party, I went to my room without another word. As I slid into bed in the dark quiet, the panic of the last hour subsided. I returned to the only thing about the night that mattered. She said she loved me.

In the morning, having ridden on that high until daybreak, I wrote in my journal:

There haven't been many good poems lately.
I've been skipping stones
And smiling too much
And I haven't learned
How to sing happy words in a song.
So there haven't been any
And I am.

Chapter 17

My father left the house before dawn on Saturday. I had woken early but idled in bed, sure that Mother would melt into a furious uproar the moment she laid eyes on me. But when I dared to enter the kitchen it was not agitation I witnessed. Instead, she was lost in thought as she stirred around the kitchen making tea. She picked up various objects and put them back down six inches to the left or right. The salt, the yellow and red box of Lipton, a stray spoon. She turned on the faucet. And turned it off again.

"Did you have a good night?" she asked, absently. "How was the party?"

Had she slept through it all? I decided to roll with my good fortune. She was so checked out of reality that my plan to go to West Beach with Rebecca actually had a chance of working. Mother put a hand to her forehead, sighed heavily and stared out the kitchen window.

"It was fine," I said, discouraging further questioning. Mother's gaze found no barrier at the glass, continuing out over the fog-hung hills to the west.

"What's the matter?" I asked.

She hesitated. "What isn't the matter?"

"Are you thinking of Ma?"

"I'm always thinking of Ma," she said, "but your father...."

"What..."

"He's just always leaving that's all. And I wouldn't mind having a little emotional support. You're always… somewhere else. Ingrid is studying for the SAT. And Katrine… is just a lot of work and now he…" Her gaze fell on the counter where an open bottle of booze was telling tales. She closed it up and put it on the shelf.

"Are you hungover?" I asked.

"So what if I am?"

"I guess I would be drinking, too, if I lost you, Mother," I said. It was true; I couldn't imagine my life without her, even if she held the reins too tight.

"You could have fooled me," she said, "You don't even hug me anymore."

I got up from the counter stool where I'd noncommittally perched, and went to her, bending slightly to put my arms around her five-foot frame. I let her hug me tight. She pressed me into her like a child, placing two fingers at the back of my neck as if supporting the weight of an infant's head. Perhaps she was remembering. I stiffened with resentment and ended the hug, stepping back.

"Hannah and I are going to West Beach today," I said.

"What for?"

"We just want to."

"Take Katrine with you. I need to go to the store."

"Mother, please, not this time. She's such a pain. We just want to go to the record store. She'll be bored."

"For how long?"

"I don't know, a couple hours?"

She sighed, looking like she might whither.

"All right."

I wasted no time running to the bedroom phone to inform Hannah of her alibi status. I glanced down the hallway to make sure Mother hadn't followed me and dialed the number I had memorized in the first grade. Hannah's twelve-year-old brother answered the phone.

"Can I talk to Hannah?"

"I don't know," he said, "can you?" and then yelled as loud as he could, "HANNAH! ANNELIESE IS ON THE PHONE!" There was a pause and a shuffle.

"Hey, Liese! What happened last night?" Hannah's bright voice was like a tonic.

"Jade is a bitch is what happened. And you shouldn't have brought Chase because I got in trouble for it."

"Why would you get in trouble because of Chase?"

"Search me. But she called my dad and told him to pick me up. Anyway, who cares. Can you do me a favor?"

"Sure. Sorry about last night."

"I want to go to West Beach with Rebecca and help her with some stuff. I told my mom I'm going with you."

"Why can't you just tell her you're going with Rebecca?"

"My mom doesn't want me hanging around with her anymore. It's a long story."

"Oh... Ok, Sure. Are we having a *sleepover*, too?"

"What?"

"Just thought I'd ask."

"No! We're only going for a couple hours." What did she mean by that? I puzzled a moment considering coming clean with everything.

"Call me when you get back so I know the coast is clear," she said.

"I will."

I hung up the phone and dialed Rebecca's shop.

"Rebecca's Dancewear," she answered in her professional sing-song.

"I can go with you...." I offered. I imagined a smile blooming on her face.

"Meet me here," she said.

I hung up, gulped tea, dressed and hurried to the car. Peering blankly at the empty driveway, I remembered the Honda still parked at the studio and ran back inside to call her again.

"Good Morning, this is Rebecca." That voice, always just outside of exhausted, perhaps lazy, more breath than vibration...but I was impatient.

"My car is still down there..."

"I'll come get you. Meet me around the corner."

I waited twenty minutes before slipping out the front door again, relying on my mother's preoccupation. She hadn't noticed the car missing, and Ingrid, studying, had no plans to leave the house. I turned right at the bottom of our street, hidden now from our windows, and waited on the corner. Soon, her small beige car pulled up to the curb. I hurried like a fugitive and dove in beside her. A cloud of clove smoke enveloped me. She smiled broadly and leaned in to kiss me. Waves of heat flooded my veins. "Let's get out of here," I said, anxious to leave my neighborhood. She hit the gas hard and I slunk down low into the seat, thrilled by the ease with which we carried out our conspiracy.

The cold December fog clung to everything in the beach town. The boardwalk, the streetlights, the dense sand, the seagulls, all exuded a heavy wetness. I breathed deeply, exhilarated by the chill and my freedom. We followed the boardwalk along Main Beach with its deserted basketball hoops and sentinel white lifeguard tower.

"You cold?" she asked and put her arm around me as we walked.

"Not anymore," I said.

The boardwalk ended at a cluster of rocks that hid tide pools full of starfish and sea urchins. We climbed sharp black, volcanic spires, avoiding barnacles and abalone clinging under slippery sea moss. Towering sandstone boulders separated a small cove from downtown. The usually bustling strand was deserted for the season except for birds and an occasional jogger who wouldn't bother to venture here. On the cliff, thirty feet above our heads, the Boom Trim Bar piped Christmas music and cars rolled by on Highway One. But in this space, Rebecca and I were alone. We sat on a flat, wave-smoothed rock, leaning our backs against the cliff. Briny sea spray blew in on the wind, dampening our hair and our faces. I could not stop smiling. I was in my element. Rather, I was part of the elements: ocean, cold-hard stone, wintertime, passion overflowing. The fog was turning into light rain.

"Kiss me," I said.

Rebecca trailed her fingers down my cheek before lacing them through my hair to pull me in close to meet her. That kiss was not like before. Not simply the press of lips on lips. Not the duty-bound mechanics of Merrick or the quick stolen moments of contact laced with fear. This kiss was in no hurry. It tempted, surrendered, bloomed and serenaded. It promised and hoped and languished.

"I need you," she said.

"Don't you get it?" I said, "I have always been yours." I felt like a child poised at the top of a very tall playground slide. I was about to sail over the edge when she pulled back.

"I still wish you had a man first," she whispered. My moment of victory was at hand.

"About that..." I said, barely moving from her.

"About that...?"

I could have strung it out, made a game of it, but considering the way time had treated us I decided to be blunt.

"I did what you and Christopher told me to do." She pulled back, frowned. "I'm not a virgin anymore," I said, a hint of triumph in my voice. "And I've decided. I want you."

Rebecca was quiet. She slid rain-wet trails of hair from my face with the tips of her long fingernails and looked at me squarely. "When?"

"When I was away." She didn't believe me.

"Who was he?"

"No one you know. I know him from school. Just a willing participant." She looked down at our hands, then out to the ocean. Had I called her bluff?

"Liese, even if you did, you can't... don't ...*love* me."

I struggled over her words, my carefully crafted world unraveling. "How can I not love you?"

"What we're doing... it's just pleasure... it's not... forever."

"It is whatever it is." I cast my eyes to the water to keep from crying. If I looked at her, all composure would be gone.

"Are you sure you want this even if I can't be everything you want me to be?"

"I want whatever you're willing to give me." Now I met her gaze.

"Okay, then." She simply put her arms around me. In that embrace there was something of sorrow. Or possibly pity. Just for a moment the last three months avalanched down my ribcage and a tremor played an arpeggio down my spine. "It's cold isn't it?" she said. But I wasn't cold. Breathing replaced words. Waves anticipated. Crashed.

"Whatever happens," she said, taking my hands, aqua stare melting into my brain, "I'll never have another woman to replace you."

On a cold, salty rock that became my altar, she took me to places I had never been before. And perhaps, never would again.

* * *

Of course, I should have been more careful. In whom I trusted, in the volume of my voice. I should have looked to see who might be just out of sight, not lurking, but simply existing within earshot of secrets girls will tell when they're drunk on love.

"So how was Saturday?" Hannah asked me. We had just come from Dudley's class. Happy and spent, we sat in the dressing room and peeled off our pointe shoes. The skin of our toes still stuck to the inside of the canvas lining. We traded sharp gasps, accepting the sting, blotting the blood. Hannah called this *the agony of de feet.*

"Saturday was... interesting." I couldn't help the smile that accompanied the anticipation of divulgence.

"You never called to tell me you were home."

"Yeah, I'm sorry about that. I guess I forgot. I was pretty distracted."

"What's with your mom and Rebecca anyway?"

I wanted to jump onto the dressing-room bench and declare my love for Rebecca to the whole studio. To dare anyone to stand in my way. It wouldn't wait any longer. Hannah was my best friend. If I couldn't tell everyone, at least I could tell her.

"One day, a long time ago...," I started, then changed tactics. "Remember when we were freshmen and I liked that guy, Troy Mack? When we had just started high school and I was upset because he didn't ask me to the Winter Formal?"

"I guess so."

"Well, that night at the studio I had told Rebecca about it, and she said we should all become a big pack of lesbians and leave the men out of it."

"What? Seriously?" Hannah was laughing. This was a preposterous notion.

"I said the same thing," I laughed along, "and then Rebecca said, '*well maybe not all the men, but when it comes to love, why leave out 50 percent of the population?*'" By now Hannah was dissolving into peals of laughter. I waited for her to calm down to a chuckle.

153

"I decided she's right, Han."

Hannah stopped laughing. "What are you saying?"

"I'm saying I love Rebecca."

She looked at the floor. "You love her... like that?"

"Like that." In that moment I knew I was risking my oldest friendship. A friendship with history full of campouts and milestones and birthday parties and school drama. More than that... I was risking the person who had accepted me and had my back no matter what. I was risking someone whose ability to make me laugh had left me gasping for breath on many occasions. She had been as necessary to my life as Ingrid.

"God, that's a relief," Hannah said at last.

"How is it a relief?"

"When you told me you weren't a virgin last year, and you wouldn't tell me who you were with, I thought you were seeing Chase behind my back."

"Oh god, no!"

"I did. And I thought back then, that even if it was true, it wouldn't stop me from being your best friend. I'll always be your best friend, Liese."

"Even now?"

"Yeah. That's nothing. But do you think you're actually gay then?"

"No, I just think I fall in love with people. Not bodies. I don't need anyone's label."

"That makes sense. I'll see you at school tomorrow."

She gathered her things and went out leaving me to realize I had been the one whose mind had been closed. Dancers flowed around me like a river as I sat in the middle of the floor, unmoving. Liberated of my secret. A thing of energy. And love like magic.

* * *

What no one knew was that Rebecca was different when we were alone. I watched the smoke curl from the dwindling end of her cigarette in the living room of her rented condo. Hannah had been happily conspiratorial when I'd mapped out my deception and so far, all had gone as planned.

Rebecca got up from the torn leather chair where she had slumped before the old pine table. The table was a record of sorts and had been in her house for as long as she'd been on her own. Soft, unfinished wood had yielded to the pressure of ballpoint pens, random pencils, in the hands of visitors who left their mark in its surface. In the center of the table was a drawing in black ink of a gnarled oak tree, its branches reaching and twisting across the wood grain. Under the illustration, in perfect block letters, were the words Rebecca's Tree with a date next to it. I quickly calculated 6 years gone by.

"Who drew that tree?" I asked.

"My ex-husband," she told me. I thought of her married, briefly domesticated, clawing at the bars of a cage she entered in a moment of romantic naïveté. "It didn't last long," she said, "but he loved me."

I sat on an old orange couch, something from Goodwill perhaps or a hand-me-down from a distant relative and watched her crush the cigarette in a brass tray. I pulled a woven sepia shawl, made last summer by a creative Irish aunt, around my shoulders and scrunched my knees to my chest, still dressed in studio garb. It was cold, but my shivering wasn't only about temperature.

"I'm sorry, darlin'," she said to me. "I thought we would have the whole evening."

"It's okay." I looked away.

I had planned this night meticulously. My alibis in place, my stories straight. My lies formalized. Memorized. Patiently woven around half-truths.

"I understand," I said, when she didn't respond. "You need the money. I'll be here when you get back."

"You'll wait for me?" she asked.

"Of course," I said. "I'll wait all night and more." I felt the heat of tears building up behind my eyes which I willed myself not to spill.

"Oh, Liese," she said, leaning down to kiss the top of my head. I could smell the lingering sweet clove of her extinguished cigarette. "I might be a while."

I tipped my head back from where I sat so I could look into her face. She studied me for a moment without speaking. Her lips always looked like she'd been crying. I fixed my eyes on them. Knew how they felt. Wished I could curl into her arms and sleep.

"I'll try to be back by midnight," she said and grabbed her keys from the table. When the studio was between performances and didn't need costumes, she drove a limousine to make rent. But tonight? I was still reeling from her casual announcement. As if it had been any other night. When the front door closed, her black Labrador Retriever padded over to me, sniffed my ankles, and hauled himself onto the couch, placing his chin on a paw.

"She'll be back," I told him and draped my arm across his bony spine. We sat just like that, for a long time, staring together at the front door.

It could have been anyone, but I knew it was Rebecca when the yellow phone on the kitchen wall startled me. I got up from the couch and answered it. Food-caked dishes toppled in the sink. Red wine circles made a kaleidoscope on the vinyl countertop. Something on the old linoleum floor stuck to the bottom of my feet.

"Rebecca's phone," I said into the receiver, and wasn't surprised to hear her voice, gone not 20 minutes from the house.

"Listen, Liese, I forgot to tell you..."

"Where are you?" I interrupted.

"I'm calling from a payphone at the gas station. I had to fill the limo."

I waited. "So, I forgot to tell you," she said, "my friend Lenny is dropping by tonight."

"While I'm here?" I asked. "Who is he?"

"He left something at my house."

"You want me to let him in?"

"Yeah, he's a good guy."

"What did he leave?"

"Don't worry about it, just let him in. He'll grab his things and leave."

"Okay. The dog misses you."

"Give him a kiss for me."

I hung up and stared at the door some more. She didn't say exactly when Lenny was planning to come, whoever he was. I went back to my spot on the living room couch. For all my nerve-wracking manipulation of events, all I had to show for this moment was an empty room, a sad dog, and a pending stranger.

I wandered down the short hall into her bedroom. A low queen-sized waterbed was draped in a crocheted afghan, the kind with multicolored squares made by patient, sedentary grandmothers. This one was black with gold and orange patterns in the center of each square. I knew she had a grandma, once, who always mistook her for her sister.

I sat on the frame of the waterbed avoiding the inevitable sinking, sloshing sensation. Against the wood-veneered wall was a row of books on a black lacquer shelf, dust accumulated in front of their spines. I pulled one from its place, looking for clues. I wanted to know who she was outside of the studio. What kind of a child was she? How did she become the woman she is now? I wanted to know the parts she kept hidden behind her boisterous, carefree laughter, cocaine, and cannabis. I wanted to understand why she was hiding. To bring her out. To fix her.

A blue vinyl cover with gold emboss was a classic or some other relic with literary intention. Next to it, a cartoonish book called *Baby Devine* obscured the edge of a photograph, breaking the pattern of book spines. Maybe I shouldn't, I thought. Maybe she put it there to forget it. But just as easily, she left it there to preserve it, or to remove a crease with the weight of books pressed against it. I slid it out with a tinge of anticipation then immediately froze, entranced by her ice blue gaze staring out. I wondered who was holding the camera. Who seduced that stare from her and made her feel the way she looked in the photograph, with the sun catching the top of her hair, a blue plaid button-down cotton shirt, her mouth forming a word, her eyes, like a challenge, her hands, long nails, silver-bangled wrist, elegantly resting on her knee. In this photograph, she was not rushing out the door or embroiled in a project or bemoaning a million stresses. In this picture, she was content, and I realized I had never seen her this way.

There was a knock and a double doorbell. I jumped, dropped the photograph on the bed, and ran down the hall. Bruno had beaten me to the door. He barked and growled low. Through the peephole, I could see a man with curly brown hair, a prominent nose, and black glasses. He looked like an artist. Or maybe an actor. Unafraid, I twisted the bolt lock and opened the door. He was surprised, then confused. "Lenny," I said.

"Yes... hello... is Rebecca home?"

"She's not. She told me you'd be coming by," I said, and stepped aside. He accepted the gesture, walking by me and into the room.

"You left something?" I asked.

He was confused again, thought for a moment. "Oh, yes, my... my pipe," he said. He headed down the hall to an empty-ish room and I followed. I hadn't thought to explore it before. It was sparsely furnished inside—a mattress on the floor, some loose junk mail, an ashtray full of cigarette butts, a single spindle chair. Dark red curtains covered the window and cast a strange glow. Bruno was at Lenny's heels sniffing behind him.

"Stop, Bruno," I said, embarrassed for the man.

"He knows me," said Lenny. "He's just saying hi."

Lenny fished a glass pipe from between the mattress and the wall—the kind with a shallow bowl where you tamp marijuana leaves, then pitch a flint, lighting while you suck the flame through the leaves. I knew this because I'd watched Rebecca do it: hold her breath, offer it to me. Exhale in a blast.

Lenny planted his rear-end on the mattress and extracted a Bic from his pocket, then a plastic zip-lock from under the mattress like these gestures had been repeated hundreds of times. I sat on the spindle chair, ready for him to cue the next scene.

"Are you Rebecca's new roommate?" he asked. "I guess I didn't leave the place too tidy. Sorry 'bout that."

Rebecca never mentioned a roommate. "No," I said, "I'm a dancer where she works."

"I should have guessed," he said, surveying me while he lit his pipe again. "Will she be back tonight?"

"Much later," I said. "She's driving."

He nodded and handed me the smoldering pipe. I shook my head. The light was all but gone from the sky, the strange glow replaced by almost darkness.

"So, you just hangin' out then?" he asked.

"Yeah," I said. He nodded, studying the remains in the glass bowl.

"Been dancing long?" he asked.

"My whole life, just about," I said. "What about you?"

"I'm no dancer," he laughed, "but no stranger to the theater either."

"No?"

"I'm directing a production at the college. Working with the acting class there."

I understood now. He was tall, gangly, pale. Dark brown hair and black glasses that contrasted with his skin that never saw the light of day. Holes in the knees of his 501's. Like a million directors.

"I like your shawl," he said, and reached for the intentionally frayed edge. "So interesting. I've never seen one like it."

"You won't, either. My aunt copied it from a tv show."

"Ah, a costume designer, is she?"

"Sort of," I said.

He moved closer to me and placed his hand on my shoulder as if to appreciate the weave.

"Are you and Rebecca ... friends?" he asked.

"For years," I said.

"Close friends," he declared, rather than asked. He lets his fingers brush through the length of my hair as if I were a fond niece. Familiar. Affectionate.

"You could say we are close," I said and met his eyes. I was not afraid of this man. He was in his early thirties. Natural in front of a crowd. Confident in his ability to control an audience. But I was not one of his fans. Not one of his students. I recognized his desire before he did. Or before he wanted me to.

"Well, why wait for her though," said Lenny, "when I am right here?"

He lifted the shawl from my shoulders, dropped it on the back of the chair.

"What do you want to do?" I asked.

"We could chat," he said, amused.

"Might as well," I said. "Bruno is depressed for one thing. He doesn't feel like talking."

He chuckled, patted Bruno's head. Lenny was not unattractive. If I'd not been in love I might have seen him differently. And besides, I was angry with Rebecca. Of all nights, she had to work this one? I was not important enough to turn it down just once? I was pouting to myself when he stood and scooped me off the chair like a child, sliding one hand under my thighs, the other behind my back, and levitated me to the mattress.

"We're going to talk in bed?" I said flatly.

"You look tired," he said.

Actually, I was tired. And cold. And fairly hungry. I lay back on the mattress trying not to think about the age of the sheets, the state of the pillowcase, and closed my eyes. I didn't open them when I felt his breath on my face. Or when he grazed my bare shoulder with his fingertips.

"You want to sleep?" he asked.

I nodded my head on the pillow, eyes closed tight, like a child shutting out monsters. He sucked the pipe and I waited for the heavy exhale. The room filled with the sweet scent and I breathed it in. I was vaguely aware when he settled his weight next to me. His arm reached around and he fit his body along mine, then stopped moving. I waited, aware of every inch of him. When nothing more happened, I relaxed.

* * *

When Bruno barked me awake, I was alone. I sat up, disoriented, hearing keys in the front door. It took a moment before I could locate myself, on a smoky mattress, in a room belonging to a stranger. Rebecca's stranger.

I flew from the mattress, guilty for what I might have done, and relocated to Rebecca's room. On the bed, the photograph I'd plucked from between books still stared, accusing. I whisked it back to its shelf and rolled onto the waterbed, careful to still the sloshing.

She didn't come in right away. I wondered if Lenny was still in the living room or if he'd snuck out while I slept. The digital clock on the bedside table said 2:00 a.m. Still cold, still hungry, I pulled the black grandma-afghan over myself and tried to quiet my breathing. Such an odd thing, to hide from her, when all I ever wanted was for her to see me.

Her footsteps advanced down the hall, clove smoke drifting in before her. She came to the bed, leaned down to see if I was sleeping.

"Liese?" she said. I opened my eyes, legitimately bleary.

"What time is it?" I asked so that she had to tell me.

She didn't. "I'm sorry it's so late," she said.

"Bruno's glad you're here," I told her.

"And you?" she asked.

"I could take it or leave it," I said, then rolled onto my back and saw what the photograph saw. She sat on the edge of the bed, staring at the bookshelf. I wondered if her eyes picked out the small edge of emulsion sticking out from between the books.

"I was hanging out at the Hollywood sign tonight when the ride was over," she said, "smoking with another driver."

"Yeah?" I said. But I wondered how she could just sit and smoke with strangers while I waited for her all night.

"Yeah," she said. "And I told him my lover was waiting at home for me."

I rolled towards her, covered her hand with mine, relishing the title bestowed upon me. The colors of our nail polish made weird pop art where our fingers entwined, my pink over her red. I imagined sketching our hands, together, just like that.

"You know what he said?" she asked. I shook my head. "He said, '*Keep it under 100.*'" She laughed.

I smiled but my heart wasn't in it. "You know what I said to him?" she asked. Head shake. "I said, '*Not a chance.*'" I took this as an apology but was not convinced.

She joined me on the bed and covered my body with hers so that I melted into the waves of the waterbed, heat rising between us, spreading to the ends of my toes, the tips of my fingers, the back of my neck. She wore a man's black suit, a white button-down shirt, a black bow tie. She hadn't worn these things when she'd left. She'd had on blue jeans and a red tee shirt with a wide neck that slid from one pale shoulder. She'd worn rubber flipflops that slapped lazily against the floor when she walked. Somewhere between here and Hollywood she'd morphed into a limo driver. I imagined her chatting up her passengers as they guzzled booze in the back seat. Before the end of the drive, they would be her best friends.

Her lips pressed soft into mine in the dark, her blonde curls falling over my cheekbones. I wrapped my arms around her back and rolled to the side so we faced each other.

"I missed you tonight," I said.

"Did you meet Lenny?" she asked.

"He came and went," I said.

"He's a good guy," she said. "Lived here for a couple months when he was down on his luck."

"He said as much," I said, a shadow passing between us.

"I need a shower," she said. She crossed the room to the small, adjacent bathroom. Her man's suit fell to the floor and she beckoned me from the bed. I rose and went to stand beside her, watching our reflection in the bathroom mirror.

We were the same size. The same height. "Get undressed," she said. The same pink.

Hot water steamed the small room, and the mirror. Our bodies became bare shrouds in the glass. She stepped into the shower stall, graceful, soft. Not edgy, like me. She poured liquid amber soap into her hands, hydroplaning over my bones and muscles in the rush of water.

Still wet, she crossed the room to the bookcase, letting her towel fall to the floor. Her body glowed like a Maxfield Parrish painting in the light that spilled from the bathroom while steam whorled into the cold bedroom. She pulled the *Baby Devine* book from the shelf. The photograph stayed put between the blue book with gold leafing and a thick black leather-bound something. A Bible, maybe. She didn't notice the photograph.

"I want to read this with you," she said, and turned on the bedside lamp.

The book was a rhyming poem with childish illustrations about a baby who is born for show business. I hated it right away. The distorted images and ghoulish nursery rhyme pretended to be something they were not. Like clowns.

"You read this side of the page and I'll read this side," she commanded.

"Out loud?" I said. It was awkward and silly. The fat, distorted baby wore lipstick and pink high heels.

Rebecca read the first page in singsong rhyme. I choked out the next to appease her. She closed the book without turning the page. "I thought you'd like it," she said. "I thought you'd think it was funny." Her disappointment felt strange. Something microscopic shifted in my unconditional admiration.

"It's just weird," I told her.

She leaned back on the bed, pulling me with her. "Thanks for waiting for me," she said. But there was a strange pall between us now.

She traced the edge of my hip bone with a long fingernail.

"What am I gonna do with you?" she asked.

"I don't know," I said.

"I find that very hard to believe," she whispered into my ear, her fingers trailing down my stomach.

I caught my breath and she knew, then, she was still mistress of me. And I was mistress of the place where photographs stare into book covers and old roommates appear to smoke in the dark.

* * *

A day passed. I'd gone home early from "Hannah's house" and slept for almost a whole day. When I returned to the studio, to her shop, she was sitting at the long white desk and I struggled to read her expression. I recognized a sort of challenge, like the one in the photograph I took from between her books. That stare had something to say and it might be full of rocks or butterflies—you'd never know which—but you were soon to be pummeled by it.

I thought for a moment that she knew the picture was missing. Before I'd left that morning, just 36 hours ago, I had reached for it, just to see it again, while she'd brewed coffee in the kitchen. But she'd started down the hall and I'd shoved it into my dance bag, which hung from my shoulder as I prepared to leave. It's the only thing in my life I've ever stolen. And even then, I might have put it back if I'd had the chance.

From behind her desk she said, "How do you like my shawl?"

At first, I didn't understand what she meant. I was still thinking about the photograph, now tucked between books on my own shelf. In my own room. She extended the sepia material away from her shoulders like bat wings and only then did I recognize it. "I found this in Lenny's room," she said. "Any idea how it got there?"

The night, its cold and hungry elements, stirred up a dust devil and I was instantly numb: the sound of her house with no one in it, the waiting game, the lonely dog, the stoned stranger. Dirty sheets and red curtains. A hard chair with a spindle back. A mattress on the floor. The click of black and white minutes passing on the flip clock. The long-awaited keys in the lock.

"None," I said.

Chapter 18

On audition day it didn't occur to me to be nervous. We had been studying the *Coppélia* mazurka for a week. I wasn't familiar with the entire ballet, but I knew there would be two leading roles and one of them would surely be mine. That Sunday morning, dancers buzzed in and out of doorways, talkative and frenetic, practicing *pirouettes*, readjusting pointe shoes.

Candidates from all over the county were invited to try out for Dudley's productions but usually they stuck to their home studios. Two girls we had never seen before milled about awkwardly, hanging tightly together. They were just a bit younger than we were. Ample cheeks puffed above theatrical smiles, dressed in pastel, childlike leotards with attached skirts. We would never dare to wear such a thing to class, let alone to audition. With experience, ballet taught that less is more when it came to attire. Anything that disrupts the line of the body would be considered frivolous and silly.

"Who are they?" Hannah asked me under her breath, careful not to take her eyes from the knot she re-tied in the satin ribbon of her pointe shoe. I scanned the room for anomalies and landed on the two interlopers leaning too casually against the barre.

"I don't know but they aren't ballet dancers."

"I saw Wesley talking to them earlier. Maybe he knows." Wesley was out on the dance floor, whipping out *fouetté* turns, his eyes locked in the mirror. Whip-spin-whip-spin-whip. He ended with a double *pirouette*, cleanly and calmly resolved in an open fourth. With his hands, he added that subtle twist of the wrist, signaling the mirror-audience that he was ready for his share of applause. From the clamor of pre-audition mayhem, he received a smatter of claps, and, from the barre at the back of the room, a whistle. Hannah and I looked up, for we had already guessed the source of the sound. Who did they think they were, taking such a familiar attitude with Wesley? He turned to them, rear to the mirror, and bowed deeply, ever the harlequin. I could feel Hannah's arched eyebrow without looking at her, just as she could sense the roll of my eyes. Wesley shuffled his soft-shoed feet across the slick maple wood, toward the girls at the barre.

"Ladies," he said, and lifted the hand of the brunette, gracing it with a courtly kiss. A snicker from Hannah.

"Seriously, Wesley?" I said for her benefit.

Jade and Dudley entered the studio from Ricky's side and called us to order.

"Welcome, all!" shouted Dudley, clapping his hands twice. We settled quickly for him. Jade busied herself at the stereo, shuffling libretto papers and album jackets, her back to us.

"Before we begin, my loves," said Dudley, his smiling eyes surveying the room, "I'd like to introduce you to two lovely dancers who will be joining our production of *Coppélia*." If the room was quiet before, now it was silent. We all had wondered, but no one asked. "Megan and Alexis, raise your hands please." As if we didn't know where to look. The girls each put a hand in the air and smiled broadly. They gazed directly into the sea of faces like divas holding court. Not so much a challenge as a refusal to back down from any of us who might offer one.

"Megan and Alexis have come to us from the musical theater department at the high school of performing arts," Dudley continued, "I am told they sing like angels and Ricky says they dance like the dickens!" Reserved chuckles. A few hands waved politely in their direction. Low-energy greetings emitted shyly from several throats. Dudley cleared his, and continued, "For those unfamiliar, *Coppélia* is a romantic comedy choreographed in 1870 by Arthur Saint-Leon, who first staged it in Paris. The wonderful music is by Léo Delibes, a French composer of the same era. I have no doubt you will be enchanted with it as I am. We'll audition the boys first, since there are only a few of them. Thank you, gentlemen, for being with us today. Girls, you may use Studio B to stay warm. When I call you back in we will audition the *corps de ballet* pieces, followed by the solos. Questions?" The room murmured but no hands went up. "Off with you, girls," he said and we flowed into Studio B, leaving the boys to the scrutiny of Jaybird and Dudley.

The door to Rebecca's shop stood open, inviting. I couldn't keep my eyes from wandering in that direction. Hannah watched me watching.

"Is she here today?" she asked.

"I don't know." I had been practicing the art of subtlety.

"*Coppélia* is a ridiculous ballet," she said.

"What's it about?" I didn't really care.

"Some moron falling in love with a doll."

"Creepy."

"Dudley's right, though, I do love the music," she waited. No response from me.

"Liese...?"

"Yeah?"

"Just go talk to her. It's all you can think about anyway." I don't think Hannah minded Rebecca, but she was put out by my inattention. I got up and casually walked to the door leading to the shop, closed for Sunday.

The small room was quiet. I stepped down into soft carpet and wove my way among racks of costumes. My footsteps made a sound like someone following and I turned to look back into the studio. I expected to see Hannah there, grinning, ready to tease. But she was at the far end of the room, easily relaxed into lateral splits, her elbows on the floor. Her attention was focused on Bridget's incessant *pirouettes*. Bridget, who was dripping sweat into a puddle at her feet, focused intently on the mirror, whipping her spot around twice, three times, and falling each time, her control now awash in nerves.

I turned back to the shop. The lights were off and morning sun angled into floor-to-ceiling glass windows, warming the small space despite the early spring cool. Rebecca's empty chair was swiveled outward, gaping, away from its desk. I walked to where she usually sat and absorbed all that was her, strewn about the desktop: clove cigarette butts in a white ceramic ashtray. Piles of sales receipts. Costume pattern catalogs. A slowly wilting white rose in a glass vase, the water mostly evaporated. The aqua desk phone, so often pressed to her ear, sat like a spring of potential energy on its cradle. Suddenly, it rang shrilly, shattering the quiet. I jumped and stared at it, unsure of what to do. One ring. Two. I decided to let the answering machine do its job. I had been holding my breath, creeping like a spy in her space, alone. I flopped into her chair to stare out the window into the hills. Mustard weed had begun again, blossoming the hills in soft yellow. The answering machine clicked on.

A male voice: "*Rebecca, hey, it's J.T. Thanks for last night. Had a great time. Free next weekend? Call me.*" The machine concluded with a long beep. I sat unmoving, staring outside like a fish in a bowl. Above my head, suspended from a small suction cup stuck to the window, a long glass prism caught the light and shot rainbows around the room. Colors ricocheted off sequined costumes hanging on a rack and sprayed the white walls with violet and blue. J.T. ... Had she mentioned him before? Who was he to her? The clock on the wall ticked and I sat hypnotized by the echo of his voice in my head until Hannah jarred me awake.

"Come on, Liese, we're up," she called into the empty space where I sat nursing an unfamiliar new pain.

"Coming," I said and followed her into the chaos of Studio A.

Dancers lined the walls leaving the floor empty. Jade announced the mazurka we all knew from class, which would serve as the audition piece for the *corps de ballet*.

"How are those new girls gonna get through this?" Hannah asked into my ear.

"Guess we'll find out."

Jade called for groups of eight, and we arranged ourselves according to friends. The new girls did not move from the barre. Though as a soloist I didn't intend to be part of it, I loved the mazurka. Its old European roots stirred somewhere in my German blood. Hannah and I grinned through the simple flow, the odd rhythm, with strange accents thrown into the third beat. Not quite a waltz and not a polka either. The mazurka toyed with sound and the choreography played back with it. The dance was familiar and comforting, like a handshake between friends, a jump-rope rhyme. Concentric circles unwinding and weaving ended in a triumphant posture, knee to the floor, the peasant celebration complete. We returned to the barre immensely pleased. Several more groups auditioned for the *corps* but the new girls stayed put, smiles glued to their faces.

"Anyone not auditioning for female solo roles is excused," Dudley clapped again for attention. A sea of dancers filed out of the white barn doors leaving Hannah, Bridget, Tiffany, me... and the new girls. Hannah and I exchanged skeptical glances.

"Are they even on pointe?" she asked me. If I had been a cat I would have been in full, stiff-furred arch, all hiss and claw.

"They'd have to heft a bit of weight to get up there," I said. Megan and Alexis went to the dressing room and came back with pointe shoes covered in perfect satin, exposing limited use. Megan took her time, arranging and rearranging, fitting and tying. Alexis fussed awkwardly with lamb's wool, stuffing it first into the tip of the shoe, then spreading it over her toes, trying to hold it in place as she slid her foot into the starched vamp. The rest of us stood, warm and already *en pointe* from the mazurka, ready to take in the choreography Jade would throw at us for the solo auditions.

"Okay, listen up!" shouted Jade, taking over from Dudley. "I want one thing from each of you. We won't be learning choreography today." We exchanged glances around the room. "Instead," she continued. "I want as many *fouettés* as you can perform, *en pointe*, until you can't do anymore. One at a time." Hannah groaned. The same whip turn Wesley had been practicing at the beginning of the day, but for us, from *plié* to *pointe*, took a fair amount of strength. It is that moment of choreography that never fails to bring an audience to applause. A trick of momentum and centrifugal force balanced on a two-inch platform. Sure of my impending success, I stood ready to be called and was not disappointed.

"We'll start with Anneliese," said Jade. I took center floor and waited for the music. She chose a classical march, 2/4 time, perfect for the quick snap of the head, force reaching down and out, then sharply up and in.

I turned once, pushing into the floor, spotted the mirror, whipped around and caught the rhythm easily. I wasn't counting, just initiating and completing the mechanics, a spinning metronome. With each spot on the mirror I could see the line of dancers behind me: Hannah's face, willing me on, Tiffany's easy smile, Bridget's slight frown, Wesley's giddy agitation. I was lost in the pure sensation. Even daydreaming. The pleasure of motion and a steady train-track beat. After what felt like a long, easy minute there was a zip and the music stopped.

"That's enough, thank you." I rolled out of my performance, deflated, and looked at her. "We know what you can do," she said. "Hannah, you're next."

Hannah had struggled for a decade to stretch the tendons from metatarsal to shin, placing her toes under the low front of a heavy couch, then straightening her knees to deadlift it, the immense weight on her ankles. But her joints did not budge. Even a minor misalignment of the body will send a series of *fouettés* off the mark.

I backed up to the barre and threw an encouraging smile into the mirror. She concentrated on a steady launch and Jade set the needle on the record, beginning the march once again. Hannah pushed off and labored through the first and second revolution, stayed upright for a few more and ended, gracefully bowing out. She joined me at the barre.

"That went well," she laughed.

"Who the hell wants to be the girl who gets jilted for a doll anyway? Worse, who wants to be the doll?" I said. I was only half joking.

"I don't care which ballet it is. Just once, I'd like the solo," Hannah said.

Jade called Tiffany, followed by Bridget. I had the clear lead if Dudley and Jade were choosing based on *fouettés*. Each dancer sustained four, maybe six, rotations before her ankle could no longer support the up and down demands of the whip-turn. I began to wonder what the *Coppélia* solo was like, and whether I would be dancing with Christopher or maybe even Wesley if there was not much lifting required.

"I have to get these things off my feet," Hannah said. "It's been hours." We crossed the room to peel off our shoes.

"Megan and Alexis, would you like to try together since we're running short on time?" Jade's voice boomed into the room. We stopped in our tracks and turned back in the doorway. The new girls exchanged the first tentative glances we had seen on their faces all day. They quickly trotted center and took the prerequisite fourth position, waiting for the march to begin. They were easy with eyes on them. No stage fright. All confidence and presence. Wesley gave them an encouraging cheer and Megan smiled back at him. I don't know what I expected. Perfection? Not even close.

Technique? Not the sublime lines of ballet, refined to the last detail. But determination? Yes. And charm? Check. Megan and Alexis turned it on for the judges whose usual poker expressions now revealed subtle enchanted smiles, as if they were the charmed audience for a couple of Minnie Mice. Both girls had a solid build that allowed them to take the rigor of the movement at least for a short time. They had pulled it off, I thought, in an amateurish way.

"Thank you for coming, everyone! Results will be posted in the studio next week," Dudley shouted so that three rooms could hear. The volume of chatter increased and busy activity resumed. The room emptied of dancers who drove off in cars, strolled across the parking lot to a café or sat outside to wait for rides. Dudley and Jade remained in the studio to hash out our fates.

"I better get going," Hannah said, "I have to get at least a 3.5 this semester. My mom wants me to start applying to universities and I have a paper to write."

"Okay," I said, "And Han, don't worry about today. It's a stupid ballet."

"I'm not worried," she said, "but I know I won't get a solo."

"That's not true. You never know."

"Well, you seem to. And you know what's not fair?"

"What?"

"You still don't even care." She let her heavy bag fall to the floor and regarded me. "You don't have to work for it. You were born with perfect feet."

"Oh come on, I do too work!"

"Well, I guess we'll see next week if there's justice in the world."

"I'm sorry, Han. You know I wouldn't even be here if it weren't for you."

"Yay." She gathered her things and left.

I stared after her. She was right. For me, ballet was dogged competition, an adrenaline high from pushing beyond the point of exhaustion, a release for all of my pent up, overflowing emotions. But Hannah had tortured herself for perfection, prized the glamour, the beauty and the stage. And perhaps I hadn't realized that she loved it all as much as I did. Maybe more.

Out in the parking lot, the engine of her old red and white '72 Oldsmobile revved a little louder than was probably necessary, and she was gone.

In no hurry to go home, I went back through the studios, cutting a wide berth around my teachers, seeking the dim quiet of Rebecca's shop. I imagined her doing everyday things. Buying milk, dog food for Bruno. Did she think of her work here when she was off somewhere alone? Did she think about Christopher and Jade and Ricky? Did she think about me? I sat again in her chair pondering the cryptic message from J.T. on the answering machine. There was something about his voice, his tone, that told me he truly liked her. And if he was that confident and flippant, maybe she truly liked him.

Since our day in West Beach near Christmas time, Rebecca and I had spent one strange night, and then had seen each other only in passing, stealing quick contact in studio doorways or trading stares over a sea of bunheads. Always she met my pleading questions with a frantic whisper, "I miss you, Liese, but I've been so busy...." I could not conceive of what could keep her so preoccupied when I had thought of little else. For instance, that day on the rock. I could almost feel Rebecca melt into me, become part of me. Didn't that make us complete together? I didn't need anyone else. Wasn't I enough for her?

How much of yourself could you give away and still remain yourself? I wanted to let go of everything holding me back. To disappear into love.

I picked up the stub of a pencil lying on the desk and searched for something to draw on. I was restless, and my hands wanted to be occupied so I could think clearly. The back of a yellow sales receipt provided a blank canvas. I sat kindergarten-style in the office chair and doodled. I sketched a foot, the bones and sinew. I realized my muscles were aching. I felt the way the calf muscle left the Achilles tendon as I graduated the line to the knee, the hip. My pencil hopped to a blank space to the side of my foot sketch. I left it to its deeds while my mind wandered back to the beach, looking for details: in the water, the sand. In our body language. In Rebecca's words. And back farther, to the dark studio at the Christmas party when she had asked me to move in with her. The day in Los Angeles when she rescued me from Étienne and the long ride home. The terrifying chances we took in the car in my parents' driveway.

And finally, the night alone in her condominium and the stolen photograph. Other days, too, I had etched in my memory, with every sight and sound, every word and nuance of expression.

I stared at the new drawing I'd made while lost in the past year. It was a face—but not Rebecca's. Small glasses framed the dark eyes above high cheeks, a smallish nose. The thin upper lip of the Celts was stiff and pursed. Laugh lines fanned out from the corners of the eyes, but the eyes themselves did not smile. The brow was slightly furrowed and I stared into the face until recognition woke me. It had been months since I'd seen that face. Now it looked back at me from a scrap of paper. Looked into a world never fathomed in life. A world where my heart was hostage in a trap of its own making and nothing could be done to free it.

A very slight tapping sound came from somewhere overhead. I searched for its source. Above me the crystal prism swayed slightly on its thread, just enough to knock into the glass. The front office door was shut and locked. It was a calm day. Even if the industrial doors of the studio were open, there would not be wind enough to come through the adjoining door, turn a corner and cause the crystal to sway.

Stillness washed over Rebecca's shop. "Ma?" I asked the air above me. The crystal prism continued its tiny impact against the glass.

I stared into the dim room searching for some sign of the presence I felt. The costumes hung undisturbed, dotted with glitter and light. Scattered rainbows rippled lightly on the walls as the prism knocked on the window, as if asking admittance. I closed my eyes to find that tunnel into oblivion I had discovered as a child. This time it was not so easily accessed. Instead I groped, cloudy and vague, staring into it like the ocean through a thick salty mist. Ma was nowhere in the opaque emptiness.

My shoulders loosed their tight hold on my neck as I thought simply to receive her. Open and still, I remained in Rebecca's chair, existing in the room with Ma, wondering how she found me in this place she had never been. Had she also been in the studio while I flowed through my turns? Did she witness Hannah's defeated expression as she lamented her struggles in the dressing room? Or did she simply respond to the pain in my heart, leaning in close, quietly singing "Never mind?"

Chapter 19

I was a child sitting in a grove of mustard weed. Yellow flowers taller than my head buzzed with hundreds of honeybees.

"Be still," said my father, "they won't bother you." I looked at my sister, who calmly obeyed. I sat, too, not daring to itch my nose or move the hair from my eyes.

"They're doing their job," he instructed, "watch them." Ingrid and I followed the bees with our eyes, from flower to flower, listening to their rapid-winged vibration as they accepted our intrusion into their world. "They're collecting pollen for the queen," he told us.

I watched a slight smile play on Ingrid's lips. The kind you might plaster there for the sake of someone else, rather than an artifact of true emotion. I tried to feel if she was frightened but sensed no agitation from her. She was simply very good at being Victor's daughter. A sea of bees is not a place to challenge authority, and if Ingrid wasn't scared, I would not be either. Ducks quacked in a lake at the crease of the valley. Hills of mustard stretched around us in a yellow diorama. Time didn't matter. Only the bees and my sister and my father's voice, deep and low.

The six a.m. alarm pierced my room and I woke to bright spring sun on my seventeenth birthday. And no wonder the bee dream came again. It was always in March. I wondered if it was a tale my imagination told me, or something that actually happened. Perhaps the three of us sat in that field on my birthday many years ago. I asked Ingrid once but she had no memory of it. Still, the brilliant detail, the mezzo-pitched buzzing near my cheek bone, the sun-warmed scent of mustard flower and the ridiculousness of yellow causing a slight ache behind my eyes was all so perfectly rendered, I couldn't imagine it was anything but a keen memory. And if it was a memory, I had resolutely held to it, wishing to live it again and again. Did the bees have a message? Or was it simply my father's calm demeanor in the midst of potential disaster? Something I could rely on in an unpredictable world, where I could no more control the events of life than I could my own heart and mind.

I threw off the covers and dragged myself out of bed. Ingrid was already up and beaming peppy energy in the hallway between our adjacent rooms.

"Happy Birthday," she said. "How was the audition?"

"It was good," I said. We shared the bathroom mirror, brushing our teeth over one sink.

I threw her a hand towel and continued to the kitchen, headed for the kettle.

I was always happy on my birthday and this morning I was also confident. Ingrid's unusual sparkle was infectious, and I shrugged off the fog of my dream. Even the persistent Rebecca-shaped ache that had taken up residence in my heart seemed, for once, a distant concern.

"I already boiled the water," Ingrid called, following on my heels.

"You were up before me?" This never happened.

"I'm wearing your skirt today," She announced.

"Which one?"

"The long black one."

"How do you know I wasn't going to wear it?"

"I don't. But you love me and you don't mind."

I threw her a mock-frown and made tea for us both.

"Aren't you going to ask?" she said, teasing me.

"Ask what?" I handed her a steaming mug of black tea, the English way, a bit of milk, a smaller bit of sugar.

"Yesterday was an important day..."

"Why was yesterday important?" I planted myself on a counter stool and she sat beside me.

"I got a letter from La Jolla." She shoved it in front of me on the counter. The admissions letter from the university congratulated her on her success and welcomed her into its esteemed halls.

"You got in!"

"I got in!"

"Of course, you did," I laughed.

"I'll be living down there in the dorm," she said, "and you can come on the weekends to visit me."

"Ingrid, you'll have roommates and new friends. You don't want your little sis hanging around while you're off doing college things, do you?"

"Well, yeah, I kinda do."

"I will come. As long as I don't have rehearsal," I said.

"It's gonna be a blast!" Ingrid said. She trotted off down the hall to raid my closet.

"Don't spill tea on my skirt!" I called after her.

Already Ingrid was often away with other seniors, visiting college campuses or attending parties thrown by beloved teachers to say goodbye to the class of '83. Our universe had begun to shift. My final year without her would be bitter-sweet. On one hand, I would no longer be the little sister. And I would have our car to myself while she lived on campus. But it was difficult to imagine waking up at home with no one to compete with for the shower, or the tea kettle at six o'clock in the morning. No one to run off with my favorite skirt. It was difficult to imagine pulling solo into the parking lot past the High School Dolphin marquis. Or to walk alone through the hall by the giant whale, painted before Wyland was famous. I stared into my tea cup. It was brewed with a tea bag instead of loose leaves. I thought briefly of tearing it open and letting them settle to the bottom. Perhaps I could divine a bit about the year ahead. But I was confident I would get by. And perhaps it would be good for her to forge an identity apart from me, as I had done at the studio. She had seemed sad when I assured her she would meet new friends, but I knew there were adventures in her future and I was a tad jealous.

The school day could not move fast enough. I stared at the clock in each class, hearing nothing in the words droning from my teachers. Crowds of teenagers moved like a current through hallways where I stood like a stone, anchored in place, out of my element. I wanted to be at the studio, already preparing for barre, stretching and warming muscles, awaiting familiar voices, throwing the mass of my *grand jeté* into the sprung pine floor, feeling it rebound as I took off on the other side.

Through the final period of the school day, I wondered if Dudley would have the *Coppélia* roles posted at the studio and, if he did, how I would deal with Hannah's disappointment. I had never felt it as keenly as I had after the audition. I was sorry for her frustration but didn't take it personally. How could she blame me for her troubles? She had managed to duck out at lunch, leaving me to my chocolate donut alone. I had saved one for her. I would bring it to her at ballet tonight.

After school I dropped Ingrid at home and went straight to the studio. Intentionally early, I pulled into the industrial complex, choosing the spot next to Rebecca's beige Toyota. The fading bumper sticker on the back said *Dancers Know All The Positions*. It wasn't many years ago I had to ask why it was funny. "So, um, we know a lot of positions," I had said to Ingrid when Mother dropped me off at ballet class, "first, second, fourth, fifth... why would that be a bumper sticker?"

Already in high school then, Ingrid had rolled her eyes at my innocence. "It's referring to *sex* positions," she said, "a *double entendre*."

"Double what?" I had asked.

"You'll find out when you're older," she sighed in that exhausted one-year-older-sister way. Now, through the windowed wall I could see Rebecca in her office chair, aqua phone pressed to her ear, laughing. I wondered if J.T. was on the other end. I had no desire to compete with who or whatever held her attention. I went into the studio door instead, to see Dudley. He, too, sat at his desk, frowning a little. He looked up only briefly as I came into the office.

"Is it that late?" he asked, his pen flying across the schedule in front of him.

"No, I'm early," I said.

"That's my girl. Always leave yourself time to stretch before class." He kept writing.

"I was wondering if the cast was posted yet, actually."

"Ah, yes, well, it is ready. Not posted." Now he stopped writing and looked up.

"Can I see it?"

"I thought maybe you and I could talk first." The expression on his face was unfamiliar. Was it concern? Trepidation?

"Okay. What about?"

"Well, you see, Jade and I... well I actually... and Jaybird, too—we..." He rubbed his forehead.

"What's wrong, Dudley?" His nervousness made me anxious. Always in the back of my mind was the fear that he knew about Rebecca and me. He took his spectacles off his eyes and squinted.

"My love," he said, peering at his desk, "if we were doing, say *Giselle*, there would be no question you would be my lead." Now he looked up.

I stared at him. What was he saying? I was the clear winner of Jade's *fouetté* competition. He had to know that.

He continued, "*Coppélia* is a happy character. She is all smiles and campy melodrama."

"*Coppélia* is the doll part, right?"

"Yes, you see, she spends the whole first act sitting like a statue on a balcony while the chap called *Franz* tries to convince her to come down to him. Not a terribly challenging role, really, at least in the first hour."

"Don't worry, Dudley, I didn't want that part. I can't imagine dancing like that. Mechanical. Like in Nutcracker?"

"The choreography does have some similarities to Marius Petipa's, I suppose." He wiped his glasses on his perpetually white tee shirt and put them back on. He didn't want to be sidetracked.

"But the other lead, the girl who is jilted by the guy — for the doll?"

"*Swanilda*, yes. *Swanilda* must be innocent and frail," he said, dramatic intonations anointing his words, "She must be slight and pure. You are *Giselle*, or *Juliet*, but you are not *Coppélia*... or even *Swanilda*." He let his words hang in the air between us. "I'm glad you came early," he said, his voice grandfatherly but full of undeniable authority, "I wanted you to hear it from me. Not a piece of paper on the wall." I had no words for him and he expected none. "Sometimes," he continued, "we choose dancers based on other things, besides technique, you see?"

"I see," I said. but I didn't. *Who danced better than I did on Sunday?*

"That's my girl. You've had your share of the limelight, no?"

"Yes," I said, my confidence drained away. "So, who, then?"

"You'll find out with the rest of them. No spoiling the surprise."

"Right," I said, sucker-punched. "So, I'm in the *corps de ballet?*"

"Yes and, well, there is a beautiful short piece, the *Dawn* solo. Jade thought you would make it lovely, and I don't doubt it."

"I will," I managed.

I dragged my wounded pride through the barn doors, through the dressing room, into Studio A. Staring into the still, empty space, I concentrated on echoes of Sunday's audition. Who were the two new girls? Open audition or not, they didn't act like ballerinas. They didn't look like us either. Tiffany had held her own in the solo audition. Bridget, with her perpetual frown, was no *Swanilda.* Hadn't Wesley acted strangely with those girls? How did he know them? And Hannah's defeated tirade in the dressing room...Well, she would be vindicated. I thought, for a moment, that one of the roles might be hers. But she was not slight or innocent either. I continued through Studio B to Rebecca's interior door, hoping to catch her between phone calls. In truth, all I wanted was for her to wrap her arms around me. To let me cry on her shoulder. I could be innocent and frail, couldn't I?

I stepped down into the room that had vibrated with color and spirit on Sunday. Today, it was just Rebecca's office. The same costumes, cigarette smoke, wilted rose. The crystal above Rebecca's head hung undisturbed on its nylon thread. Intent on the surface of her desk, she didn't hear me come in.

"Hey," I said quietly.

"Hey, angel," she said, "how are you?" Her breathy voice, and that fearless endearment. The room spun for a moment.

"We had the audition for *Coppélia* on Sunday..." The wound was fresh enough to eclipse even her gaze, which now took me in as if to memorize me. I felt like a still life, there in the middle of the room. She got up from the desk.

"I know! I'm sorry I couldn't be here," she crossed the small room and stood in front of me, laced her fingers together at the back of my waist.

"I went to the garment district in LA with a friend on Saturday to look for costume material for the production." She kissed my forehead. "And we stayed out so late." She laughed. "We got sooo drunk in town!" She looked at the ceiling, her goofy, big smile radiating mischief.

"Who did you go with?" I asked.

"You remember I told you about my friend, J.T.?"

"No, I don't think so," I said. "Who is he?"

"He's a really great guy, Liese. We've been hanging out a lot lately." Our faces were so close I could feel her smoky breath against my nose. "I think I could even fall in love with him," she said. Words had very little friction when passing off her tongue, so of course the impact when they hit was enough to knock me down. She pressed her lips lightly into mine, connecting our foreheads to make a tent. "You'll like him," she said.

I stared at the floor, breathing carefully through my mouth so she wouldn't hear the very un-*Swanilda*-like sob building in my throat. Behind the wet blur in my eyes I could see the winter beach, rain, and white-tipped waves rolling against the flat black stone where I had, I thought, given her everything.

"It's my birthday," I said, sniffing and pulling myself into composure.

"Seventeen," she said.

"You'll be twenty-seven in August."

"Always in August." Her fingers traced each bone up my spine, sending a shiver to my shoulders.

"I'll be legal next year," I said. She placed a hand on my head and smoothed my hair down my back like a cat.

"Next year," she repeated, and kissed me again.

Protests raced through my head but I trapped them there, refusing to let them escape into words. No one born can be so forgetful. How could she just toss me off like I was nothing?

"I'm not *Coppélia*," I said, instead.

She stepped back from me. "It's true," she laughed, "you are not *Coppélia*. And Dudley told me. I'm really sorry. Happy Fuckin' Birthday, right?"

There was no stopping it now. The dam broke. Tears fell.

"Oh Liese," she said, "you can't win 'em all."

"You really think that's what this is about?"

She took my hand and led me to the office chair by the window, plopped down, and pulled me into her lap like a child.

"Liese, you and I will always be friends. But we can't be more than friends." I put my head into her neck, catching another ungraceful sob in my throat. "You can cry, darlin', don't hold it back for me."

So I didn't. "How could you do this to me, Bec? You said you loved me."

"I do love you, Liese. Don't you think it ripped my heart out to make love to you and then have to shove it all down like it never happened?"

"No, I don't think it did rip your heart out. I don't think you gave a crap, actually. Not if you can just replace me with J.T. It's all just a game to you. And I don't know if I can just be your friend. Not anymore."

"Listen, J.T. is someone I can have. Someone I can run off to Los Angeles with and no one will ask any questions. I need that," she said. "I haven't replaced you with J.T. You will always be important to me. You don't understand now, but you will. I promise."

And there it was. Even Rebecca had resorted to child-speak. I stood up to go. As I walked away, she grabbed my hand to pull me back.

"Let me go," I said.

And she did.

Chapter 20

"If I didn't know better I would say they had something on someone," Hannah said. We stared at the audition results posted in the studio hall. We had tumbled through the week in anticipation but I had kept quiet about Dudley's decision to keep me in the shadows.

"How is that even possible?" I was sort of laughing.

It was absurd of course. Two nobodies drop into our studio on audition day from god knows where and suddenly they're commanding lead roles. They didn't half embody Dudley's usual choice. They were bold and fleshy and not at all what you'd call light on their feet. And Jade? Who was more conscious of body weight than the queen of white Lycra? You had to be made of bones alone to look good in that stuff. She didn't accept extra weight on herself and she didn't accept it from her dancers. Not usually, anyway.

Since Dudley broke the news the week before, the sting of rejection had faded. I hid behind the cocky confidence that my solo, however minor, would prove to the audience and all involved what a farce the audition had been. Still, I would have expected any name next to a coveted solo besides the one we now beheld. My disappointment renewed itself and screwed into my ribs.

Megan and Alexis burst through the door with Wesley, laughing like old friends. Not just old friends but old friends who expected good news. Hannah and I stepped away from the wall, allowing the three rabble-rousers a clear path to glory. Megan ran her finger down the list of names while short, stubby Alexis peered over her shoulder on tiptoe. She tossed her bobbed blonde hair behind her like a teenaged Marilyn Monroe.

Megan's shrill screech startled everyone as she hopped up and down like she'd just won Publisher's Clearing House on late night TV.

"I got *Coppélia*! Oh my god, Oh, thank you, Dudley, wherever you are!" She turned and hugged Alexis, who struggled free to search for her name.

"And I am your beloved... or rather... you are my beloved," said Wesley, turning from the list. He knelt, arms spread wide to receive her.

"Oh, *Franz*," said Megan, "I wish I could get down off this blasted balcony and kiss you my *darling*!" She fell into his embrace and they commenced a frenzy of campy, squeaky smooching on the floor.

Alexis stood back, hands on her hips. "Okay, okay, you two, break it up," she said.

"What did you get, Lex?" said Megan from her Wesley-tangle on the ground.

"I'm just a *villager*," Alexis said. But she wasn't in the least bit put out.

"This is gonna be a blast," said Megan. "Can you believe the three of us are dancing together in the same show again?"

Hannah gave me a raised eyebrow and we both looked at Wesley.

"Okay you guys, you guys, seriously, stop with the looks," Wesley said to us. "Megan and Alexis were in *West Side Story* with me! Last summer at the Civic Light Opera! We had so much fun, I invited them to try out!" Megan grinned up at us, big white teeth spread across her face.

Hannah and I nodded our dawning comprehension. But that didn't explain why Megan was cast as *Coppélia*. Dudley was getting screwball in his old age.

"I guess she's kind of campy," Hannah said in my ear, "Maybe there's a method to his madness." Megan sprang up and took both of Alexis's hands. They jumped in a circle like a couple of hyper six-year-olds. Wesley dove into the middle of them and yelled, "Ring around the Rosie!"

"Just back away slowly," I said to Hannah.

"Wait, I never even found my name." Hannah wove her way back to the wall and ran her finger down the list. "As if I don't know I'm a *villager*." I followed and peered over her shoulder. Dudley had placed our names alphabetically with our roles in a tabbed-away column.

"Holy shit," she said, "I don't believe it. He also gave me the *Prayer* solo. What even is that?"

"Feel like playing Ring around the Rosie?" I asked.

"Shut up. What did you get?" She scrolled to my name and traced across, where she read, "*Villager, Dawn* solo."

"I don't know what that is either," I said, "Guess we'll find out."

Hannah studied me for signs of disappointment. I didn't let on that I'd been prepared for this, my moment of shock tempered by a week of slow acceptance.

We went into the studio to warm up for class.

"What do you think of Tiffany as *Swanilda*?" She asked me. No one had even mentioned the winner of the other lead role presented on Dudley's list. *Swanilda* was the serious role.

"I think she'll be great," I said. Tiffany was appropriately slight and good-natured.

"And she's never had the lead before," said Hannah. She approved on Tiffany's behalf.

"I do love the *corps* choreography," I said. "It's eight minutes long and challenging as all hell." I was determined to feel, if not good, at least okay about the production. What did I care anyway, about the show? I just wanted to be on stage while Rebecca manned the curtain rope. I just wanted to exit a scene, frenzied and exhausted on my way to the dressing room, and be tugged back into a dark wing for a costume adjustment. And for the kiss that would follow.

Chapter 21

We called this beach "Hole in the Fence" because that's how you get there, still to this day. South of Pacific Crest, Pacific Coast Highway runs along the train tracks to San Clemente where sixty-foot sheer cliffs rise sharply on the other side of the road. A chicken wire fence detours pedestrians from crossing the tracks to the sand, but those of us who grew up there shunned the long walk to the parking lot entrance. We would hop the track and climb through the chicken wire where someone, tired of the obstruction, had thought to bring wire clippers, creating an entrance big enough to climb through if you tossed your blanket, surfboard, and bags of charcoal over the top.

Suspicions at home were mounting as I became careless. I had allowed Ingrid access to my notebooks and told all to Hannah. But also, several new eleventh grade friends not associated with the academic crowd, those with piercings and magenta hair, chains clipped to their jeans, made me feel less alone in my strangeness and we traded tales of eccentricity on the stadium bleachers after school. My family closed in around me, threatening to impede my most intricately planned, delicately balanced ambitions. I wanted to escape Ingrid's questions about college applications, Mother's angry quips about the company I kept, my father's gathering dark clouds of temper. When there looked to be no escape from another year of turbulence, I started to pitch hope into honesty.

After all, Mother always told me that family would be there when friends jumped ship in troubled times. Despite the tension between us, I wondered if I could trust the bond that was older than any friendship I'd known, except maybe Ingrid's. So, with a bottle of wine in a paper bag and a corkscrew, I invited my mother into my world.

"I want to tell you something," I said after class one evening, "but not here." She was cutting onions the way my father taught her, crisscross patterns pressed into the bulb with a sharp, serrated knife, then turned on the side to slice down. Little cubes of perfectly cut onion fell onto the chopping block. She pushed her glasses up her nose with the back of her hand. She knew better than to press for details. If tensions rose, I would shut down, call the whole thing off. I knew by the half-open door of my cabinet, the missing church key, that she had been in my room looking for clues to the life I kept separate from her. I also knew that she was more likely to keep her cool, #1, in public, and #2, with a glass of wine in her hand.

"Not here?"

"I'd rather talk to you alone." Making her feel special, confided in, was part of my plan.

"Where should we go?" she asked, moving on to breadcrumbs, assembling her meatloaf.

"The beach, I think. Bring some wine and we can hang out and talk."

"Well, that would be alright I suppose," she said. "How about Saturday?"

"After ballet, yeah," I said. "In the evening." For the next couple days, I rehearsed the way I would say it. Rebecca and I are in love. But that wasn't the truth and I was going for honesty. I love Rebecca. Close, but that wasn't my point. I am a lesbian? Was I? What was the maddening force shoving every waking thought into divining ways to be near her? And besides, I could not implicate Rebecca. I was still seventeen, though the year was fading. This would be about me, alone. Family accepted you for who you were, didn't they? Mother would love me anyway, and I wouldn't have to hide anymore. Get past this moment of terror, and things would start to get better.

On Saturday evening, I led the way over the tracks and through the gaping wire hole with an old quilt bunched under one arm. Mother passed me the paper grocery bag containing our wine before climbing through. A row of fire pits dotted the strand. We hadn't brought wood with us, but we threw our blanket among the fire rings because here you could smell the smoke mixed with salty ocean breeze as others lit them all the way down the beach.

Just north of where we sat, the jetty at Doheny created perfect, surfable waves. Boys from school, long blonde hair stringy with salt, jogged by us to the water's edge and dove in, racing to get behind the breakers. The sun began its plunge into the horizon, blasting orange across the surface of the Pacific. I pulled the corkscrew from the bag and unwound the bottle's metal collar.

"Did you bring some cups?" Mother asked.

"Nah, we can pass the bottle."

"Okay." She laughed at this like such an act might hearken back to some wilder times.

I poked the tip of the screw into the soft cork, gathering my thoughts. With each turn of metal into the bottleneck, I bought time, planned my confession. Should I just come out with it? Make small talk? Let her go on about life for a while? Harmony between my parents had been scant lately. I decided that was the safest approach, allowing time for wine to calm her nerves. Despite the forethought, my opening line was weak and transparent.

"So, how have you been?"

"I've been okay. Is that what you want to talk about?"

I popped the cork all the way out. "Not entirely."

"Your dad has been gone a lot lately. I'm a little down, I guess."

I handed her the bottle and waited for her to go on. "He travels even more than usual with the new promotion." She took a swig.

"He was promoted?"

"Well yes, didn't you know? Before Christmas."

"Oh, yeah," I said. But I hadn't known.

"They're always sending him to Europe and now he's going to Egypt and Malaysia. He'll be gone the entire month."

"You'll have us," I said.

"I know, but you guys aren't around like you used to be."

"There's always Katrine..."

"There's always Katrine," she echoed.

"It won't be long 'til Ingrid's gone. You guys will miss each other."

"We will, but La Jolla isn't far away." With my father traveling and Ingrid away at school, Mother, Katrine and I would have to form a separate nucleus. The thought made me squirm with obligation. Mother drank a few healthy gulps and passed the bottle to me. My nerves required a little sedating as well. I sipped. The deep red Cabernet was warm in the cooling ocean air. The breeze picked up. Smoke drifted downwind from a nearby fire. We were quiet while we passed the bottle, enjoying the final sliver of sun on the water and the welcome haze of alcohol.

Mother broke the silence when the light disappeared. "So, what is this about, Anneliese?"

I took another healthy gulp of wine. Now or never. "I think I might be a lesbian," I said, staring straight ahead. I felt Mother's entire being stiffen into a pillar of ice.

"This is about Rebecca." she said, her voice full venom.

"Why is everything about Rebecca?" I asked, trying desperately to keep my cool.

"Because everything is about Rebecca for you." She matched my tone.

"This is not about Rebecca."

"Then who is it about?" There had to be a culprit.

"It's about me," I said. She was stoic, silent. I continued. "Look at our family. There's you and Ingrid and Katrine and me and your sisters, there was Ma.... Everyone in our family is female except Daddy and he's been a jerk lately. You always tell me how strong the women in our family are. They're all creative and wise and wonderful, according to you. All men seem to care about is sex."

"Isn't that what this is about? Sex? You don't have to be a lesbian if you just prefer the company of women."

"It's not about sex. It's about understanding. I don't get men. Or the ones I do know creep me out and make me nervous." Poor Merrick. So much for honesty. He didn't fit any of those descriptions. And he had fallen for me in spite of himself last summer, singing drunken anthems on my front lawn in the middle of the night, to Ingrid's great entertainment.

"Then perhaps you ought to get to know more of them and drop this ridiculous obsession with ballet. The only men there are ..."

"Don't say it, it isn't true. Dudley isn't gay." She was baiting me but I would not bite, yet.

"What makes you think you're a lesbian if it's not about Rebecca?"

"Because Rebecca is not gay."

"Rebecca is whatever she wants to be." *Bingo.*

"Why can't I be whatever I want to be?"

"Because you are my daughter!" Her cool began to evaporate and she turned to look me in the eye.

"If you love men so much, what's wrong with you and Daddy then?"

"Don't bring me into this. This is not about me!" She gulped the wine and jammed it back into the sand between us where I retrieved it and did the same.

"What could you possibly know about being a lesbian anyway? Your father is going to have a fit."

"I was hoping we could keep this between us for now."

"That's asking an awful lot."

"What I know," I said, "is that sex with women is gentler than sex with men." My mother's revulsion was palpable.

"Oh, so now you know what it's like to have sex with a man?"

"I'm not a virgin, Mother." More wine on both sides.

"So, enlighten me, Anneliese, how is it done?"

Now it was my turn to be repulsed. I was not about to entertain a freak show audience. My extremely left-leaning mother, who had gone on in my youth about the strength of women, about our hard-earned rights, about our innate strength and ability to love, suddenly wanted to bury everything I had become under tradition and social expectation. I was disappointed. But not surprised. This was not her world.

"What would Ma think?" There was a sob in her voice now.

"I don't think Ma would mind, actually." To this my mother said nothing. She couldn't honestly disagree.

"I don't want to hear this anymore," she said, rifling in the quilt for the cork and shoving it into the empty bottle, "Let's go."

"We're a little buzzed to drive right now," I said, getting to my feet.

"I'm fine," she said and gathered up the quilt as it rained sand.

I picked up the bottle and hurled it to a trash bin and we dragged ourselves back through the sand, through the hole, across the tracks where the Honda sat waiting on the highway. In the car she gripped the wheel with both hands and gritted her teeth, staring out the window. I said nothing and fixed my eyes on the water out the passenger window, awaiting her next attack. Instead, she grabbed the stick shift like she meant to kill it, popped the clutch, lurched us onto the highway, flipped a U and took us home.

Chapter 22

I stood in the wings and pressed the tip of my pointe shoe into a box of crumbled rosin. Sufficiently sticky, I ground it into the black wood stage. We had never danced at the University theater and it was definitely not constructed with ballet in mind. Drama, perhaps, or orchestra, but not movement. The varnished planks would surely send me sailing if I hit the satin edge of the shoe, instead of the squared platform at its tip.

I had arrived early to walk the stage alone. I needed to understand its entrances and exits, the placement of the lights, the edges of the apron, without the hot spots in my eyes and the expectations of an audience. Even the pacing of other dancers running pieces in the empty theater, or set designers, yelling across the vast space about props and musical cues, would be too much for my fragile concentration. The janitor had opened the green room door for me in the alley and I'd woven my way to the wings in the dark. We had a 2:30 call and I would be alone for another half-hour.

I walked center stage and looked out into rows of folded theater seats. Those seats would soon hold five hundred pairs of eyes. And five hundred judgments. I would have five hundred opportunities to communicate a moment that might persist in a single memory. The *Dawn* solo was less than three minutes long, but I was determined to make it three minutes of perfection.

Masking-tape crosses marked the center of the rhombus-shaped stage. I measured the opening choreography within them, picking up speed to match my mental tempo. As I rounded a corner, I lost my footing and stumbled. I investigated the floor for slick spots but it was simply the frictionless contact of satin against veneer. How on earth would I stab the tip of a shoe onto this surface, my weight and momentum behind it, and expect to stop on a dime? Or even a silver dollar? The slightest tilt and the shoe would skate sideways. I would have to be absolutely sure of my target. I paced across the stage as I ran through the more challenging choreography. About half way into the piece, there would be a crescendo, and powerful movement to match. It required a step into a spin, *piqué en attitude*. There were times I failed to find the fulcrum of this movement even at the studio. My confidence was beginning to drain. To build it back up, I tried the allegro, the final *grand jeté*: a series of steps that gain momentum, becoming higher and longer, until the final leap. As I landed, I heard the heavy slam of the green-room door and dancers began to fill the edges of the stage with armloads of costumes and quiet chatter. Ricky met me at the edge of the stage, concern in his expression.

"What was going on out there?" he asked. So, I hadn't been alone after all.

"The floor is too slippery," I said as I passed him by. I didn't want to talk about it. I relinquished the space to the entourage that would fill it within moments. Spins and stretches and jumps would ignite the room with energy. I needed to remain calm so I ducked into the dark wings intending to stretch.

Black floor, black walls, black curtains, I was invisible—lying prone, watching the lighting technicians change gobo filters, practice following spotlights, trade cycloramas. There was the Renaissance European Village scene, with its half-timber window boxes, balconies and snaking vines. Then, the giant clock with three-foot-high Roman numerals, and the fountain in the town square. Tonight, we would build a story, all of us together.

For three months we had worked to blend many pieces into a continuous, moving experience. Even Megan seemed to embody *Coppélia* well enough to convince me she could move like a doll, if not a ballet dancer. Alexis was awash in other *villagers* so she did not have to pull much weight on her own. There were moments in the Mazurka when I danced beside her and I am being honest when I say I had lost my resentment somewhere in the rehearsal process. Megan and Alexis were good natured, humble, and easy to work with, and I was happy to watch Tiffany bud into a soloist. It is for these reasons that I am certain I was misunderstood when I counseled Megan, two years my junior, not to try for heroics.

Megan's solo required the kind of *pirouette* that could be a slower single revolution or a quicker double turn. From where I watched in the wings, I could see her trepidation building just as mine had. On her inexperienced toes, pointe shoes looked like blocks of cement. The character she played hid the awkwardness. She tried the *pirouette* she knew would be her biggest challenge. With furtive movement she pushed into a single rotation. I held my breath. Her landing was graceful enough. *Good. That was clean. You'll be fine.* I watched her set up again. With a determined focus into the empty audience, Megan pushed into the floor and went for the double. Catching the edge of her shoe, she fell, palms splayed on the floor, shoulders hunched in shock. I got up from where I lay hidden and galloped to the little heap that was Megan, center stage.

"Just do a single *pirouette*," I said. "It looked fine the way you did it the first time."

"I'm supposed to do a double, though," she said. "It's in the choreography that way."

"A clean single is always better than a sloppy double," I told her. That statement was a mantra among us. But Megan hadn't been among us long enough to understand. She hauled herself off the floor and backed up into the wings, eyes still upon me until she reached the curtain where she turned and ducked into the shadows.

I continued to lie low until show time. Hannah and Tiffany, Bridget and Wesley, a dozen others cavorted in the green room, sipping Coca Cola, scarfing bananas and M&M's, guzzling coffee. I could not participate. For the first time, I was nervous to perform. I had never understood stage fright and now it threatened to sabotage my three minutes.

Back in the dark, my back against the wall under the curtain rope, I thought of Jaybird and Dudley. I didn't want to disappoint them. Dudley would think I wasn't trying hard enough if I slipped. If I held back, he would know. He would think I was being lazy because I wasn't dancing the lead. I wondered if Ricky would spread the word among the dancers about the absolute lack of traction we all faced. I knew Rebecca was surrounded in a tumble of boisterous dancers with last minute costume adjustments. I didn't think of Megan again.

By the time the curtain rose on *Coppélia* that night, I had nurtured a calm focus. In Act I, I danced the mazurka, concentrating on the character of the *villagers* rather than the slippery floor. For the first time since I'd known him, Dudley had paid as much attention to acting as he had to choreography. We were slow, at first, to shed the ballerina mask. That faraway gaze, the slight smile Dudley had described as "a walk in the meadow," had been nurtured from our earliest studies. You could be straining for all you were worth, fighting tired muscles, biting back pain in your lungs from over-exertion, terrified or embarrassed from a fall or misstep, ready to die, nothing could show on your face but serenity. "The audience will never know," he said to us, "if you don't tell them." And above all, you keep going. You fall, you get up.

I had learned my lesson about dancing in the *corps* from *Romeo and Juliet* at the Westwood in Los Angeles. This time, I knew the choreography without hesitation. I watched in my peripheral vision for the dancer to my left and right, staying in line, ready to move as one, like the little fish that dart without plan or announcement, their unity the key to safe travels. I understood, perhaps for the first time, that being a *corps* dancer was more difficult than being a soloist. Only in the *corps* were mistakes so glaringly obvious. Perhaps the audience would not recognize a less than accurate execution of movement, or a step out of order, from a soloist, but the most checked-out old uncle, dragged to a performance against will and better judgment, would have no trouble identifying a *corps de ballet* dancer who interrupted the line, started out in the wrong direction, stepped three to everyone's four, or continued moving when all were frozen. I danced with a new respect for the entire troupe.

As we exited the village scene, I began the mad dart to the dressing room to change into the *Dawn* costume, a monstrosity of ivory taffeta and tulle. I was not a fan of tutus—the short-legged among dancers never are. As I burst through the heavy stage door, attendants caught its weight to keep it from slamming. On stage, a love story unfolded between a girl and a boy, a boy and a doll, light-hearted, frustrating, and lovely.

I rushed through the green room, down the hall, and skidded into the dressing room. Shoving aside heavy costumes on the rack, I searched frantically for the *Dawn* tutu among brown felt *villager* vests and long translucent blue *Waltz of the Hours* skirts. It wasn't there. Frantic, I spun around the small room checking backs of chairs, under counters. Finding no trace, I sprinted back to the green room, breathing heavily now, my cool unraveling, pointe shoes skidding on the industrial grey carpet. Several dancers stretched on the floor and I jumped the obstacle course of their legs.

"Have you seen Rebecca?" I shouted, as I scurried by like a madwoman. They regarded me coolly.

"She's around," called one, "look backstage." The sound of low chuckling followed me down the hall to the stage door. I calmed myself enough to open it quietly and peered inside. Several startled faces stared back at me from the silent wings; there had better be a good reason for opening the stage door during a performance. Under the hot white lights, I could see Tiffany and Wesley dancing their opening *pas de deux*. I looked around frantically for Rebecca. She was nowhere. As I was about to back out the door, an insistent arm slid around my waist and yanked me into the dark. I turned to see Rebecca with the *Dawn* costume over her arm.

"Hurry up," she whispered, "give me your dress." She began unhooking the back of my *villager* costume. There was no time for the dressing room now.

"Where was it?" I snapped at her, struggling to stay quiet. "Why wasn't it on the rack?"

"Excuse me, your majesty, I had to fix the hem. It was falling."

"Now? You had to fix it now?!"

"Look, Liese, Dudley only mentioned it when I got here. You were busy on stage when I came in, or I would have let you know. Step in." She had opened the two-dozen hooks and eyes that ran up the back of the bodice and held the tutu in front of me. Wearing only the requisite tights by now, and naked from the waist up, I turned to the wall in the dark and stepped inside trying not to fall over and cause a ruckus backstage.

"Hold on to me," she said. I didn't want to. I balanced on the rocky sole of one pointe shoe. During the months of rehearsal we had avoided each other, speaking only when necessary. My wounded expression had sent her eyes to the floor as often as I had thrown it her way. We had spoken no more of J.T. or of our troubled attraction to each other.

"Don't be an idiot," she said.

"It took me three months and all afternoon to be ready for this," I said, "and I was ready, but now I'm panicked and I might as well not go on."

"Or maybe you just want to be pissed off at me." Still behind me, her hands moved quickly, fastening the hooks. "Breathe in," she said. The bodice was so tight I had to collapse my ribs a bit. When the hooks were set I could breathe again, as long as I didn't gasp.

"Of course, I'm pissed. The floor is slippery and I'm nervous and the last thing I needed was to have to run all over hell for ten minutes looking for my costume. Couldn't you have waited with it in the dressing room?"

"So now I'm your lady in waiting? I was where I needed to be and you don't get to decide that." She finished fastening the bodice, grasped my shoulders, and turned me to face her. "You aren't the only dancer here, or haven't you figured that out yet?"

"Thanks for fixing my costume," I said, sarcasm thick and oozing.

She tried to meet my eyes but I looked beyond her to the stage. "Knock it off," she said. "Now."

The crescendo began. Shrugging her off, I moved into position at the edge of the stage. With eight seconds counting, I leaned over to check the knots on my ribbons one last time and felt her sharp slap. No time to react, I entered the pool of light, still stinging in more ways than one, and measured center. Time stood still as I looked into the audience, quiet but for the rustling of programs. The warm moonlike spot cast a spell of calm over me.

The audience was not there to judge, but to share what I could offer. My nerves fell away and I gathered the coming three minutes back under my control. I would not waste a second of it. Not for Rebecca. Not even for Dudley and Jade. And certainly not for the roles I wasn't given. If I slipped, I would get up again, but I would not hold back. I thought of Ma. She had found me when sadness had taken root in my heart. I hoped she would find me again tonight, while joy was seeping in to replace it.

The floor ceased to exist. The stage became my bedroom, its window, watching cars on the highway as they disappeared between the hills, so absolute was my peace. Hundreds of eyes upon me were no more than stars in the sky, words on a page, rolls of undeveloped film. I was in an isolated world, forty feet wide and just about as long, with a few more minutes to live.

Nervousness, a tense posture, is the enemy of ballet. In my minor solo, I felt as if I'd conquered it. My brief time in the spotlight wound to a close and the *Dawn* music was rinsed away by the beautiful violin strains of Hannah's *Prayer* solo. She entered stage left as I disappeared right. Every ounce of panic and frustration forgotten, I remained in the wings to watch her dance. Her strong grace exuded confidence and I wondered if she felt awash in the same spell. Memories spun through my mind as Hannah presided over that small slice of time.

For a decade we had danced together, both in the studio and on the stage. When we were new to pointe, Dudley had set the choreography of Le Patineur for us, the skater's waltz. We performed together in matching green velvet dresses, white fur cuffs on our wrists, white fur collars. My dress still existed in a box somewhere in the back of my closet. I hoped hers did, too. In that moment I realized that Rebecca had made those costumes, when Hannah and I were ten years old. I'd barely known her then. I decided the skater's dress would remain among the treasures of my past and follow me across decades to come.

When the *Prayer* solo ended, Hannah exited to my wing. I delivered a high-five and we ran for the dressing room to morph back into *villagers* for Act II.

"So, what did you say to Megan?" Hannah asked me. She yanked at her awkward tutu.

"To Megan? Nothing. Will you unhook me?" Hannah started on my bodice.

"Everyone was comforting her backstage. Apparently you made her cry."

"What the hell?"

"Yeah, they all think you're a witch. What else is new?"

"Han, I didn't say anything to Megan!" I replayed the afternoon encounter in my head, searching for the offending words.

"Apparently, you told her she did sloppy doubles." Hannah put the back of her hand against her forehead and pretended to faint with the emotional assault of the words.

"Hold on a minute. Who is saying this?"

"Megan told everyone. She cried to Ricky and fell into his arms and Wesley was trying to calm her down and you are persona non grata." There was a hint of scandalous glee in her voice.

"That is totally unfair! I was only trying to coach her a little. I told her a clean single is better than a sloppy double, not that her doubles are sloppy!" Hannah shrugged and I added, "Even though they are." We laughed as we donned the brown peasant dresses, adjusted long ribbons in our hair. We hung our solo tutus back on the rack and went to stretch in the green room with a bag of peanut M&M's between us.

Wesley walked by as he left the stage door. It was intermission. "Nice going," he said to me as he continued to the dressing room. Ten paces behind him, Tiffany and Megan followed, jolly in the throes of stage success. As soon as their eyes fell on me, their faces went sour and they stomped the rest of the way through the room.

"Somebody's in trouble," Hannah sang.

"This is nuts. She's twisting what I said. Do you think I should talk to Dudley?"

"I'm sure he knows already."

"I so don't need this," I said, "I'm going to talk to Wesley."

I found Wesley in the guys' dressing room with his leg up on the wall, stretched into a vertical split. He looked over his shoulder.

"Oh, hey, Liese, did you come to tell me I suck?"

"Wesley, I didn't say anything mean to Megan, I just gave her advice."

"....That's...not how she made it sound."

"Then she's lying."

"So you're calling her a liar now? Just because you didn't get to dance the lead doesn't mean you can be a bitch to the person who did."

"Wesley, you know me better than that."

"I thought I did. Maybe I don't."

"I have no problem with Megan dancing *Coppélia*. I just thought the stage was slippery and she shouldn't try to do something she isn't comfortable with. I wouldn't!"

"Like you're the example we're all supposed to follow?" He pulled his leg off the wall, put his dance bag over his shoulder and headed to the door. "She can do the double," he said. "She did the double tonight. She'll do it again tomorrow. Stay off her back."

"You are all full of crap," I said, and went back in search of Hannah and M&M's, but she, and they, were gone.

"*VILLAGERS* ON STAGE, NOW!" Rebecca yelled from the stage door.

Once again, I was rushing. I stepped inside and the heavy black door closed behind me.

"Liese, Liese, Liese...." she said close to my ear. "What am I gonna do with you?"

"This is all a big misunderstanding. It didn't happen like she said." I fixed my eyes on the stage, still refusing to look at her.

"I'm staying out of it, but you need to think about your words before you spit them out, know what I'm saying?"

"Bec, we've been repeating that phrase to each other for years."

"Then consider your audience. Megan hasn't been here for years, and for your information, her parents have donated a heap of money to the studio. In fact, pretty much everything you see here is thanks to them. The backdrops, the lighting, the audio equipment, the costume material. They even paid to have the programs printed. So go easy."

Realization washed over me in waves. The audition. The way Jade and Dudley coddled Megan and her ever-excited friend, Alexis. The solo assignment. Everything began to make sense.

"You don't say..." I said. "That is very interesting."

"What's that supposed to mean?" She knew what I meant.

"How did they even know Dudley needed money?"

"I don't know, Liese, but given the fact that you didn't follow through with Étienne's little fashion show last year, I don't see that he had a lot of options."

"So that was my fault, too?" With five minutes to curtain, rage, mingled with triumph, bubbled in my veins. Soon, I would be back out there in the *corps*, performing among them, Hannah and Alexis beside me, Wesley, Tiffany and Megan center stage. We would maintain our character-faces, but our eyes would pitch a volley of darts. With this new knowledge, I would not shrink from their accusations. To hell with all of them. This cast was a fraud and I was done with it. Dudley's words rang in my ears, "*Sometimes we have to choose dancers based on other things, besides technique, you see?*" Indeed.

"I know that look," said Rebecca, "and I think you better cool it."

"Don't worry about it," I said.

"Can't you just dance and have fun, like everyone else?"

"Oh, I will have tons of fun," I said. The *corps* populated the stage and I plastered an enthusiastic smile on my face and joined them. The music began.

Before the final curtain that night, Rebecca carried an armful of roses to the line of exhausted dancers, placing them in the hands of each soloist. I felt suddenly out of place among them: their heavy breathing beginning to calm, their eyes flickering in stage light, their smiles genuine and tired. In one night, I had become more truly a dancer than I had ever been. And just as quickly, I was releasing this place, these people, this life. Rebecca grinned as she greeted each dancer with flowers. Her expression was unreadable as she approached me. Roses changed hands, cheeks were kissed. Applause faded into white noise as we retreated in unison behind the red velvet curtain. It fell slowly, eclipsing the audience before our eyes.

In that moment, the real world returned for the cast of *Coppélia*. They celebrated and cheered and hugged and laughed. They posed for pictures. Dudley and Jaybird mingled, congratulating. Ricky and Christopher, who had doubled as prop masters and set designers, wove among them distributing flamboyant hugs. Moments of elation and clumsy mistakes were traded and re-lived. But I remained frozen, an observer, apart. I moved like a spirit to the wings, thinking only to gather my things and retreat home to the quiet of my bedroom. It would be some time before the cast left the stage, now shrouded by the curtain. The audience headed for the exits, the parking lot, their cars, their worlds. Later, the dancers would gather at a cast party and this madness would continue into the night. I wanted to be alone.

The green room was an abandoned disaster of candy wrappers, ribbon, hair pins, makeup, costume bags, leg warmers, and Coke cans. I wove through the mess to the dressing room and sat in front of a bulb-ringed mirror to release my hair from its headache-inducing twist. The intercom, usually connecting the stage to the dressing room, had been silenced. My ears rang with sudden quiet and I stared at my black-lined eyes, thinking of Dudley. What could I say to him now? I was not the girl he knew and he was no longer the grandfatherly man who raised me to dance. I had failed him. We failed each other.

Heels clicked hesitantly on the tile floor in the hall. In the mirror, I watched Rebecca approach the dressing room door. She stood behind me. Her hands floated to my shoulders, and, without ceremony, her lips brushed my neck.

"Are you going to hide from everyone?" she whispered.

I tried to mask my surprise, to sound casual. "Do I have a choice?" I shivered, anyway, at her touch and covered her hand with mine. I stared at her image in the mirror. Her aqua eyes had softened. Something like sorrow seeped through her fingers, now gripping my shoulders with a message of their own.

"It isn't your fault, Liese," she said. "Dudley, the money..." She slid the strap of my leotard off my shoulder, kissing where the fabric left. "And this bullshit with Megan, it will blow over. You worry too much. Like me, I suppose."

No longer satisfied with reflections, I turned to look at her. Leaning awkwardly now, she slid her fingers through my hair and pressed her kiss into me. I could have sworn she was breathing life back into my soul. This time, though, I was careful to understand the fleeting nature of the comfort she offered.

"I miss this," she said.

"Me, too." I was holding my breath as she kissed me again, desperately restraining all that threatened to pour out of me and into her, like a wild thing bucking on a leash.

I believe we would have heard Megan coming if she hadn't already removed her pointe shoes on stage, or perhaps in the greenroom. Barefoot, but for tights covering her feet, only her short, sharp gasp startled us awake. We stared at each other, the three of us paralyzed as she stood in the doorway, gaping at the spectacle of Rebecca and I, engaged in what could not be explained away.

After a few seconds, she laughed. "Wow, Sorry, you guys," she said, composing herself as if she couldn't have cared less. "Guess I should have knocked, right? I'll just grab my stuff and leave you two alone." She plucked her dance bag out of the corner of the dressing room and made a hasty retreat.

Rebecca stood and stared at the empty doorway. "That wasn't good," she said. I didn't respond. "I mean it was really, really... stupid of us."

"I guess we can't expect she'll keep her mouth shut," I said.

"No, I don't suppose we can."

Still in shock, I began to gather my makeup and pointe shoes as Rebecca headed for the hallway.

"I'm going to help strike the set," she said, returning to her business persona, "Leave your costumes on the rack."

"I will."

She lowered her voice. "I'll see you later, okay?"

"Later." I didn't watch her go. I could not leave fast enough. With my arms full of the paraphernalia of theater and the roses crunched on top of it all, I left through the alley door where, a lifetime ago, the janitor had let me in.

Chapter 23

Regular classes resumed the following week, and I left school for the studio, as I had done for all but six of my almost eighteen years. But there was an odd sensation in the pit of my stomach—an insistent buzzing in my brain, warning me, telling me to be on my guard. I was tense, defensive and ready to face a foe. Dudley was behind his desk but he got up instantly when I came in and sat on the old brown couch, patting the seat next to him.

"Early as usual," he said, "good thing. We need to talk."

There would be no buffer zone, then. No delaying the inevitable. No softening of blows. "What about?"

"Do you have any idea what I am about to say?" He was nervous.

"I might have some idea," I said. I had several, actually.

"I will let you tell your side, but I must tell you mine first."

"I'm listening." My heart began to pound.

"A few months back, just before we auditioned for *Coppélia*, I was in my office speaking with a—a benefactor...," he began. I listened, terrified of where he was headed. "This lady and I, we were just on the other side of that wall there." He pointed at the thin matting that separated the office from the dressing room. "And just beyond that wall, you were having a chat with Hannah. Do you recall the day?"

"I've had many chats with Hannah in that dressing room, Dudley." My feigned innocence annoyed him.

"Let's get to the point," he said. "You told Hannah about Rebecca. About your feelings for her."

I bit my lip, squinted my eyes shut. I had believed we were alone that day. This was not a conversation I ever wanted to have with Dudley. Not in a million, trillion years. I looked at the floor, then at him. "I got sort of messed up in Rebecca," I offered.

"To say the least," he said, and trained his eyes on me despite the psychic shield I was throwing up between us like a thousand layers of glass. "I was standing here and the woman was standing with me," he continued, "and it all came gushing out of you." Silence from me. Dudley continued. "Now, that alone might not have sealed your fate..." I looked at him now, dread becoming reality, "but her daughter was our *Coppélia...* Megan." I hoped my expression revealed contempt. "And Megan saw something at the theater that made her mother very upset when she heard the news." I was stone-still beside him, but squirmed inside, wishing to run from the studio and never return. "And, do you know what she said to me, after the show the next day?"

"No," I offered the only syllable I could muster.

"She said, and I quote, '*One of them has to go. I don't care which one. But if one of them isn't out of there by the time Megan is back in class, I will make sure that studio falls down around your ears.*'"

"Around your ears?"

"That's what she said. And why do I care? Because, that woman has saved us from closing our doors. And what's more, you and I both know that you have outgrown this place. I've taught you enough and it's time for you to move on to bigger things. At nearly eighteen, you should already be in a real company, if that's what you're going to do with your life. Rebecca can't leave. Her work is here, with us. It must be you. You are the one who will go."

A couple tears slid down my cheeks, but I was not surprised. And I did not completely disagree with him.

"I didn't want to involve your parents in this," he said, "as you are an adult now, as far as I'm concerned. I'm sure you aren't in a hurry to explain this to them. You can say whatever you like about why you're not coming back here. But understand," he said, "you are not coming back."

"I understand," I said.

"Do you have anything you'd like to say?"

"Thank you for teaching me to dance, Dudley."

He gave me a thin smile and his eyes allowed the tiniest glint of good humor returning.

"I wish you the best," he said.

I wondered what he had said to Rebecca, if she knew of the words I would be hearing today. My mind began to wander through the still empty studios, first A, then B, and into her shop. I wasn't going to throw myself sobbing at her feet. I just needed to know what she was thinking. I wanted everything to be normal just one more time. Just for a few minutes. But that was not to be.

"Go and talk to her," he said, reading my thought. "I've already spoken with her."

"Do you remember the day you told me we could never be more than friends?" I walked into the familiar scene, glad to catch her without a phone in her hand. She did not hesitate.

"Yes, I do."

"Did you mean it?"

"Liese... I just..."

"Just say yes or no."

"Yes."

"That is the way you want it, not the way someone else is telling you it should be?"

She looked hard into my eyes. "Yes," she whispered.

"I didn't mean what I said that day, about feeling that it was never important to you. I think I know that it was."

"It's very hard for me to separate what I feel for you," she said. "I'll always be attracted to you."

"Please tell J.T. for me that I respect him, if you love him. But I want to say to you what you said to me, that night on the beach." She waited. "*I'll never have another woman to replace you.* Don't replace me, Rebecca. Men, sure. But please, I couldn't bear it." I tried to comprehend the simple, dense weight of this new reality. She would never be mine again.

"I'm sorry," she said, "I've been so confused. Please don't hate me." She came across the room and took my hands. "Friends?"

"I don't know if I can do that. Not yet anyway."

"I understand."

"I feel like we're approaching the end of a long play. I could go on and on about it but I won't. Someday I'll write it for you."

* * *

Ingrid had left for her first year at the university. *Coppélia*, and life as I'd known it, had ended in September. I was still in bed on a warm Sunday in October. There was just a hint of autumn in the air and my senior year had begun without much fanfare. Things were more relaxed at school with most of our fates sealed by the tests we had taken, the transcripts we'd sent off to various colleges over the summer. I stared at the roses I'd tossed on my dresser the night of the final performance. Dry petals had turned dark red, almost black, like cabernet. Santa Ana winds were blowing again, making the air so dry that the white Baby's Breath, supporting what was left of the roses' delicate petals, would crumble to dust if I touched it. I could still feel the ache in my heart when the flowers had passed from Rebecca's hands to mine. The spirit of that day lived in the brittle hips and curling leaves, refusing to give up the ghost. A Spanish mirror, carved in arcing waves like a stormy sea, reflected the pathetic bouquet from behind, like something Snow White's stepmother might gaze into, proving beauty to herself, alone.

On the nightstand, the clock radio was playing something by Chopin. I heard the phone ring from Katrine's room. She didn't answer it. It rang again. If our dad had stayed in bed this morning, watching Bugs Bunny and scoffing at Televangelists, as was his Sunday custom, he was one ring away from flying out of bed to holler about who was so rude as to call on a Sunday morning. I threw back the covers and ran down the hall to Katrine's room. She was still in bed, but upright, painting her nails with bright pink polish that she balanced on a book in her lap, ignoring the ringing phone like a princess.

"Why didn't you answer the phone?" I asked, grabbing it from the cradle on her nightstand. She shrugged.

"Hello?"

"God, I'm so glad you answered." Rebecca sounded anxious and tired. She had never dared call my house. At least not in the last three years.

"What's wrong? Are you okay?"

I was still trying to fathom the sound of her voice in my ear when my mother's muffled bark floated across the hall from behind her closed door. "Who is it, Anneliese?"

I cupped my hand over the receiver. "It's Dudley," I lied. Katrine looked up at me with eyes that recognized deception. I threw back a warning glare. If she couldn't hear the voice, exactly, through the earpiece, she could tell it wasn't male.

"Look, I'm in a bind," Rebecca said. Her voice was quietly frantic. "And you've worked the shop before, right?"

"Yeah…"

"My sister…." Rebecca said. And then she was crying. I tried to remember if Rebecca had ever mentioned her sister other than in passing, and even then it was long ago.

"Tell me what's wrong, Bec."

She took a breath. "I need to get my niece, my sister, she's… her motorcycle went down and she's… my niece is only nine." I was silent. "Look, Liese, you know I wouldn't have called unless it was an emergency but I have customers coming to the shop to pick up orders and they have to have their costumes by today. I know it's hard for you to be here but I don't know what else to do. I've tried everyone else I can think of. I'm leaving a key under the flowerpot outside the door. Can you be here by 10?"

"I think so," I said, "Yes."

"Thanks. I haven't been exactly close to her these past years," she was calmer now, "but she's my sister and her daughter is alone." I hung up the phone, stunned. My mother was up and standing in her bathrobe in the hallway.

"I need to go to the studio," I said, "to help at the shop."

"Why you?" she asked, "I thought you quit that place to get ready for college."

"Because I'm the only one who answered the phone, I guess, and Dudley needs a favor."

She narrowed her eyes. "Who else is going to be there?"

"It's just me," I said, "I need to be there to deliver some orders at the shop." She turned back to her bedroom and closed the door.

"Can I come with you?" Katrine asked, blowing on her pink nails.

"No, you'll just be bored," I said. "And why didn't you answer the phone?"

"Because," she said, "my friends at school say if you answer too soon, people think you're desperate." I rolled my eyes at her.

"Why would they think you're desperate? That's ridiculous." But I knew there was some horrible, middle school truth to it. "Who did you think would be calling you?"

"I don't know," she said, "Anybody from school...maybe." I gave her a wry smile.

"You don't have to act for anyone at school," I said. She shrugged again and examined her nails. Katrine's clock said 9:15.

The parkway was empty, and the air already warm, as I drove to the studio for the first time in almost a month. The dry hills on either side were golden now. Summer's purple thistles had gone brown and their downy seeds, like hundreds of white messengers, blew away on the strong eastern wind. In five minutes, I turned into the industrial complex and parked in front of Rebecca's office. I had hoped she might still be there but the whole place was deserted. The other businesses were closed on Sunday except for the delicatessen across the parking lot.

Otto, the deli's Italian baker, came out in his white apron and waved when I got out of the Honda. I waved back. "Dancing today?" he asked, surprised to see me.

"No, just helping," I said.

"Come have sandwich when you hungry," he said and went inside.

Strong, hot gusts blew my hair into my eyes as I searched for the key under the big stone pot with geraniums overflowing. When everything else is dead, you can't kill a geranium. Its strong, knotty stems leaned over the pot almost touching the ground. Thick, succulent petals begged for water. Blindly grasping brass metal, I slid the key out and made a mental note to fill a cup in the bathroom and dump some water in the pot. The groundskeeper wouldn't be there until Wednesday.

I cupped my hands around the glass of the studio door and peered in, just to convince myself there was truly no one around. Above all, I did not want to run into Dudley and I was fairly certain the feeling would be mutual.

The day was melancholy with autumn coming on, even in the 80-degree sun. I slid the key into the door to the left and opened Rebecca's shop. The stillness, on days like this, was a startling contrast to its regular energy. Like a deserted amusement park. No music blared from the studios, no laughter from the dressing rooms, no shouting from instructors. If I were a spirit haunting the place, I would perceive the energy of dancers, sense their frustrations, feel their emotions. I couldn't help but wonder what had gone on in my absence. I flipped the light so that Rebecca's customers, when they arrived, would know someone was there. Staring around the room at the artifacts of her life, I felt like an intruder now. No longer the child in need of protection, or the girl flirting with things she couldn't have. I was on the cusp of adulthood, just months away from 18. And Rebecca belonged to someone else.

I flopped in her chair. Boxes stacked against the window were labeled for pick up. I shuffled for the matching receipts on her desk and remembered the geraniums. I abandoned the desk and went to the studio bathroom to fill a plastic cup. As I turned on the water, the phone rang and I ran for it, thinking maybe it was Rebecca, needing me again. I liked the thought of rescuing her, if I could be nothing else.

"*Rebecca's Dancewear*," I tried to sound professional.

There was hesitation, and then, a male voice. "Is... Rebecca there?" I guessed I hadn't pulled it off.

"Rebecca's out today. This is Anneliese, can I help you?"

"Hello, Anneliese."

"Hello..."

"It's J.T."

I'm not sure which of us was more surprised. My heart sank to my knees. "She's out," I said, "Family emergency."

"Since I have you on the phone," he said, weighing his words, "maybe you'd like to... talk about things?"

Talk about things? "Um, okay."

"Rebecca's told me a lot about you."

I was speechless. I'd assumed I was a secret. A dirty one, at that.

"I'm aware that you're fond of each other," he said, "that she is important to you."

"Yes," I managed.

"And I want you to know that I will take care of her. That she's not just another girl to me. And I hope I'm not just another fling for her."

The word startled me. I wondered if that made me a fling. I also felt mildly sorry for him. I'd known Rebecca for almost a decade now. I gave him six months, if he was lucky.

Before I knew what I was doing, I said the only thing in my head: "I still love her."

"I know you do. But I'm asking you to stay out of it. And to trust me. If you love her, you want what's best for her. And you are not what she needs right now."

"How do you know what she needs?" I was getting brave now, and I never backed down from a challenge.

"She needs someone she can have. And I love her, too. She will be all right. I promise."

His voice was not unkind and, despite the aching in my heart, I heard the truth in his words. She had said them herself. Accepting defeat, I simply responded, "Okay."

Chapter 24

The grainy buzz of the zipper tore up the front of the green, canvas army tent. Ingrid poked her head inside.

"You're not sleeping already, are you?"

"Nah, I'm just writing," I said. I held a flashlight between my chin and shoulder so the light beam hit my notebook.

"Quit it, we're having fun. You don't write when you're camping!"

"I do."

"Well, stop for now," she said. "We don't get to hang out anymore and I have to go back to the dorm on Monday." She plopped next to me on a pile of sleeping bags and pillows. The huge tent had been our family's shelter for many campouts. It smelled of dust and warm pine needles. The usual suspects accompanied us to the Mojave River: our parents, aunt and older cousins, their significant others. Outside the tent, a fire blazed in a stone pit. Railroad ties and logs served as benches, hosting the adults and their flasks of booze.

"What are you writing?" Ingrid asked. I liked the feeling of being alone, yet surrounded, just outside. Ingrid's company made it even better.

"I just want to remember," I said. "So, I'm writing what happened."

We laid back and looked up at the roof of the tent. Shadows of juniper trees rustled in silhouette, dropping short needles over our heads.

"What happened?"

"Everything happened. Ma. Ballet. School. Rebecca."

"Hm. Can I read it?"

"If you want to."

Outside, the wind still blew. It was a long episode for a Santa Ana. We had endured it for a week now. My father had been concerned about building a fire and filled a bucket from the spigot at the ranger's office. He kept it near the fire. Voices and laughter floated into the tent as Ingrid and I remained still, listening. My aunt began to sing: *"Away out here they got a name for rain and wind and fire..."*

My mother joined her and now their two voices, silly with alcohol, filled the campsite with the fervor of the old westerns they loved. *"And they call the wind Maria..."*

Ingrid and I laughed as the Santa Ana lent itself to the mood like a goofy stage prop. Now we heard our father's baritone begin alone, as the others trailed off.

Something grabbed hold of my heart and twisted. I looked at Ingrid. Her eyes were wet. What was it about our father's voice, alone? He rarely showed emotion, unless he was angry. This was a side we never knew. He continued, solo. From across the campground, someone with a harmonica jumped in to accompany him.

"And now I'm lost, so gone and lost, not even God can find me."

I stopped trying to control the flow of tears and Ingrid laughed at my goofiness.

"Dork," she said.

"Fruit loop," I volleyed.

"Let's go," she darted out the flap and I followed. On the picnic table, Ingrid found an open bottle of port wine. She pulled the cork and poured into two Styrofoam cups. We sat on the table, our feet on the bench, watching our parents revel in fire, wind, and song.

Epilogue

"Dance is the rival of love, for it quickens the beat of the soul."
                                              ~Jean-Baptiste Alphonse Karr

The slopes of West Beach meet the waves at a steep angle, especially in the winter. Designated, or maybe just accepted, as a gay beach, that is where they found Ricky, almost lifeless, his strawberry blonde hair a mop of seaweed, his tall, thin body, limp on the sand.

Ricky bodysurfed the way he danced, slicing through the emerald falls as naturally as the dolphins that played with the surfers. West Beach is known for its riptides. The locals avoid them and warn tourists away. Ricky was no stranger to rough seas. But that day, as he described it, he had come over the falls of a particularly steep curl and met the hard sand with the back of his neck. After that, he could not move his legs. Moving on his elbows and clawing at the sand, he pulled himself up the steep strand out of reach of the waves and lost consciousness.

His dancers went to the hospital in small groups to see him and returned to the studio with descriptions of a metal crown with pins sticking into Ricky's skull. They whispered solemnly of his prognosis. He would never dance again. Never walk again. Though we didn't know it at the time, Christopher was already weakening with the effects of AIDS. Now he was at the hospital day and night beside Ricky. I imagined the studio empty of their energies. It may have been a matter of weeks. Perhaps it was months. But it was quick. Ricky caught pneumonia in the hospital and could not clear his lungs. And in that way, Christopher lost him. Everyone lost him. Hannah reported from the studio that things were dreadfully quiet during those months.

Sometimes I think I see Christopher downtown. Or at a studio that is new to me. I think of skipping over and saying, "Do you remember me?" But it's only for a split second and then it is I who remember: he is gone. Kidney failure took him in the end. Life is tenuous and we have little control over who keeps it and who loses it. We can be careful and responsible, wear seat belts, have safe sex, don't drink too much. But life is easily taken for granted while we are living. It would have saved Christopher some pain if he had gone before Ricky—but nature is as cruel as it is beautiful.

* * *

Now, my students line the bar, stretching, waiting for the music to begin. My voice overcomes their whispers. "Let's begin," I say. They are sixteen, seventeen, even twenty. They are innocent. Asking perfection of themselves. Failing. Trying again. Willing their bodies into shapes made perfect before the mirror. Conscious of line from fingertip to shoulder, from rib to hip, they watch me for signs of approval, their breath synchronized to measures of music.

"In my class," I tell them, "you will be present and perfect and strong."

I am not a shouter. I pace behind them, correcting, suggesting, chanting in the language of ballet, a hypnotist controlling the converted. Together, they are an orchestra, a rip current, a constellation, a murmuration. "In my class," I tell them, "you are an athlete, an artist, and a technician."

But one by one, they are girls becoming dancers, their shy and mad self-consciousness shed in the doorway. Sheltered, polite, and ordered. I was no such violet. But now and then, a glimpse in the eyes of one who is careless, in the words of one who is flippant, in the tears of one whose frustration pushes her to bleed, the decades look back at me. Which one am I? The one who is too free with her heart and her words? The one who is naive and vulnerable but thinks she is a formidable stone? Is anyone here looking for symbols in every uttered syllable or overflowing with the demands of her heart? In a way, I don't want to know. I hold vigil over their improvement. I am not a friend or a mother. Not even a sister. I am never late and duck out without a word when class is done.

My students achieve, chart paths, and succeed. They carry their training to Pennsylvania, New York, and England. But as I watch them go, I wonder what experience they bring to their motion. What can be expressed from the safety of a bubble? It is the task of life to teach them joy and rage, rapture and agony, jealousy and dedication, each in her own time.

But who will be the one to teach them passion? Who will be the one whose spirit rides on every breath she takes until the rhythm of dance is her soul?

Godspeed, ballerinas.

The blue profound stage gleams with narrow girls
like moonlight in a cavern. While clear slow
waltz-notes ascend from shadowed instruments
their pallid arms precisely flow and glow,

Their trembling arched legs lift, their skirts drift wide
their bodies bend like soft blown flames until
like steadied flames they straighten and subside
making a silence ere the strings are still.

~George Dillon, *Toe Dancers*,1927

Huge thanks to Sean O'Grady, whose enthusiasm and counsel helped me stay the course. Thanks also to Dr. David Stevenson for keeping me grounded, Sherry Simpson for unparalleled powers of editing, and Dolores Schultz for believing I had a book to write. Thank you to my sisters, Heather and April, for agreeing to be in my story and for helping to pick apart our past. And, finally, thank you Paul, Pearce, and Harrison for listening to me read the whole thing aloud a half-dozen times without falling asleep.

1. Anneliese's two clashing identities is a theme that runs throughout *Narrow Girls on a Blue Profound Stage*. At home, she is a well-behaved teenager, sheltered by socially conservative immigrant parents. But in her world as a dancer, she encounters substance use, sexual exploration, competition, jealousy, envy, and recklessness. How do these two conflicting worlds shape the way Anneliese views herself? Which world has a more powerful pull on her choices? What clues from Anneliese's childhood contribute to who she becomes as a teenager?

2. Despite the age difference between Anneliese and her lover, and her age at the onset of their affair in *Narrow Girls on a Blue Profound Stage*, Sellge does not write negatively about the relationship. How does the narrator's point of view help you accept Anneliese's experiences as authentic expressions of her sexuality? Would you have wanted the author to present the relationship with a more critical eye? Do you feel that Anneliese is equipped to handle the sexual interactions she has with the older woman, or do you feel the relationship was harmful to her? Do some people reach emotional and sexual maturity more quickly than others?

3. *Narrow Girls on a Blue Profound Stage* is a work off autofiction. Far from fiction, but not entirely memoir, Sellge has changed and adapted certain events and chronologies to better tell her story and also to shield the actual people with which she interacted during her years in

the performing arts. What is your reaction to the people in Anneliese's circles, both at home and at the studio? What, if anything, would you have wanted them to do differently with regard to their respective relationships with the narrator?

4. Sellge opens and closes the book with the voice of an older person speaking in retrospect. But the story is told in the present action through the eyes of a teen-aged narrator. How might the story have felt more or less accessible if it had been told in the third person? Would you have had more or less sympathy for the characters? What might have been lost in terms of authenticity if the story had been told with a deeper degree of narrative distance?

5. Anneliese's mother seems to be a caring, if distracted, person. Why does she react so negatively when Anneliese comes out to her? What does Anneliese's mother want for and from her daughters? How might the story have gone differently if Anneliese's parents had been open and accepting of her sexual identity?

6. The three sisters in *Narrow Girls on a Blue Profound Stage* have very different personalities. What is it about Anneliese that draws her apart from the family norm? Do her sisters resent her involvement in ballet? Is her older sister, Ingrid, bothered by her relationship with the older woman? Why does Ingrid follow their parents' expectations and do you believe the story upholds theories about birth order in families?

7. There are elements of magic in *Narrow Girls on a Blue Profound Stage* that you don't often encounter in memoir or autofiction. Anneliese's grandmother reads tea leaves and then visits her as a ghost and Anneliese claims some level off clairvoyance and the ability to speak to animals. Do you believe these occurrences are a young girl's magical thinking or did they really happen? If you believe these events are in Anneliese's imagination, how might she be using these elements as coping mechanisms?

8. *Narrow Girls on a Blue Profound Stage* is layered with controversy. Yet the author seems to want only to tell the story of an innocent yet deep obsession and the need for self-expression. Are the controversies in the book, (alcoholism, unwanted sexual aggression, paranormal occurrences, and under-age sex and drug use) necessary to the story? If you were to remove all of those elements, what would be left? If you

could remove one controversial element and still tell the story, what would you take out and why?

9. *Narrow Girls on a Blue Profound Stage* takes place in a time before the #METOO movement and before non-binary sexual identity was accepted and commonplace. How might Anneliese's experiences differ if the story were to take place now? What has changed with regard to a teenager's right to sexual identity and choices, and what has changed with regard to sexual interaction that is considered abuse?

10. Which character in *Narrow Girls on a Blue Profound Stage* has the deepest effect on you and why? Who do you most identify with? Who in your coming-of-age years influenced you as deeply as Anneliese is influenced by her lover and do you consider that influence positive or negative in retrospect?

11. In *Narrow Girls on a Blue Profound Stage*, Anneliese tells her lover that her Grandmother knew about their affair, even though she hadn't actually told her grandmother. Why did Annelise believe her Grandmother knew? If Anneliese had told her grandmother about her affair with the older woman, would she have been more accepting than Anneliese's mother was?

12. *Narrow Girls on a Blue Profound Stage* braids the two identities of the narrator, that of dancer and that of family member. But the facets of each identity run deeper: in each world, she is both a lesbian and a sister, a lover and a daughter, a best friend and a competitor. At what points in the story do Anneliese's identities come together in some sort of harmony? How does it change her when it does?

Lisa Sellge wrote *Narrow Girls on a Blue Profound Stage* (originally titled *The Seamstress*) as her Creative Nonfiction thesis at the University of Alaska, but she really began writing the book as she experienced it in the pages of her journals in the early 1980s. Lisa's creative writing has appeared in *Atticus Review, Brevity Blog, 3rd Street Beach Reads Volumes 1 & 2,* and *Literally Literary.*

She is currently writing her second work of autofiction that picks up where *Narrow Girls* left off. She lives in Washington where she works as a content editor, and photographs birds with the same level of obsession she brought to ballet. *Narrow Girls on a Blue Profound Stage* is her first novel.

For memorable fiction, non-fiction, poetry, and prose,
please visit Propertius Press on the web
<u>www.propertiuspress.com</u>